BREAK
THE
FAL

JENNIFER IACOPELLI

BREAK
THE
FALL

Hodder
Children's
Books

HODDER CHILDREN'S BOOKS

First published in the US by Razorbill, Penguin Random House in 2020

First published in Great Britain in 2020 by Hodder and Stoughton

1 3 5 7 9 10 8 6 4 2

Text copyright © Jennifer Iacopelli, 2020
Gymnast image copyright © ITALO/Shutterstock.com

The moral rights of the author and illustrators have been asserted.

A CIP catalogue record for this book is available from the British Library.

ISBN: 978 1 444 95324 4

Typeset by Input Data Services Ltd, Somerset

Printed and bound by Clays Ltd, Elcograf S.p.A.

The paper and board used in this book are
made from wood from responsible sources.

Hodder Children's Books
An imprint of Hachette Children's Group
Part of Hodder and Stoughton
Carmelite House
50 Victoria Embankment
London EC4Y 0DZ

An Hachette UK Company
www.hachette.co.uk

For all the girls before and after

chapter one

White-hot sparks of agony light down my spine, scorching over my hips and into my thighs. I grind my back teeth together and clench my fists against the pain, blunt fingernails biting into the palms of my hand.

C'mon, Audrey, it's nothing. Push through it.

Pounding my knuckles against the muscles of my calves helps distract from the ache as I sit on the floor, legs spread out in a split, waiting my turn.

The only sound in the sold-out arena is the reverberating squeak of the uneven bars lifting up into the rafters. It's been like this for two days. One by one, we go up to the vault or the beam or the bars or the floor and perform while the crowd holds its breath.

I do too. If I don't, it might become too much, and I can't afford anyone noticing how much my back hurts.

Especially not him.

Coach Gibson—or Gibby to those of us on the United States Gymnastics national team—is patrolling the wells between the raised podiums, watching with an eagle eye for any sign of weakness. He's everywhere all at once, cold and analytical, taking in every hesitation, every flinch, homing in on our weaknesses.

He stands to my left, wearing a red, white, and blue tracksuit, arms crossed over the swishy material.

"How's the back, Audrey?" he asks.

"Great. Ready to go."

His eyebrows rise, and he hums in disbelief, but he never looks away from my teammate and best friend, Emma Sadowsky, swinging on the uneven bars.

Gibby can stare all he wants; Emma won't screw up. He knows it, even as he makes a show of looking critically at her handstands and the distance of her releases. She's perfection.

Something as small as a wince from me, though? That's basically admitting I'm in too much pain to go on.

Emma is a great gymnast, but even on her best day she's not better than me on uneven bars. Of course, she's head and shoulders better than me at everything else, which more than makes up for it. We've trained together since we were three, when our moms signed us up for Mommy and Me classes. Now, fourteen years later, we're at Olympic trials.

She's definitely going to make the team. As last year's national and world all-around champion, she's the favorite to win multiple golds in Tokyo. So far Emma's accomplished everything we ever dreamed of as little girls, and now winning an Olympic medal is only a matter of time.

For me, just making the team will be a miracle. The pain doesn't matter. Not really. Aside from the blissful days following a cortisone shot, my back always feels like this. The doctors said I should probably quit, but I told them to shove it. Then I apologized, and we settled for a compromise: retirement after the Olympics.

I only have a few more weeks of gymnastics left. Or, if my next routine goes wrong, just a few more minutes.

With a *thwack* of her feet against the landing mats, Emma finishes her routine with a stuck double layout, her body arched through the two flips in that satisfying way that makes my fourth vertebra twitch. Or maybe that's just from the roar of the crowd, screaming in approval for their golden girl.

Joy for my best friend floods through me as she salutes the judges and then waves to the fans. A spike of excitement courses through my body. The pain fades to the background. It's almost time to compete, and my body and mind are on the same page.

I still have a few minutes to breathe because about twenty yards away, Chelsea Cameron, the reigning Olympic all-around champion, is about to start her floor routine. They keep the routines staggered for the TV broadcast, making sure the fans at home can see everything.

"You nailed that," I say, standing as Emma jumps down from the podium, a fake smile plastered across her face. I've known her long enough to know the difference.

"I know," she says, smoothing back her hair, hands still encased in chalky grips. She's a ginger-headed white girl, and the chalk leaves a streak in her hair just a shade or two paler than her skin. I smile at that. It's usually my own dark hair streaked with the chalk and not hers. "You've got this, Rey."

"I know."

She smiles, a real one this time, and some of the tension in my shoulders loosens despite Gibby still being right here. It might seem like his focus is on Chelsea, tumbling across the floor on the other side of the arena, but I don't doubt that his attention is at least partially on me.

I swing my arms in circles and then stretch them above my head, trying to pretend I'm not completely aware of Gibby's presence, that I'm totally dialed in on the routine ahead of me. He's not much taller than I am, being a former gymnast himself, but the sheer totality of his power in my world makes him seem gargantuan.

He runs a hand through his jet black hair graying slightly at the temples. "Show me what you've got here, Audrey," he says. *Or else*, I add in my head.

Chelsea lands her final tumbling pass. Her days as a top all-around gymnast are long over, but her name still carries the weight of Olympic gold and million-dollar sponsorships. Plus, even at twenty, she's still badass on vault and floor.

I take a deep breath, pushing Chelsea out of my head. Gibby wants to see what I've got on bars, and I have to show him that I belong on the Olympic team, that I'm worthy of my dreams.

Okay, Audrey, hit this routine and you go to Tokyo.

The crowd has finally settled after Chelsea's floor, just in time for the announcer to call out, "And now on uneven bars, representing NYC Gymnastics, Audrey Lee!"

My heart leaps at the sound of my name, and a frisson of excitement spreads over my skin. If it's the last time I'm going to do this, I want to remember every detail. I lock eyes with my coach, Pauline. She's chalking the bars exactly the way I like: just a thin layer, nothing that will clump into my grips. A tight smile plays across her face, and I return it.

There isn't time for all the words I want to say to her about how thankful I am and how much I love her and how no matter what happens, she'll be like a second mom to me, forever. Actually, I'm pretty glad there isn't time to say all that. Crying right now would suck.

The crowd buzzes, but not loudly enough to drown out the thumping of the blood pounding in my ears. The light near the side of the podium is still red, so my eyes flicker over the arena, everyone's devices reflecting the glare of the lights, cameramen hovering at the edge of the apparatus, attempting and failing to be unobtrusive while bits of chalk hang in the air, clinging to everything.

It's beautiful.

The judge at the end of the row gives me a green light, the sign to begin.

Everything else fades away. I lift one arm in salute, the other out to the side, an affectation I developed from obsessing over Russian gymnasts growing up. Then I turn, eyes on the cylindrical fiberglass bars that hold my ticket to the Olympics.

I swing up and into a handstand, holding to show control, but not nearly long enough for the blood to rush to my head, and then fold my body in half, legs straddled in a V and extended fully, all the way through to the tips of my pointed toes. There's barely time to breathe during a bars routine, especially mine. It's one of the most difficult in the world, every element linked to the next in a smooth melody that flows with the creak of the bars and the twang of the wires. Up on the high bar, I release and catch, and then back down to the low, a swing around the low bar and then straight back up again.

It's not flying, but it's as close to it as a human will ever achieve. Now, a giant swing up to a pirouette and down, and then a release into a back layout, my body held stick straight with one, two, three twists, and land, controlling the smallest step, barely a flicker.

It's done.

A hit routine and a massive sigh of relief. I clap my hands together, the grips sending a cloud of dust up into the air, and salute the judges, maybe for the final time.

Hopping down from the podium, Emma hugs me before I really find my feet. Coach Pauline is next, a woman who knows me better than even my parents. Over her shoulder I catch Gibby's eye, but there's no emotion there. No pleasure or satisfaction, only an unidentifiable steeliness. He looks away.

I'd done what he'd asked, hadn't I?

Was it enough?

"C'mon," Emma murmurs as our coach lets me go. There are tears in Pauline's eyes when I pull away. Tears of joy? Sadness? Both?

I grab Emma's hand and squeeze.

"I knew you had it," she says, squeezing back.

That's what breaks me. I yank her hand and pull her close, the tears starting to gather in the corner of my eyes. "I'm so proud of you. So proud of us."

"Me too." Her voice cracks, but she sniffs past the emotion, something else she's better at than me.

Pauline slides her arms around our shoulders as we pull away. Then together, we walk toward the corner of the arena as the final competitor is announced.

"And now on floor exercise, from Redwood Shores Gymnastics, Daniela Olivero!"

The powers that be knew what they were doing when they

assigned Dani the final spot in the final rotation. Her *The Greatest Showman* routine is super popular with gym fans, and she's pretty spectacular on the floor, with insanely high tumbling and a ridiculous amount of energy throughout.

Up until last year, she was on the fringes of the elite ranks, but everything's sort of come together for her in the months leading up to the Games.

The music gets the crowd on its feet immediately. I look at Emma, and her eyes twinkle back at me. Together, we start dancing along. The choreography of Dani's routine is fabulous, and we've seen it over and over again at National Gymnastics Committee camps.

Sierra Montgomery and Jaime Pederson, two white Oklahoma girls who always do everything together, are laughing at us, but they get swept up in the song too, letting their hips sway with the rhythm.

The music comes to an end as Dani nails her final tumbling pass and the whole arena roars in approval, a wave of sound crashing over us. My pain is a fleeting thing now, a tingle at the back of my mind as every single competitor on the floor starts to give one another impromptu hugs.

I pull away from Sierra and then Jaime and try to catch my breath when I'm nearly bowled over by Chelsea Cameron. Despite barely topping out at five feet tall, she nearly takes me down on impact, her textured brown curls catching against my damp cheek. She's crying and probably not even aware of who she's hugging because we've barely exchanged more than a couple of words over the years. Dani is still hugging her coach, but eventually Emma gets her in a bear hug—as much as a girl who weighs ninety pounds can bear-hug anyone—and then she's pulled over to the rest of us.

Bittersweet tears prick in the corners of my eyes. It's overwhelming, going out and doing everything you can to prove you belong and still not knowing if it was enough.

Almost against my will, my gaze flickers to the scoreboard. I don't want to look, but I have to. The combined scores from two days of competition are displayed for everyone to see, and before I let my fate be decided by Gibby, I need to know where I stand. Though my vision is increasingly blurry from the gathering tears, I can see my name clearly enough.

1. Emma Sadowsky   118.2
2. Daniela Olivero   118.0
3. Sierra Montgomery   117.1
4. Jaime Pederson   116.3
5. Audrey Lee   115.4
6. Chelsea Cameron   110.5

Everyone finished as expected, though I'm a little surprised at how close it is between Emma and Dani. There are four spots on the Olympic team, and I'm in fifth, but all-around scores don't matter as much as what Gibby wants. Let's be real: his opinion is the only thing that matters.

Somehow in the midst of the chaos, I slip on the black tracksuit Emma and I wear. It has the New York skyline emblazoned on the back in silver glittering rhinestones and NYC GYM on the left lapel. Obnoxious, maybe, but gymnastics fashion is rarely subtle. The tears are really falling now. No matter what happens, this is the last time I'll wear my NYC Gymnastics tracksuit. From here on out, it'll be USA gear or nothing.

Stop it, Audrey. Enjoy the moment.

I try to channel Emma and push down the emotion. It only half works. Better than nothing, though. As I shoulder my bag, one of the workers I vaguely recognize as an NGC official is motioning for us to leave the floor. I shuffle in behind the rest of the girls, twelve of us about to be whittled down to four, plus two alternates.

Behind me, the announcer calls out to the crowd, "While we wait for the decision from the selection committee, please join us in honoring Olympic silver and bronze medalist Janet Dorsey-Adams, owner and head coach of Coronado Gymnastics and Dance, on her induction into the NGC Hall of Fame!"

The spotlight follows Janet up onto the floor, where there's a trophy waiting for her. It's pretty cool to be in the Hall of Fame; maybe in a few years I'll be—

"Audrey, come on!" Emma's voice interrupts my thoughts from farther down the hall than I thought she'd be.

I turn to catch up with her, but instead my eyes meet the chest of someone a lot taller than me. We nearly collide, my nose to his pec, before strong hands reach out, holding on to my upper arms lightly. In a quick leading step, we're clear of each other and he releases me. I glance up and gasp in surprise. I know him.

Leo Adams, son of Janet Dorsey-Adams and world champion snowboarder. His mom used to drag him along to competitions when we were little. We follow each other online, but I haven't actually seen him in person for years.

Wearing a sardonic grin and a THIS IS WHAT A FEMINIST LOOKS LIKE T-shirt, he's tall compared to my five feet four inches, maybe six feet or a little more. He's biracial—half Black, half white—and there's a dusting of freckles across the bridge of his nose.

"Hey, Leo."

I inwardly cringe at not having a better opener, and, like, what if I remember his name, but he doesn't remember mine?

This could be bad.

A smile lights up his face, though, and I find myself matching it. "Audrey Lee," he says. *Oh, thank God, he knows who I am.* "Careful. Don't want you to lose your spot on the team for being clumsy."

I let myself smile. "It might be worth the risk."

What the hell, Audrey? Are you flirting? Must be the high from the competition, and it's made you completely insane.

"Audrey!" Emma calls again from down the large corridor, her voice bouncing off the concrete walls. She frantically waves me toward her, but I hesitate. She and the rest of the girls are disappearing into the locker room.

It's weird. I've entered some kind of alternate universe where the adrenaline is still numbing my pain and my gymnastics career might be about to end and there's something totally liberating about that thought.

"I should probably . . ." I trail off.

"You should definitely," he agrees, and I laugh.

"Ladies and gentlemen, in fifteen minutes we'll be announcing the next USA women's Olympic gymnastics team!" the announcer calls out.

I take a step toward the locker room and then another. *Don't look back, Audrey; boys are for a month from now, after you have an Olympic medal. Or two.*

The door swings shut behind me. The rest of the girls are there, even Sarah Pecoraro and Brooke Cohen. They qualified last year as individual athletes. They're going to Tokyo, but they won't have a shot at the team medal like the rest of us—if we make it.

"Where were you?" Emma demands, dragging me over to two empty seats.

"Do you remember Leo Adams?"

"What?" she shrieks. "He's here? Wait, how much longer until they announce?"

She's all over the place, and I don't blame her. She's just won the Olympic trials, but she has to wait like the rest of us, and it's not like I don't need a distraction too.

"Fifteen minutes."

My phone vibrates in my bag. There are a few thousand notifications waiting for me. Being on national TV during the trials process has made social media more than a little bit insane, but I've learned to ignore most of it.

It's the last alert that catches my eye. A mention from @Leo_Adams_Roars.

I bite my bottom lip, trying to keep that same smile he prompted from emerging again as I open his account. The profile pic does him justice: the same freckles, the same smile, plus a set of dimples I somehow managed to miss moments before.

"Wow. He's super hot," Emma says, probably louder than she meant to.

"Who's super hot?" Sierra asks, head whipping around from whispering something to Jaime.

"Leo Adams," Emma supplies for her, pointing to my phone. In an instant, my brief little moment with Leo turns into the distraction we all need.

"Is that Janet's son?" Jaime asks.

"No, there's just a random guy with her last name hanging out in the tunnel during her award presentation, Jaime," Sierra drawls with an eye roll.

"Is he a snowboarder?" Chelsea asks when my thumb hovers over a black-and-white picture of him sitting on a mountain—shirtless—with a board strapped to his feet, the sun rising in the distance.

"A snowboarder who appreciates *aesthetic*," Emma quips with a perfectly shaped ginger eyebrow raised.

"He won junior worlds last year," I say casually, trying to pretend I don't check up on his career pretty regularly. I mean, it's not like it's hard. We all post at least once a day, and he remembered my name, so odds are he knows the same stuff about me. Probably. Maybe.

Dani leans around Chelsea from her seat. "Boys who look like him should always walk around without a shirt. Look at those shoulders."

I nearly have a coronary when Sierra reaches over and likes the picture for me. "Oh my God!" I pull my phone away way too late. I don't have a ton of experience with boys—forty-hour weeks at training don't exactly make for epic teenage romance—but I know enough to know that liking a picture from months ago looks incredibly desperate.

Sierra laughs, and the other girls giggle. "It'll be fine. Look."

And she's right. I finally look at the message he wrote.

@Leo_Adams_Roars: Ran into @Rey_Lee, literally! It's okay. She's fine. That uneven bars gold is still ours! #NGCTrials

A knock interrupts, and together our eyes fly away from the screen. The distraction is over. Gibby and the rest of the selection committee are hovering at the door.

It's time.

chapter two

Shallow, gasping breaths are all I can manage as we enter the arena in a line, arms raised, waving to the crowd. Their answering wall of noise is a humming buzz in the background. Not even a lifetime of dreaming has prepared me for this. My skin is tingling and numb at the same time.

Gibby is at the center of the floor, a spotlight shining on him in the otherwise dark arena. His hair is impeccable, his shoulders high, back straight, commanding everyone's attention.

"Ladies and gentlemen! It is my honor to announce to you the athletes selected to represent the United States of America at the Olympic Games in Tokyo, Japan. Along with our individual athletes, Sarah Pecoraro and Brooke Cohen, please join me in congratulating . . .

". . . Chelsea Cameron . . .

". . . Audrey Lee . . .

". . . Daniela Olivero . . .

". . . Emma Sadowsky . . ."

Gibby's voice cuts in again. "Our alternates are Sierra Montgomery and Jaime Pederson."

I burst into tears as soon Gibby announced our names in that locker room, and it's only gotten worse since. My cheeks are raw from wiping the tears away. My throat is thick, and it's impossible to get my breathing under control. For once, I don't care. Being under control is totally overrated. At least, for now.

Emma is beside me as we move up the stairs that lead to the raised floor, the arena lights blinding us. She hasn't broken yet. Not one tear or choking gasp, just the serenity appropriate for the best gymnast in the world. I clutch her hand tightly. Holding it keeps all of this real. If I let go, it might slip away into the ether. I'll wake up from this elaborate, torturously perfect dream.

It's everything I thought it would be and at the same time completely different from what I imagined. Not making the team would have been way more devastating than making the team makes me happy. It's strange to know that about yourself, that you take your failures far more to heart than your achievements. It's not exactly healthy, but it's who I am.

A resounding *crack* makes me jump as confetti explodes from somewhere above us and glittery bits of red, white, and blue paper tumble down from the ceiling, getting caught in our hair. For an awkward moment, one even lands in my mouth. There's another round of laughing and hugging as it rains down on us. Honestly, I don't think I've ever hugged so much in my entire life. It's not my usual thing, but I could totally get used to it.

"Girls, huddle up!" Chelsea calls over the din. She's been to the Olympics before and knows what this feels like, but all I want to do is soak in the moment. With my back, this is a one-time thing for me. Sierra's arm slides around my shoulders as we all come together. What must it feel like for her and Jaime? Alternates. I'm not sure I'd feel much like celebrating if I were in their shoes.

Emma's arm comes around my other shoulder and I'm in a circle with these girls, all eight of us, all together. Their names will be connected to mine forever, no matter what happens between now and the closing ceremonies.

"We're a team now." Chelsea says, having to shout. Even so, her voice doesn't carry beyond our tight circle. "It's us against the world, and we're going to come out on top."

I nod along with her words. We all do.

"Hands in," Chelsea says. Looks like someone is making a play for the captaincy. I mean, it's an easy choice. She's the oldest and the most experienced gymnast. Chelsea puts her hand out, then Emma, then Jaime and Sierra, me and Dani, and finally Sarah and Brooke. "USA on three—one, two, three . . ."

"USA!" we shriek, raising our hands to the sky and then fanning out as one, turning and waving to the crowd. The lights have come up in the arena, and I think my parents are sitting a few rows behind the vault table.

Yep, that's them, and I don't even have the heart to be embarrassed by the way Mom is jumping up and down, waving frantically for my attention while Dad smiles and claps with the rest of the crowd.

I wave back but can't go over to them, not unless I want to spring over the wall separating the competition area from the stands and give security apoplexy. I'll see them in a bit.

But first we have interviews.

The NGC worker, whom we've followed like ducklings all weekend, corrals us down from the floor. Tissues are pushed into my hands as we move back into the tunnel toward the media area. There are stools waiting for us with our names plastered behind them.

Sliding onto the stool, I try my best to wipe away the tears without completely destroying my makeup, and a few reporters wander over to me. There are predictably massive crowds around Emma and Chelsea's designated seats, but it's cool to see that Dani Olivero has got a group as big as theirs plus all of the Spanish-speaking media. She's Mexican American and speaks Spanish at home, so she can actually give those journalists a good quote. There are six empty stools on the other side of the room for the girls who didn't make it. They're still in the locker room. How close was it really? How close was I to being one of them, instead of sitting on this stupidly uncomfortable stool?

A few reporters clearly decided to talk to me first, waiting to interview our stars once the crowds thin a bit.

"Audrey," begins a tall blond woman, hair pulled back into a French twist, "what's going through your mind now that you know your comeback was successful?"

Oh, that makes sense. They're interested in a redemption story. Redemption from what? Pain, I guess. I'm still on such a high that I don't even feel it, when normally sitting on a stool without a back would be the worst. Adrenaline is my new favorite thing.

I grin and bite my lip, but can't stop myself from saying, "Don't call it a comeback."

A few reporters laugh, getting the reference. I'm from Queens, and LL Cool J's "Mama Said Knock You Out" is probably way more important to me than it is to most people. The woman who asked the question furrows her brow in confusion, and I shrug awkwardly. "Sorry. It's gymnastics. There are injuries all the time. We all go through them. I'm really happy I had enough time to rehab and get myself to a point where I could make the team."

"Speaking of the team," a tall man with long sideburns and hipster glasses cuts in, "what do you think about finishing in fifth place all-around, but making a team of four? Is that fair?"

It takes everything I've ever learned about dealing with the press to not roll my eyes. "That's way above my pay grade." I smile and shrug again. It's something my dad, a surgeon, says all the time about decisions his chief makes at the hospital. "The way the team finals work can be complicated math, piecing together the top three athletes on each event, so I'm sure that had something to do with it."

That's exactly why I made the team. I'm top three on bars and beam. Chelsea is top three on vault and floor. Dani and Emma are our top two all-arounders, great across all four events. We're four athletes whose strengths and weaknesses complement one another perfectly, adding up to three great routines on each apparatus in team finals. It's just math.

An older woman I recognize as a reporter from *Sports Illustrated* asks, "Were you surprised to make the team?"

"Surprised? I don't know if I'd describe it that way, but was I sure I'd make it? No way."

"What's it like going through this with Emma Sadowsky?"

I could kiss this reporter for finally asking a decent question.

Emma is a few stools away, fielding questions like a pro. Any skill I have at this kind of stuff, I learned from watching her. "It's fantastic, amazing, and totally mind-blowing. She's my best friend, and I don't know how I would have made it through the last year without her. Seeing her in the gym every day motivated me to keep going, and going to the Olympics with your best friend? That's ridiculous in the best way. A total dream come true."

"Do you think she can beat Irina Kareva?"

"She beat her last year." Even though I wasn't able to compete at worlds last year, it was still super satisfying watching Emma take down Kareva. Everyone thought the Russian superstar was untouchable, but Emma beat her by nearly a point after Irina faltered on beam.

"Kareva posted a video of a triple-twisting Yurchenko last week. That gives her a huge difficulty advantage over Emma if she can hit it."

That's a ridiculously big *if*. No woman has ever landed a triple-twisting Yurchenko in competition, and in that video Kareva's looked pretty terrible. It's the only thing I don't admire about the Russian team. Their gymnastics can be beautiful, but they always seem to be chucking vaults way beyond their abilities. Not that I'm going to say that on camera. "Guys, again, that's way above my pay grade."

"You and the other girls were just verified on social media. How do you feel about that?"

The first thing that comes into my head pops out of my mouth. "Have you seen who they give those check marks to?" The reporters laugh, but there's an NGC worker side-eyeing my flippant answer from over her shoulder. "I'm kidding. It's amazing. Totally a dream come true."

I don't even know what I'm saying anymore. The adrenaline is starting to wear off, and a sudden pain flares in my hip. I've been sitting still too long if the pain isn't localized in my back. My eyes fly toward the NGC worker at my side, who somehow understands my need to be finished with these interviews.

"Sorry, everyone," she interrupts, pushing through the group, "but Audrey has to get some treatment on her back before she stiffens up. Thanks for your questions. The girls who didn't make the team will be made available to you in a few minutes."

I slide off the stool and pick up the bouquet of flowers that I received after the announcement. Mom will be excited. She always feels like I'm missing out on normal teenage things, so she'll be thrilled to press these flowers into a memory book like it's a prom corsage or something. Olympic team or prom? Yeah, that's not even close.

Speak of the devil. As soon as I leave the media room, I see my parents with the other girls' families. Dad's head of dark curls towers over everyone else, and Mom is tiny beside him, her long black hair hanging down her back. If I were ever allowed to take mine out of a bun, it would look just like hers.

People are constantly curious about the three of us. Mom was adopted from South Korea as a baby, and I definitely take after her in the looks department, so if it's only me and her, people will just flat-out ask where we're from or what we are, like it's somehow any of their business and not super fucking rude. When Dad and I are out together, people just assume I'm adopted. Then my last name, Lee, adds another layer of confusion, because it comes from my Dad's English ancestors, but that's going way back.

"Audrey!" Mom yells when she finally sees me and they push

past the security guard in front of them. Almost instantly, her arms are around me, pulling me in close. "I'm so proud of you, sweetie!"

"You were fantastic, Rey," Dad adds in his deep rumbling voice. His large hand cradles the back of my head, drawing both me and Mom into a group hug. It's a perfect moment. It's the moment I've dreamed of since I was old enough to understand what the Olympics were. It hasn't been easy on them, watching me all these years.

I wince when Mom squeezes a little tighter. Clearly, she feels me tense and pulls away immediately. "Do you need to go see the trainer?"

Nodding, I smile past the pain. "When we get home, I need to get a cortisone shot. Dr. Gupta said it should last me through the Games if I made the team."

"Go on," Dad says and motions toward the trainers' room across the hall. "We'll meet you back at the hotel. The NGC is throwing you girls a party."

My eyebrows lift at that idea. I don't exactly associate the NGC with parties—more like early curfews and surprise bed checks at three in the morning—but, hell, it's the Olympics, so why not?

"I'll see you guys over there." I hand Mom the flowers and give them each a fierce hug before I turn toward the trainers' room.

The other girls, everyone except Dani, are headed in that direction as well, some hugging their parents too, but most headed straight for the treatment—massage, heat, and ice—that will push down the pain for the rest of the night.

"Where's Dani?" I ask Emma, who shrugs uncomfortably and then makes a beeline for a training table.

"She's still giving interviews," Sierra says, rolling her eyes. There are tear tracks on her cheeks, and I know those weren't tears of joy. She's an alternate, caught in a weird vortex between making the team and not. I guess I can forgive the eye roll and the sharpness in her voice. "Apparently, she beat Emma in the all-around today. They're treating it like some kind of miracle."

Wow, I hadn't noticed she'd outscored Emma today, even if Em's two-day total was higher.

"I mean, it's sort of a big deal," Jaime says. "Emma's national and world champ, and she beat her."

Sierra scoffs. "Yeah, because scores at trials *definitely* always hold up once we get to international competition."

That's not a bad point. I'm pretty sure all of our scores were inflated at least a little bit today. Judges sometimes get caught up in the Olympic hype as much as the rest of us.

I follow them into the trainers' room, and Gibby waves me over to an empty table. Josh, one of the NGC trainers, has bags of ice ready for me.

"Congrats," Josh says, sitting down on a stool in front of me as I lift myself onto the table, trying to suppress the wince as a dull ache radiates through my lower back. Gibby's right here, and seeing me wrapped in massive ice blocks is enough of a reminder of my injury issues for the man who decides my role on the team.

"Thanks," I say, smiling at Josh. He's been around the national team since forever.

"You did great work out there, Audrey," Gibby says, his eyes not on me, but darting around the room to the other girls. I'm convinced he does it on purpose, letting us know that while he's talking to us, there's always someone else who can take our place.

"Thank y—" I try to say, but he cuts me off.

"I'm sure you know that all spots on the team are conditional upon preparedness leading up to the Games."

I swallow down the panic that flares up in my chest and nod once to show I understand.

"You and Emma have dreamed of winning team gold together since you were little. She's holding up her end of the bargain. You were named to the team today, but I'm sure you know how close it was. I expect you to give me more than you have so far, do you understand?"

"Yes, of course." It's a lie. What more could he want from me? I'm maxed out on the difficulty I can manage with the amount of pain I'm in—which he definitely knows—and there's no time to upgrade even if I weren't. My bars have been consistent since I came back, and I have a good shot at a gold if I hit in event finals. And even though their difficulty scores are lower, my floor and vault have been solid all the way through the selection process.

Duh, Audrey, he means beam.

The connections between my skills have been shaky at times, and while I'm capable of hitting them, it's been tough to do it in competition with the pressure of making the team constantly looming. Plus, it's where I take the most risks with my back. The beam is punishing on the joints, whether you're falling off it or staying on. I've tried to avoid overtraining on the event, but that's an excuse. It looks like it's gonna be balance beam or bust before Tokyo. I can increase my score by two- to four-tenths if I consistently nail those connections.

"I'll do whatever it takes."

"Good," he says. Suddenly, he shifts his gaze to me and winks, the smallest of smiles appearing. "Just so you know, I'm rooting for you here."

I nod firmly and smile through the ever-growing flares of pain radiating from my spine.

Then he wanders toward Sierra, who's getting her shoulder wrapped with an ice pack that makes my back wraps look tiny. Jaime is on the table next to hers having her elbows wrapped the same way. I wonder what he's going to say to them. Gibby's a great coach, but he's definitely not above mind games and pitting us against one another. But he said he's rooting for me—that has to be good, right? It's definitely good.

I take a deep breath and see Josh looking at me with concern. "How's your back?" he asks.

I kick my legs around and settle facedown on the table. "It's fine."

"All right, then—let's make sure it stays that way for the party tonight," Josh says as his fingers probe against the sore spot near my fourth vertebra. There's scar tissue and all kinds of fun things going on between his hand and where my formerly herniated discs reside. Involuntarily, I groan in protest, instantly exposing that my back is so not fine. I screw my eyes shut as Josh continues his massage, and I hope against hope that Gibby didn't hear me. If he wants more from me, he'll get it, and I'll start with working through this pain.

chapter three

" I know, I know," I say, leaping up the bus's stairs. Everyone's attention swings toward me, mostly with laughter in their eyes, but I think I catch a twist of the mouth from Sierra. Plopping into the seat beside Emma, I sigh in relief.

"It's okay, Rey," she says, shifting over in her seat to give me room. "Peeing on demand is hard."

"It is!"

We all got drug tested after the competition, and, like always, I'm the last one done. Ask me to hit a gymnastics routine in front of thousands of people, no problem, but peeing exactly when the anti-doping monitors ask is almost impossible.

The only people on the bus, besides our NGC security guard, are the gymnasts going to Tokyo. Sarah and Brooke are in the first row. It's fitting that they're kind of removed from the rest of us. Their qualifications process was totally separate from ours, and they're not even going to train with us in the lead-up to Tokyo. After we all fly out of San Jose tomorrow, we won't see them again until we hit the Olympic Village.

I'd thought about it, briefly—competing all around the world against other individual gymnasts to earn my own spot for the Olympics instead of letting Gibby decide whether or not I would make the team, but my injury made that option impossible. Plus, Gibby wasn't exactly thrilled when Sarah and

Brooke decided to go that route, and alienating the head of the NGC wasn't high on my list of priorities the year before the Olympics.

"We don't have to get dressed up for this, do we?" Emma asks, picking at the velvet fabric of her tracksuit pants.

"Doesn't really matter now, does it?" Sierra shoots back. "Thanks to Audrey, we're already late to the party."

"Not enough time to change," Jaime says from beside her.

"It doesn't matter," Chelsea says in that way she has that makes it sound like her word is the final word on something. "It's just family, the NGC, and maybe some sponsors, and they'll all love the fresh-from-competition look."

"Will Leo Adams?" Emma teases quietly, but not quietly enough. The rest of the girls definitely hear her.

"I have no idea."

The really honest answer is that I hadn't even thought about him since Gibby had walked into the locker room and read off our names. Leo Adams is cute and all, but going to the Olympics definitely trumps a cute boy.

Jaime pops her head out from behind Sierra, her shiny blond curls rapidly escaping her attempt at a bun. "I bet he'll be there. His mom got an award, and they're from all the way down in Coronado. They're definitely staying overnight."

"It'll be cool if he's there, but I'm pretty sure hanging out with a boy the whole time won't impress Gibby."

Emma glares at me. "C'mon, Audrey. We made the team. You can relax for one night—barely a night. Just a few hours."

I actually have to physically bite my tongue to keep from

snapping back at her. The last thing I want to do is reveal what Gibby said to the entire group.

Something in my face must give away my annoyance, because her expression softens almost immediately. "I don't mean, like, dance on the bar or anything. Try to have a good time. You've been a big ball of tension for months, and tonight you deserve to celebrate."

"We all do," I agree. Of course—we *deserve* to celebrate.

"Right, and if you celebrate a little bit with a cute guy, where's the harm?"

Sierra nods. "I mean, look at Chelsea. She's got a boyfriend, and look how much her gymnastics has improved since the last Olympics."

Emma sits back in her seat and rolls her eyes. Chelsea doesn't even acknowledge the jab. Sierra's such a little troll, and sometimes she's funny, but she never seems to know where the line is.

The bus pulls to a stop in front of the hotel. There are crowds of people lined up behind barricades, and a ripple of excitement flows through the sea of bodies when they realize exactly who is on the bus. Emma slides out from her seat, and everyone else falls in behind her.

"You're right, you know, about Gibby and not letting down your guard," Dani says, her nose wrinkling. "Nothing is guaranteed. You got this far doing what worked for you."

"Exactly."

She nods in approval and leads me toward the front of the bus. Dani's only a year older than me, and I've known her since we were little, but we've never been that close. In the last couple of years, she's skyrocketed from the fringes of the elite ranks into a top contender.

The rest of the team is at the front of bus. "Ladies, unfortunately the crowds are way too big for us to manage, so I'm going to ask you to smile and wave to them and not stop for autographs or pictures. We need you to keep walking," our security guard says.

"Got it," Chelsea agrees for all of us, and he nods at her words.

"We'll go on my signal," he says, turning around to say something into his walkie-talkie.

"Girls, before we go out there, presents!" Chelsea says. Reaching into her bag, she pulls out seven little gift bags with two gymnasts flying through the air in the shape of Cs emblazoned on the front. It's the logo from her personal cosmetics brand. I remember seeing an interview where she talked about how, as a Black woman, she wanted to create totally inclusive line with tons of shades and tones. New products always sell out within five minutes of release.

"Okay, let's go," the security guard says and waves us forward.

Chelsea hands a bag to each of us as we pass her on the way to the front of the bus. She won two Olympic golds at the age of sixteen, and since then she's been in movies and music videos. She's famous in a way that I'm pretty sure I never want for myself.

"Thanks." I take my bag from her, and she smiles and pats me on the shoulder.

"No sweat, Rey."

The driver pulls the lever opening the bus door, and we're hit with a wall of shrieks and camera flashes. I follow Dani down the stairs, just ahead of Chelsea. The lane the hotel created with metal barriers for us to walk through isn't wide enough to keep the fans from reaching over and touching us as we walk by. The crowd surges against the barriers. I slap a few outreached hands and try to keep a smile on my face, but my blood is pumping hard, and the urge to flee is tingling down toward my toes as my body starts to overheat at the way the crowd closes in around us. I bend my shoulders in and duck my head, trying to stay as small as possible.

Once we're in the hotel, it's not much better. A lot of the fans are guests too, and the lobby is a total crush. I follow the security guard's shiny bald head because he towers over almost everyone in the madness, and finally we reach an elevator that the guard needs a key card to activate. I assume that means we're going somewhere the rest of these people can't get to, and the relief that courses through me is way too real. I suddenly feel a ton of sympathy for every celebrity in the world. There are very few people who would recognize me walking down the street, and I'm more than happy to let Chelsea and Emma take up the spotlight. It seems like I'm the only one, though.

"That was incredible," Sierra breathes out, and Jaime laughs, a huge grin plastered across her face.

Emma's cheeks were flushed. "A total rush."

"Insane," Dani says, but her eyes are wide and joyful.

Chelsea smiles. "Get used to it, girls. Your lives just changed forever."

I'm not really sure I believe her, but then the doors to the elevator open, and another crowd—this one made up of friends and family and sponsors and NGC and United States Olympic Federation officials and coaches and former Olympians—turns as one toward us in a large room, where the music is rocking and drinks are already flowing. For a moment it's silent, and then a huge cheer erupts, along with thunderous applause.

Gibby slides forward out of the crowd, his usual tracksuit long gone, replaced by dress pants and a collared shirt. I've rarely seen him out of his official gym clothes, and the transformation is astounding. He looks so much less intimidating—almost normal, like someone's dad. He smiles at us and then lifts his arms, and the crowd quiets. "Ladies and gentlemen, your United States Olympic gymnastics team!"

"Hear, hear!" someone shouts, but it's impossible to see who it is in the blur of faces.

Raising his glass, Gibby says, "A toast to Emma, Chelsea, Dani, Audrey, Sarah, Brooke, Sierra, and Jaime!"

It feels weird standing there as the group of adults lift their glasses toward us, but then it's over, the music rises in volume again, and we're drawn into the party.

Emma nudges me with her sharp elbow. "Ow, what?" I ask, eyeing one of the trays of food being passed around. I'm pretty sure they're serving pigs in a blanket, and while I follow a strict diet, those little appetizers are one of my weaknesses.

She nods in the opposite direction of where the waiter with the snacks disappeared into the crowd, and the stupid smile on her face tells me what I'm going to see before I even turn around. We've never not given each other crap for having a crush on a guy. Not that I'm saying I have a crush on Leo. I barely know Leo.

Her phone buzzes in her hand, and she glances at it quickly, but clicks off the screen just as fast. "Go," she says. "Our parents are on the other side of the room. I'll cover for you. Your hair looks great. Your eyeliner is flawless, as usual. You are an *Olympian*. Now go knock him off his feet or snowboard or whatever."

I smile and raise a hand to my head in salute. "Yes, ma'am."

When I turn around he's only a few feet away, smiling that same grin he had back at the arena and holding a small plate with pigs in a blanket on it.

"Can I have one?" It's probably not the smoothest opening, but whatever, I'm hungry.

"All yours," he says, holding out the plate, and I take one, popping it into my mouth. It's awesome. Delicious buttery goodness surrounding God only knows what goes into a hot dog. He'd even put some deli mustard on it. I might have to marry this boy.

"I love those," I say after I've chewed and swallowed.

"Well, you've definitely earned it. God, it's been forever, hasn't it?"

"Years, maybe, like, four or five."

"Clearly, you've made good use of your time since then," he says, motioning around the room. "Olympic team on your first try—pretty impressive. I knew you'd make it, though."

I laugh a little. "Yeah? That makes one of us. I was so nervous until he said my name. I'm still nervous, actually."

"You don't seem nervous."

"Maybe I'm good at pretending, then, because *nervous* doesn't even begin to cover what I'm feeling right now."

His smile fades a bit, and suddenly he looks serious. "I get it. Your whole life leads up to this one moment, and then it finally happens—you run into a tall, dark stranger just like you always dreamed you would."

And at that I *really* laugh.

"Seriously, though, congratulations. You're going to blow everyone's mind in Tokyo. I know it."

"Thanks. I just can't believe it's real, you know? After the surgery and all the work I did coming back."

"Yeah, I saw that," he says, biting his lower lip and looking a little sheepish as he rubs at the back of his neck. "Not to sound like a creeper, but I follow you, so, like, I saw the pictures and videos and stuff from after your surgery and then when I got hurt . . ." He trails off.

I cringe. I'd forgotten about the picture of a cast I saw in his feed a few months ago. "How long have you been out?" I ask, motioning to his knee.

"Four months. I've been doing PT for a bit now, and the doctors cleared me to surf, so I've been doing that until I'm good to go on hard surfaces. If I decide to come back at all."

My ears perk up at that. "You're not sure if you're . . ." My phone buzzes in my tracksuit pocket. "Sorry." I glance at it fast.

It's from Gibby.

Celebrate tonight, but remember what I said.

My eyes fly around the room wildly. Emma, her parents, and mine are in the corner, along with Emma's agent. Sierra and Jaime are with their parents, everyone talking over one another, probably about how they should have made the team instead of the rest of us. Chelsea is with her boyfriend, looking like the rest of the world doesn't exist. Dani's near them, checking her phone just like I did. Maybe he texted her too?

"Everything okay?" Leo asks, bringing me back to reality. Or maybe the text is reality and this part is something else, something I shouldn't be doing.

Then Dani clicks at her phone, pockets it, and turns to Chelsea and her boyfriend saying something that makes them both laugh.

"Yeah." I shake my head and smile. "Everything's fine."

"No worries. Listen, do you want to talk somewhere a little less . . . in the way?" he asks, motioning toward the far wall. It's glass and leads out to what looks like a balcony.

"Absolutely."

San Jose isn't the most picturesque city in the world, but like any other city, it lights up at night, and it'll always hold a special place in my heart. It's where my dream finally came true.

I lean my arms on the wrought-iron railing and turn to him as he comes to stand beside me, the warm air swirling around us.

"So, you were saying, about coming back?"

He shakes his head. "Yeah, Beijing is still two years away, so . . ."

"You still have some time." *But not a lot* is what I don't say. It takes months to get back into competitive shape at the elite level. I had surgery almost two full years ago, and it took until this past April for me to get back into real competition form. Overall, it took a little under eighteen months.

"Yeah. I've been rehabbing in my mom's gym, but I've been thinking about maybe going to school instead."

"Where?" College has always been part of my plans, but since the Olympics would have coincided with my graduation year, it's been on the back burner for a while.

"Stanford."

"Really? They recruited me heavily before I knew I wouldn't be able to compete, but I've always thought maybe I'd go anyway to study, I don't know, something that's not gymnastics. Do you think you're going to go?" I ask, finally cutting off my own ramble and feeling my face flush.

Calm down, Audrey; let the boy get a word in.

"I don't know. If I go in the fall, I won't be able to train, so . . ."

"That's a big decision."

He nods. "Yeah, it is." Then, after a long pause, he says, "What about you? Any plans after the Olympics?"

I cringe. "I really try not to think about it."

He snorts. "I get that. Retiring at seventeen is not really a thing most people do."

"Exactly."

"Audrey, are you going to introduce us to your friend?"

For once I'm wincing and it has nothing to do with my back. That's Dad's voice, and Mom is probably with him. What's the protocol for this? He's probably going to freak. I turn to face them, totally not sure what I'm going to say, but then Leo is striding toward them and extending a hand to my dad. Their handshake is firm and quick, and the next, with my mom, is the same.

"Mr. and Mrs. Lee, I'm Leo Adams. It's nice to meet you both."

"Leo, I believe I met your mother a few minutes ago," Mom says, shaking his hand as well. "She's lovely."

"Thanks," he says and smiles at them and then back to me. "I'll leave you guys alone. You should celebrate together."

"No, no, don't let us interrupt," Mom cuts in, taking hold of Dad's arm. "Audrey, we'll see you tomorrow morning for breakfast. Text me when you get back to your room *with Emma*." And with that, they're gone, back through the glass doors and disappearing into the party.

Well, that wasn't exactly subtle, and I close my eyes tightly as my parents walk away.

"Your parents are nice."

I turn back to him, opening my eyes in shock. "Thanks." Suddenly, I'm tongue-tied. The conversation flowed so easily before, and now I have no idea what to say.

My phone buzzes, thank God. Glancing at it will make the silence way less awkward. It's from Emma.

Party! Us & men's team. Meet me in our room to change!

I look up at Leo, who's putting his own phone back in his pocket. He smiles at me, and something in my stomach unknots and my shoulders loosen. I should be nervous, but being near him just makes me relax. Is that weird? It feels like it should be weird.

"Do you want to go to a party?"

"I—uh—actually, I can't. Mom and I are flying out tonight."

"Oh." Like everything about seeing him, my disappointment feels totally disproportionate to the amount of time we've spent together.

"I can walk you over there, though, if you want?"

"Actually, walk me back to my room? I'm apparently supposed to change out of this."

"That one you share with Emma?"

We laugh. "Yeah, that one."

"Sure, let's go."

We're almost entirely silent on the elevator ride up to the seventeenth floor, where most of the NGC is staying. When he reaches out to push the close-door button, the soft scent of whatever body spray he wears floats over me. It's light and airy and completely suits him.

35

I've spent my entire life around guys who smell like gym chalk and sweat. This is a total novelty. When he leans away again, the back of his hand brushes against my arm, and immediately a shiver slips down my spine—the first pleasurable feeling I've had in that spot in a long time.

This is nuts.

Is this what dreams coming true feels like? You make the Olympic team and meet a really hot guy who's into you all in one night? *Soak it in, Audrey, because life doesn't get much better than this.*

I've nearly gathered up enough courage to say something, *anything*, though I have no idea what, when the bell dings and the doors open. All the way down the hallway, on the other side of the elevator bay, the deep, pulsing bass of whatever music is playing reverberates in my chest. That must be the party. With a tight smile, I lead Leo out of the elevator car and in the opposite direction from the party, digging into my jacket pocket for my key card.

"This has been . . ."

"Wild?" he fills in for me, and I laugh.

"Extremely."

"It was really great seeing you again, Audrey," he says, and I'm about to respond, but he barrels ahead. "I always . . . When we were kids, I always kind of had a thing for you."

"Only when we were kids?" I ask, teasing him just a little, like I have the upper hand, when really, I'm completely freaking out that this is happening. Whatever *this* is.

"I mean . . ." He's rubbing at the back of his neck, but smiling too. "You were pretty smoking with those big hair ribbons and hot-pink leos."

"That's an impressive memory." I lean in a little closer. "Can I tell you something?"

He nods and licks his lips.

I swallow back the intense pang of something underneath my skin and say, "When we were kids, I always kind of had a thing for you too."

"Yeah?"

"Emma and I used to freak out if we saw your mom's gym entered in the competition because we knew she'd bring you along."

We just stand there in silence, letting our mutual confessions settle around us. We wouldn't have been able to act on it in the past; we were just kids, and neither of us would have had time for a long-distance anything—but now?

His hand reaches out, fingers closing lightly over my wrist. His hand is so much bigger than mine. "Is it okay if I . . . ?" he asks, gently bending down but hesitating.

For a moment my brain goes haywire, not understanding what he's asking, but then my eyes meet his and it clicks into place. I nod, and he closes the last inches of distance between us, but before his lips can brush against mine, the door down the hall opens and a wave of sound spills out.

Leo falls forward, his forehead resting against mine, and he exhales. The connection is still there, our eyes locked together, but the moment is over. People are streaming out of the room, and I am not doing this—whatever this is—in front of an audience. He seems to get that without me saying a word, and he pulls back and steps away. My wrist tingles at the loss of contact.

"Damn," he says, the disappointment clear in his furrowed brow, but then he's smiling, that confident grin nowhere to be seen, replaced by something almost shy and a little bit sheepish.

I lick my lips—they feel way too dry right now—and he groans in the back of his throat.

I laugh. Not at him, but at the crowd of people still flowing out of the room, making privacy impossible.

He chuckles too. "I really have to go. My flight is in two hours, and my mom will kill me if we miss it," he says, bouncing on the balls of his feet.

"Have a safe trip home," I say, trying to make it a little easier.

It doesn't work.

"Listen, I know the next few weeks will be insane for you, but we'll text, okay? And then . . . I don't know, come visit me at Stanford or wherever I am with your medals or something. I don't know. Just—"

"That sounds amazing," I cut off his ramble.

"Yeah?" he asks, his smile widening in what looks a lot like relief.

"Definitely."

He's barely down the hallway when the door behind me swings open and Emma grabs my arm, pulling me into the room. She chucks a ball of what I assume is a dress at my head, and I just barely catch it before it hits me in the face.

"Did he kiss you? I couldn't see through the peephole."

I'm not even a little bit outraged. I would have spied too. "Almost," I say, pulling off my tracksuit and getting out of my leo fast before carefully sliding on the dress. It's actually one of Emma's, a light gray mini with small straps at the shoulders and a cutout at the back where it ties together, leaving a diamond of skin exposed.

I turn for her inspection, and she nods before reaching out and adjusting the tie at the back. "Okay, you're good. And me?" she asks.

Motioning for her to spin around, I assess the gold spangled, almost flapper-style dress she's in and then I laugh. "Did you seriously give me a silver dress to wear while you wear gold?"

Her eyes fly open wide, but then she giggles. "Just preparing you for that bars podium."

"Oh my God! Okay, you look great, let's go."

We slide into almost-fancy flip-flops and grab our phones and race down the hallway together. The bass from the music is still pounding away, and when the door flies open, Chelsea is on the other side, taking our hands with a wide smile and leading us into the suite.

Emma links her fingers through mine, and we head straight for the group of people dancing. My pulse matches the quick beat as Emma and I find the rhythm of the track and start dancing and singing and laughing along. It's dark in the room. Though the cityscape shines in through the windows—the same view Leo and I looked out over just a little while ago—it's tough to make out who is who in the sea of bodies, but that doesn't matter. I'm going to the Olympics with my best friend, and even if it's just for tonight, I'm going to celebrate.

chapter four

" I made the Olympic team."

That doesn't sound real.

"I'm going to the Olympics."

Nope. Still sounds fake.

In the bed I woke up in yesterday, where the words I'm saying weren't true yet, it's really hard to make my mind accept this new reality.

"I'm an Olympian."

I blink away the last vestiges of sleep and roll over, only to be met with the sight of Emma's body launching across the space from her bed to mine.

"We're Olympians!" she shrieks, landing at my side, her red hair flying into her face.

Yeah, that one sounded real.

She lifts her phone and leans her head against mine. "Smile, Rey—we're going to Tokyo," she sings as she records, and I let a smile spread across my face. Her thumb swipes against the screen. "Perfect. Steve said I should post at least three or four times a day leading up to the Games. Oh! I forgot, while I was totally running interference with the parents for you and Leo yesterday, Steve was chatting up your mom and dad. He wants us to do some promo together before we leave for training camp."

Steve Serrano is Emma's agent. She signed with him after world championships last year, giving up her amateur status and going professional. Technically, I'm pro too. It was an easy choice to make once we realized I wouldn't be able to compete in college.

My phone buzzes somewhere near my head, and I dig it out from under my pillow, where it ended up after we crashed back into the room last night, totally exhausted in every possible way.

It's a direct message from Leo.

Not sure if I made it clear before. It was really great talking to you last night.

And then beneath it, it's his number, his actual phone number, which feels kind of serious.

"Who is it?" Emma asks, rolling over and squinting at the screen and then letting out a small squeak.

"What do I say?"

I pull up a new blank message.

"Tell him that he missed a great party," Em suggests, "and that you wanted to dance with him."

Yeah, that sounds good. Normal, but kind of flirty, without being too much. I type it out and press send.

I swipe out of the message and look at the time. "Ugh, I'm going to be late. I'm supposed to meet my parents."

One foot gets tangled in the sheets as I leap out of bed, which causes my back to spasm, but I ignore the pain. Wracking my brain, I try to remember what Gibby told us to wear to the meeting, but realize he said we'll be getting our new Olympic team clothes there, so for once it doesn't matter what we wear. I follow Emma's lead, yanking on a pair of shorts and an NYC GYM T-shirt, then throw my hair up into a ponytail, slide on a pair of flip-flops, grab my phone, and race out the door.

The door where Leo almost kissed me last night.

I'm an Olympian, and I had an amazing almost-kiss with a really hot guy last night.

This is going to be a good day.

The lobby restaurant is relatively empty. It was a long night for everyone, even the fans. Most people probably won't be up for a few hours, but I spot my parents at a table near the windows.

"See you later," Emma says, sliding away from me. Her parents and Steve are at the other end of the restaurant. Chelsea and her boyfriend are in a booth in the corner, and she shoots me a quick wave before looking at whatever papers he's showing her. I wave back and then head for my parents.

"Morning, guys!" I slide into the chair beside Dad. They already got me an egg-white omelet with veggies and a huge glass of orange juice.

"Morning, Rey," Mom says, smiling widely. She and Dad stare at me for a long moment.

"What?" I ask, looking between them. "What is it?"

"You're an Olympian," they say together.

A brilliant chill runs through me from head to toe, and I smile with them. It's been a fourteen-year journey, and my parents have been with me every step of the way, through state championships and elite qualification, through NGC camps and international assignments, through injuries and surgeries and doctors and physical therapists and finally Olympic trials.

The pride radiates off of them in their smiles.

"So, that boy, Leo, he seemed very nice," Mom says, her eyes twinkling at me with mischief.

"Mo-om," I protest. It figures she'd want to talk about Leo and has no problem being awkward enough to do it in front of Dad.

"What? He seemed nice, didn't he, Greg?"

"Lots of people seem nice," he grumbles before picking up his coffee mug and hiding behind it, but I can tell he's still sort of smiling.

"He is nice, but he also flew home last night with his mom, like, less than an hour after you met him."

"Who is nice?" A new voice joins the conversation and I flinch. Gibby is beside our table, smiling down on us.

"Coach Gibson," Dad says, reaching out to shake his hand. "Good morning."

"Morning to you folks too. Audrey," he says, nodding. "Just wanted to check in and make sure you're all doing well and congratulate you again on what you've achieved as a family."

"Thank you," Mom says, grinning and looking to me.

"Thanks," I say.

"I know Audrey has a lot more to offer than what we saw this weekend. But I don't mean to interrupt. I'll let you folks get back to your breakfast, and, Audrey, I'm truly excited to see you at training camp."

And with that he's gone. I force myself to take a deep breath and then let it out slowly. That wasn't so bad.

"He's excited you're on the team," Mom says, her smile spreading wide across her face.

"Yeah." I don't really want to share what he said last night about beam and needing more from me. My parents are happy and proud. I can deal with Gibby's mind games on my own. "There's still a lot of work to be done, though."

"There is," Dad agrees through a mouthful of eggs. "And speaking of, I got in touch with the airline this morning and had you, Emma, and Pauline moved to the red-eye tonight."

"Thanks," I say before taking a large bite of my breakfast. We didn't want to assume anything when we booked our return flight from trials, so we figured the hassle of having to change our travel arrangements was better than jinxing my chances of making the team. I'm not superstitious exactly, but Olympic trials didn't seem like the time to tempt fate.

I take another bite of the omelet and then a large sip from the orange juice. "I've gotta go, guys." I lean over, kissing Dad on the cheek, then stand, stepping around the table, and give Mom a quick hug. "I'll try to meet you in the lobby before you leave for the airport, okay?" I should have enough time between the team meeting and everything else to say goodbye. "Just in case, though, have a safe flight, and I'll see you at home," I say, giving Dad a big hug and then another one to Mom.

As I turn to leave, I look for Emma, but she's already gone. Chelsea is getting up from her table as well. We naturally gravitate toward each other as we exit the restaurant and make our way to the conference room.

"It still hasn't sunk in," I whisper.

She smiles at me, almost the same way my mom did before. "Don't try and force it. One day it'll hit you that all of this is real."

"And then I'll have a nervous breakdown?" I ask, with a half laugh.

"Totally. I was walking down a street in LA with Ben"—that's the boyfriend—"and I literally burst into tears. It was, like, six months after Rio."

"You're kidding?"

"Nope. Just started sobbing right there on the sidewalk. No idea where it came from, but it all hit me at once. For now, though, go with it. You've been to big competitions before. You went to worlds two years ago. Treat this like that, and then you can freak out about it all after!"

"You make it sound so easy."

"Oh, it's not, but I've got your back from here on out. It can be tough for women of color in this sport. We're held to a different standard sometimes. If anything weird happens, come to me. We'll figure it out together."

We're at the door to the conference room. It's the longest conversation I've ever had with her, I think. Over the last year, I've tried to pretend like I'm not super intimidated by her success, but I'm not sure I've pulled it off completely.

"Ladies, take a seat," says the same NGC worker from last night who saved me from those reporters.

Emma is already there sitting beside Sierra and Jaime. When I slide into the seat next to her, she shoots me a tight smile. This is it. Our journey to Tokyo begins now.

Gibby steps up in front of us, and we instinctually straighten to attention, our backs pressing up against the chairs. We've all been spoken to before about letting our posture slip, and the last thing we need is to get reamed over casually slumped shoulders.

"Okay, I think that's everyone," he says, and the NGC worker shuts the conference-room door. Everyone is here—all the bigwigs, the board of directors, reps from our major sponsors, our coaches, everyone.

I smile at Pauline, who gives me a sharp shake of the head in response. That's odd. Pauline is usually all fake smiles at meetings like this. Even when she's in a bad mood, she doesn't want to give off the vibe that she's annoyed with us in case it makes Gibby think we've done something wrong. I survey the room again, and then it clicks.

Dani's missing.

"Hang on," Chelsea says from beside me. "Where's . . ."

Gibby cuts her off with a raised eyebrow, and she sits back, still looking confused.

"Ladies, before we get started, I have an announcement to make. I am duty-bound to inform you that the results from your drug tests just prior to the start of trials arrived last night, and unfortunately, Dani Olivero has been suspended from the team for a violation pursuant to the joint anti-doping policy of the NGC and the USOF."

The anti-doping policy?

Holy crap, Dani failed her drug test.

Gibby's still talking, and I refocus on him. "As you know, we have a zero-tolerance policy when it comes to violations of this nature. Thus, she's been removed from team as per USOF guidelines."

He hesitates and looks us over, holding eye contact with each of us for a moment. When he reaches me, I keep my expression blank, the same way I do when we line up before a practice or competition. Showing no emotion is better than showing the wrong one. Not that I have any idea which is the right one. Shock? Anger? Disbelief? Confusion? They're all swirling through me, but he'll never know that.

Once he seems satisfied that we've all understood whatever it is he was trying to impart, Gibby smiles and says, "As heartbreaking as this news is and as disappointed in Dani as we are, there is still some joy to be found in all of this. I'm thrilled to announce that Sierra Montgomery, due to her phenomenal abilities and years of dedicated training, has been promoted from alternate and named to the team. Congratulations, Sierra!"

His hands come together once and then again, applauding her, and we join in. My hands mechanically clap over and over, but my brain hasn't quite caught up with the information it has to process. Dani suspended. Sierra promoted. Just like that. One dream dead. Another alive.

Sierra lets out a noise from her throat that's somewhere between a squeak and a scream. "I . . . I don't . . . Thank you," she manages to choke out after a moment. Her hand is holding Jaime's so tight her knuckles are white. Jaime's face is frozen in what looks like an epic internal battle between excitement for her best friend and the totally natural resentment of still being an alternate.

"You've worked hard for this, and you deserve it." And with those words, his expression lightens almost immediately, his shoulders relaxing. "So, today we will proceed as planned with our photo shoot and outfitting, but obviously we've canceled the press conference so none of you have to handle questions about these changes.

The NGC and USOF will release a joint press announcement to take care of that. However, if, somehow, anyone does ask you anything about this situation or the NGC investigation, please direct them to our media relations department and stick to *no comment* beyond that. We operate the way we always have. What happens within the NGC stays in the NGC. Understood?"

"Yes, sir!" we chorus together, the same response we use whenever he addresses us as a group. The high of last night and this morning is gone. My heart starts to race worse than it ever has before a big routine, or even last night when Leo almost kissed me. A lump slides up into my throat, but I swallow it back down. Showing weakness isn't an option, not now. Not ever.

———

"What do you think she was taking?" I whisper as we all stand together on a grassy hill just outside the hotel. It's a perfect day, blue skies and warm summer rays, but the mood around the team is anything but sunny. Ahead of us, Brooke and Sarah are posing for the NGC and USOF photographers. They're getting pictures of us for the press releases about to be sent out around the world.

"Probably a diuretic," Emma says. "She lost a bunch of weight in the last year or so, and it lines up with her results starting to improve. It makes sense."

"There is no way Dani was doping. She's too smart to do that," Chelsea bites out from between her teeth.

"Smart doesn't matter. We were all desperate to make the team, Chels. She tried to give herself an edge, and she got caught."

Chelsea shakes her head. "I'm telling you, there is no way. The results were probably a false positive. This will be cleared up when the results from yesterday's tests come in."

"He said she's off the team, though," I say. "Like, it doesn't feel like there's a lot of wiggle room there."

"She cheated," Sierra joins in, with Jaime on her heels, "so I'm not giving up the spot that should have been mine in the first place."

Chelsea whirls around, but the photographer calling us over stops her from saying whatever was about to fly out of her mouth. She just quirks an eyebrow at Sierra and then spins away, leading us to where they want the four girls on the team to pose for a group shot.

Over the next hour, we take pictures in every combination possible to make sure the NGC has photos ready to go, no matter what happens between now and the actual competition. We each sit out one of the group shots, and it really hits home that despite everything we've been through to get to this point, nothing is guaranteed, especially now that Dani is gone.

We're brought to a room where we fill out paperwork for the US Olympic Federation, which will be sent on to the International Olympic Federation. It's full of basic information like our birthdays and our favorite hobbies and TV shows, along with more personal medical information in case something happens to us while we're in Japan.

I'm glad I said goodbye to my parents earlier, because I definitely missed the time they left by more than an hour. And then suddenly all of us are in an elevator, the same one I took upstairs with Leo, and it's completely silent. Seven when there should be eight.

I pull out my phone and quickly type a message to Dani I've wanted to send since we first got the news.

Are you okay?

For the briefest moment, there's a small bubble with a ". . ." and then nothing. She saw the text and maybe even started to type a reply, but then decided not to answer. Or someone stopped her from answering.

By the time I look up from my phone again, Emma and I are at our door and she's letting us in. The room is a bit neater, but still mostly the mess we left it in that morning. There's stuff everywhere— makeup strewn across the bathroom counters, training clothes, street clothes for the small amount of time we actually got to spend not in the gym, leos and the special underwear that goes beneath them, regular underwear and bras, what looks like an entire slab of half-empty water bottles, and a lot of towels.

"Em, did you text Dani? She's not answering me."

"No," she says and yanks her suitcase off the luggage rack in the corner of the room, tossing it on her bed and throwing her clothes into it. "C'mon. We have to pack. Pauline said we have to leave for the airport in less than an hour."

"Em, seriously? I know stuff never bothers you, but how are you not freaked out by this?"

She sighs heavily and plops down on the bed beside me. "I *am* freaked out by it, but I don't want to think about it. Like, I know it sounds selfish, but I can't focus on Dani because the Olympics are nearly here and I'm supposed to—I'm supposed to win everything, and if I don't focus on that, I can't . . ."

And there it is. The moment when making the team isn't enough. It's the truth, though. We're not going to the Olympics for the experience. We're going to win. Her shoulders are drawn up near her ears, and her eyes are faraway. She's getting in her own head, and that can be a scary place, so I crack a joke to break the tension.

"I mean, you can *try* to win bars, but we both know how that's going to turn out."

Emma snorts. "Sorry, you're going to have to settle for silver there, Rey."

"We'll see."

I check my phone again. Dani still hasn't responded.

"If I got kicked off the Olympic team, I don't think I'd be answering my texts," Emma says, rolling over on her side and propping herself up on her elbow.

"You're not even curious?"

"What are you going to say if she answers?"

"I . . ." I trail off. I have absolutely no idea.

"Exactly," Emma says when my silence stretches out long enough. She sighs and reaches down to grab my hand. "You know what I think?"

"What?"

"I think we should think about all of this after the Olympics. Preferably on a beach somewhere with cabana boys who bring us drinks with umbrellas and the only gymnastics we worry about is whether or not you'll be doing any with Leo Adams back at the hotel."

"Oh my God," I protest, grabbing one of the pillows and thwacking her right in the stomach. "You're seriously deluded. I just met him."

"We've known him for years."

"That's not really . . . I mean, liking posts isn't *knowing* someone," I protest. It might feel like it is, but it's really not.

The words are barely out of my mouth when my phone blings.

It's a message from Leo—a picture of him, his green eyes still a little bleary from a long night of travel. I grin and quickly snap a shot of myself, crinkling up my nose and making a funny expression.

"Is that him?" Emma asks. "Twice in one day! Take a picture and tell him I'm stealing you from him." She mashes her mouth against my temple in the worst fake-romantic moment ever. I follow her instructions and send it, which results in a bunch of laughing emojis.

"It sucks he had to leave last night. Not that you would have had time to hang out with him today, though." She flops back onto the bed with a sigh. "God, I won Olympic trials yesterday, and you totally managed to top it." She's laughing, but there's a note of honesty in her voice. It's an odd feeling. I'm not sure if in all the time I've known her, Emma has ever been jealous of me.

"I promise you, cute boys absolutely do not top winning trials, and we'll find you a super-hot guy on that beach we're gonna go to after Tokyo."

"We better. I am never, ever going to look as good as I do right now. We are physical specimens, and we need to take advantage of it before we eat ourselves into oblivion postgymnastics."

A knock sounds at the door. "Ladies, are you all packed? Our car will be here soon!" Pauline calls from the hallway.

Together, we leap from the bed and stare at each other in panic. Then, as one, we start tossing the weeks' worth of clothes into our bags, not even bothering to check what belongs to who. We'll figure it out when we get home. One week of training back in New York, then it's off to NGC training camp, and from there, on to Tokyo and the Olympic Games.

chapter five

Sweat runs down my back in rivulets, and my chest heaves as I try to catch my breath. My lungs are screaming for air, and my back is throbbing. I grit my teeth and twist around, stretching the tight muscles as much as possible, trying to free up my range of motion. I had physical therapy this morning. Now, just a few hours of pounding later, the pain is back.

At least training is almost over.

The balloons and streamers from this morning's send-off party are still hanging up in the corner of the gym. One balloon escaped from its bunch and is bouncing up in the rafters of the hangar-size building that I've trained in since I was four years old.

Emma's floor music is tinny through the crappy gym speakers, but it's actually better that we can barely hear it. During competition, you never know what will happen with your music. It might start at the wrong point or skip or cut out altogether, so it's better to learn not to rely on it for your cues.

"You got it, Em," I yell as she steadies herself in the corner for her first tumbling pass. Pauline has us building our endurance for the Games as much as possible, and that means multiple full floor routines each session.

I rotate my neck and twist my hips, trying to stretch away the ache exacerbated by four tumbling passes and a minute and a half of choreography. My breathing starts to return to seminormal by the time Emma's reached her second tumbling pass. The pain isn't gone—let's be real, it's never really gone, not without cortisone—but it's manageable, enough for another clean routine.

"Make that a one-tenth, not a three-tenth, step!" Pauline corrects. Emma doesn't react, but she definitely heard the critique. It's been Pauline's mantra since we got back from trials: building endurance, minimizing deductions.

Emma lines herself up for her final tumbling pass, hesitating for a moment to take a deep breath, then runs into a roundoff back handspring double pike with a small step back to steady herself.

"Good!" Pauline calls, pulling her long blond hair up into a ponytail, her attention still focused on Emma's last bit of choreography before Copland's "Hoedown" comes to a crashing end. "Looking more and more like gold every time!"

Emma rises from the floor and salutes the judges for the day—the group of the junior girls who threw us the party. Pauline asked them to watch, providing slightly more pressure than a normal routine run-through.

"Okay, let's go, Rey," Pauline says, done with her ponytail and moving to change the music in the ancient CD player from Emma's to mine.

While Emma's floor routine is true Americana—even though hoedown music for a girl from the Upper East Side is a bit of a stretch—mine is almost blasphemously balletic. It wouldn't be out of place on the Russian team.

Modern American gymnastics has embraced pulse-pounding music, big choreography, and songs the crowd can clap along to.

Me? I prefer to stun the audience—and the judges—into silence, maybe make them shed a tear or two.

Most of my routine's difficulty comes from my dance elements. Tumbling wasn't my strength, even before my injuries— well-executed leaps and turns were always more my thing. If I hadn't fallen in love with flipping through the air, I'd probably have ended up across the East River at one of the city's ballet schools.

"C'mon, Rey," Emma pants between sips of water.

"Let's go, Rey!" the juniors shout in unison. I force a smile onto my face, wanting to make sure the kids know I appreciate the support, but it's tough to expend energy on anything beyond keeping the pain at bay.

With a deep breath, I move into my starting position, arms hanging at my sides, head down, breathing slowly to keep my heart rate as low as possible before the routine speeds it up. My music begins, an orchestral arrangement of "Moon River." I let my arms flow around me for a moment as the harp strings lead the music into its melody, but then I'm dancing into my first tumbling pass. It's a two and a half twist into a front full, and it's hell on my back. I put it at the beginning to get it out of the way before the rest of the routine scrapes away my endurance along with my tolerance for the sting of stopping a twist twice in quick succession.

"I'm not seeing your connection to the music, Audrey. Sell it!" Pauline demands.

I resist the urge to roll my eyes in the middle of the routine. It's tough to show an emotional connection to the music when your back is as screwed up as mine, but I push past it and try harder.

I need that performance factor to woo the judges into a slightly higher execution score.

My routine is nearly at an end when she says, "And now push," before I power into my final tumbling pass, a double back. I crunch down a bit and hop forward, but I'm able to control the landing before lifting my arms with the final notes of the music and tilting my head back gracefully.

"Beautiful," Emma says, applauding when I salute.

The muscle memory of the motion keeps me from wincing as I lift my arms to the junior girls who are cheering for me, but once I'm off the floor, the pain flares to life again.

"You need more lift in the double back," Pauline critiques, "but overall that was lovely. A solid leadoff routine for quals." Her words don't exactly inspire confidence; a leadoff routine in qualifications means they're banking on my score not counting. My floor is almost useless to the team once we get into finals.

"Both of you get some water and then on to vault," Pauline adds, releasing us for a short break.

The kids scatter back to their training as Emma and I grab our water bottles and move in the general direction of vault.

My phone buzzes. Emma is fiddling with the cap to her water bottle, so I glance at it quickly.

It's from Leo, a mirror selfie, his bathroom clearly visible behind him. He's got a gigantic bruise across his rib cage and he's definitely not wearing a shirt. I swallow against the way it makes my heart race.

There's a message too:

Serves me right for thinking about you when I'm surfing.

I bite my lip, my thumbs hovering over the keyboard. I want to respond like I have all week. He hasn't texted me too much. Just enough to reassure me that he's interested. It's a relief, to be honest, that he understands why I can't talk all the time. He gets me. I want to make a flirty joke back, a clever retort or maybe some kind of double entendre or a kissy-face emoji. I want him to know I'm interested too, really interested. That I've had this weird long-distance semicrush on him for years and that I want to get to know him for real and maybe actually kiss him at some point.

I've never felt this way about a guy. Sure, I've thought guys were hot, and I've kissed a few, but, like . . . more? That's never something I've considered. With Leo, though, I really, really want that. I want to talk to him about things that matter and go to concerts and shows and bad movies and dinner. I want to do other stuff too, stuff that's currently making my cheeks heat up.

It's kind of crazy how intense these feelings are, but maybe it makes sense. He gets my dreams and knows just how hard I've worked for them. I've never met anyone who understood that before. Even if we haven't known each other, for real, for very long, it feels like we have, at least in the ways that really matter.

I guess it's true. The first step to recovery is admitting you have a problem. I have a Leo Adams problem. Then again, should a guy with sparkling green eyes and an adorable grin, a guy who looks like he does without a shirt on and can make my toes curl with the brush of his hand against mine, ever be defined as a problem?

I don't think so.

A kid blasts off the springboard onto the vault and jars me back to reality.

"Break's over, ladies," Pauline says, and I send back a quick heart emoji before tossing my phone aside.

"Who was that?" Emma whispers.

"Leo," I whisper back, and she lets out a happy squeak before we turn our attention to Pauline.

"Both of you, full run-through like you're warming up in the arena. A timer, then the one and a half, Rey. Emma, a timer and then the two and a half."

Putting our water bottles down after another quick sip, we both race for the end of the vault run, just like we will in competition. The key to vault is to get as warm as you can, as fast as you can. There isn't a lot of time to work up to your full difficulty like we'd normally do in training sessions. You've got to get your shit together fast.

"Air awareness, girls! Impress me."

I shake out my ankles and then take a deep, steadying breath before striding at a measured speed down the runway. I vault a simple timer, letting my body flip just once through the air before landing on the mat and bouncing to kill the rest of the power. It feels okay—I mean it hurts, obviously, but the normal hurt—and I move back to the board to adjust it so Emma can go next.

"Good, Rey. Nice block on that one. Almost like old times."

I was never a spectacular vaulter, but I'd been consistently landing a double and working my way up to a two and a half when my back let me know it wasn't on board with that upgrade to the famed Amanar vault that every elite gymnast aspires to land. There wouldn't even be double twists anymore, replaced by a comparatively easy one and a half that I need to nail almost perfectly to avoid getting hammered by the judges.

It's a pretty well-accepted reality in elite gymnastics that the lower the difficulty, the harsher the judges will be on execution. Sometimes it's a self-fulfilling prophecy. An athlete might have lower difficulty because she's not a good enough gymnast to execute more complex skills and routines, but after studying it pretty carefully over the years I've come to realize that it's mostly just the judges being pretentious dipshits.

I move back to the end of the run as Emma vaults her own timer and wait until Pauline resets the springboard before I go through my vault routine again.

A deep breath, up on my toes, and then forward to the horse, a roundoff back handspring and block backward off the vault. I tuck my arms into my body, making myself as aerodynamic as possible as I spin, and then I'm opening up. It's a blind landing, but I know exactly where I am in the air. I hop forward once, then stand tall and salute. That was a good one, but it hurt like a bitch.

"Nice! Bet it didn't feel great, though," Pauline echoes my thoughts, and I fight back the laugh.

I nod once, not wanting to dwell on the pain. "You want another?"

"Yep," she says. "If this were Tokyo, that would have been the warm-up."

As I walk back to the end of the run, Emma salutes with confidence and launches herself down the runway into a beautifully executed two and a half, with a small step forward for control.

"Yes! That was it, Emma!" Pauline yells with a sharp clap of her hands. "You bring that vault to Tokyo, and Kareva won't be able to touch you—with or without her triple."

They set up the springboard again for me, shifting it a little farther away from the horse.

Emma gives me a thumbs-up as I prep one more time, a graceful salute, toeing the perfect spot on the run to begin and then a back handspring into the one and a half. This one is a little overcooked, with a sharp lunge at the end that will cost me at least three-tenths in execution. *Damn it.*

"Well done," Pauline says, but her eyes are narrowed and her mouth is tight. There isn't much point in correcting it. As the weakest vaulter on the team, I'll probably only go up in qualifications, when we're allowed to drop our lowest score. Still, doing your best work in warm-ups is a waste.

I rise up and down on my toes. My back doesn't feel any worse than before. "I'm going again." Pauline opens her mouth to argue, but then closes it and doesn't protest, so I spin away and make for the end of the run.

"Audrey, that last one was fine," Emma says, taking a long drink from her water bottle.

"Just one more," I whisper.

This rotation I do a timer and then a full and then finally the one and a half, and the final vault is much cleaner than my previous attempt.

"Good job, Rey," Pauline says. "It's noon. You two are done for the day."

I shake my head, distracted. I want to go again, make sure that this combination of warm-ups is what will work. "Nah," I say, walking away again, twisting back and forth at the waist. The pain is the same, no better, but no worse, so I push it to the back of my mind.

I've gotten really good at that over the last two years. I'm fine. I can go again.

———

"I just wanted to go one more time," I grumble from my seat in the pedicure chair in the salon around the corner from Emma's apartment. It's tradition to get mani-pedis before we head out to a major competition. The salon is super chic, way nicer than the one my mom and I go to back across the river in Queens, but Emma's treating, so I wasn't about to argue.

"And she let you go three more times. You *always* want to go one more time," Emma retorts from the chair beside me. "It's how you ended up with that whole situation to begin with." She motions vaguely to my back. She's right. I know she's right, but there's just so little gymnastics left in my future, I want to do as much of it as possible before it's all over.

"And I know how you feel, Rey—you want it all to be perfect—but haven't you learned by now that it's impossible?"

I send her a side-eye and mutter to myself.

"What's that?"

"You know me too well," I repeat, louder this time.

Our phones buzz simultaneously. It's the group chat we've got with all the other girls. Sierra sent a video of her bars routine.

I click out of the clip before it even ends.

"She's just trying to psych you out," Emma says, shrugging.

"I know, and I refuse to take her seriously. She's not better than me on bars."

"It's Sierra—like, what do you expect?"

"I expect my *teammate* to stop passive-aggressively hinting that she's going to beat me out for a spot in the bars final."

"Well, it's the only event final she has a shot to make, you know?"

"Yeah, just that and the all-around," I shoot back, trying not to sound bitter. With Dani out, Sierra is the next-best all-around gymnast we have, and while I've resigned myself to the fact that an all-around medal probably isn't in my future, it still hurts to think about.

"Excuse me?" a little voice asks from beside Emma's chair. The woman doing Emma's nails tries to shoo her away, but Emma shakes her head.

"Hi," she says, smiling down at a little girl, probably, like, seven or eight, with a piece of paper and pen in her hand.

"Can I have your autograph and will you take a picture with me?"

"Sure!" Emma says just as the pedicurist finishes the last stroke of polish on her pinkie toe. She gingerly gets down from the raised chair, signs the paper for the little girl, and then poses for a picture. The girl's mom takes a few shots with her phone before she quickly draws her daughter away.

"You're so famous," I tease as we head over to the dryers to lock in the polish for at least a few days before training completely destroys it.

"It's so weird," she says. "Like, a few people recognized me after worlds, but now, after those commercials launched . . ." She trails off. Emma is the new spokes-athlete for Nike. There are a bunch of billboards around the city with her face on them and a whole series of commercials airing during the lead-up to the Games.

"My best friend is a star, so it's my duty to give you crap about it."

"I expect nothing less," she says, and we dissolve into giggles.

Emma snorts and checks her phone. "Did your parents look over the proposal Steve sent?"

"Yeah, and they're good with it."

"Wait, what? You're going to sign with him? Why didn't you say anything today?"

I shrug helplessly. "I don't know. It's cool, but it's only, like, during the Games. You need individual success to really get people interested."

Steve is going to represent me too. Obviously, since I'm distinctly *not* the national or world champion and *not* favored to win the all-around in Tokyo, no one's exactly banging down the doors to put me on billboards, but there are a few companies who'd like to sponsor me.

"Maybe I should just *let* you win bars."

My eyes flash to her. "Don't say things like that. It's bad luck."

She groans. "Jeez, I was *kidding*."

An awkward twisting in my gut doesn't let me drop the subject. "Okay, look, it's fine to joke about competing against each other, and maybe it's a little bit goody-goody of me, but, like, after what happened with Dani, I don't want anything else tainting this experience. That's the whole point of the Olympics, isn't it? To go out there, do our best, and see who comes out on top."

Emma stares at me for a good five seconds in silence, and then she nods.

"Yeah, definitely. That's the point."

chapter six

"You seem tense," Dr. Gupta says as he prods my lower back with his gloved hand. The analgesic gel is cold against my skin. The spot has mostly gone numb, but getting the rest of my body to relax after being in near-constant pain since the effects of my last shot wore off is a losing battle. The injury is chronic; it started more than five years ago, and the pain will never really go away as long as I'm training. Even then, I'm probably in for a life sentence of dealing with issues there.

But gymnastics is worth it. The Olympics are worth it.

Mom laughs from her seat in the corner of the exam room. "Have you ever seen her not tense?" she asks, and Dr. G laughs too.

"Stop mocking me and make the pain go away." I deliberately add a whine to my voice.

"Unclench first," Dr. G orders with a snort. "You know the drill."

Breathing in deep and then letting it out, I try my best to release the tension from my muscles. It's far easier for him to do his job if I'm relaxed.

I watch the screen to my left as the needle is inserted and the miracle drug is applied to my lower back. Dr. Gupta always puts a local anesthetic into the injection as well, and thus my back goes pleasantly numb almost immediately.

"Good," he says, nodding to the technician operating the ultrasound machine. "Give yourself a minute, and then try and stretch out as much as you can."

"Thanks." I roll over and then sit up, letting my shirt fall back into place. The relief isn't instantaneous. It always takes a couple of days before cortisone really works on me.

"Yes, thank you, Dr. Gupta," Mom says, standing up to shake his hand.

"No thanks necessary," he says, pulling off his gloves and tossing them into the trash can. "Bring back some medals and take a picture with me to put on my wall."

Dr. Gupta is one of the best doctors in the state. A ton of pro athletes—including several of my beloved Yankees—see him regularly. He has a wall with pictures of all of them with Super Bowl and World Series rings, plus a couple with the Stanley Cup. I have one up there with my medals from world championships two years ago (a team gold and uneven bars silver), but an Olympics picture would be even more epic. Two gold medals are the dream. One for the team, another on uneven bars. Two medals to hang around my neck so I can pose with Dr. Gupta as he points at them with pride.

"Good luck in Tokyo," he says with a wink before leaving the room.

I stand, still bracing myself on the exam table, and slide my sandals back on to my feet. I should probably be wearing sneakers for the support, but honestly, I always make sure to put together a look for my trips to Dr. G's in case a Yankee or two is wandering around for treatment. I'd die of embarrassment if I ran into Aaron Judge while wearing schlubby clothes. My gold strappy sandals and matching gold sparkly nail polish set off the gold shimmery tank and hunter-green shorts I meticulously paired together last night. I reach down to touch my toes and then twist at the hips. Moving around after a shot is necessary to make sure the medicine gets where it needs to go.

"You ready?" Mom asks, hooking her bag over her shoulder.

"Yep!" I grab my phone and take a quick selfie with my thumbs up.

@Rey_Lee: Dr. G says I'm ready to go! Tokyo here I come!

And then a quick message to Leo with a picture of the gigantic needle that just went in my back because he's a boy and he'll be impressed.

Predictably, he replies immediately with *Awesome!!*

I already said goodbye to Dad this morning, and Mom is taking me straight to JFK to meet up with Pauline and Emma for our flight out to Los Angeles.

There's a car waiting for us at the curb with my luggage already inside: two huge suitcases full of everything I'll need. The trip to the departures gate isn't long—Dr. Gupta's office is only twenty minutes from the airport.

Mom holds my hand for the entire ride, and every once in a while she squeezes it. I squeeze back. Weirdly, I feel like I'm the one giving reassurance to her, rather than the other way around.

"You know how proud we are of you, right? No matter what happens," she says, squeezing my hand a little tighter.

"I know." I try to push away the feeling that she really means *Even if you don't win.*

We hit a little bit of traffic on the ramp leading to the drop-off curb, and I squeeze her hand again. She looks away, craning her neck to try and see past the driver's head at whatever traffic is holding us up.

My throat thickens at the idea that I'll be away from my parents for so long—almost a month. It's weird because that's never bothered me before. When I went to worlds two years ago, the separation was as long as this one will be, but this feels different, like it's the end of something beyond my gymnastics career.

No. Stop it. Thinking about that is a bad idea, Audrey. No thinking about how there are only a few weeks left of gymnastics, a few weeks until you have to figure out the rest of your life. That the Olympics will be the most important experience of your life, and you have to do it without your parents by your side.

Sniffling away the emotion, I turn to the window, using my free hand to wipe away a tear that escapes. I can't cry. If I cry, then Mom will *definitely* cry, and that'll set off Emma's mom, and we'll all be sobbing messes in no time with Pauline rolling her eyes at us being *sentimental*, her least favorite thing. So I swallow back the tears, and with a few deep breaths I smother down the emotion.

We finally reach the curb, and Mom gives my hand another squeeze. The driver leaps out of the car and opens the door for us. Emma and her parents are already on the sidewalk with her luggage. Her parents don't really work, per se. They both come from old money—like Sons of Liberty and the Daughters of the American

Revolution old—and their penthouse with Central Park views speaks for itself. My parents—a cardiologist and a CUNY professor—do pretty well, but the Sadowskys leave us in the dust.

"How was Dr. G?" Emma asks, her eyes dancing with mischief. "Are you all fixed?"

"Yep, good as new. I'll be busting out Amanars by the time we land."

The driver brings around our luggage, and horns blare in protest at our prolonged stay on the curb.

I pull Mom into an extra-long hug.

"Take care of yourself, sweetheart. Text me as soon as you get settled at the training center and let me know how the first day goes."

Nodding, I pull away and smile up at her as Emma finishes her goodbyes. Our parents get back into the cars, all of them wiping at misty eyes. We stand with Pauline, watching the black cars pull away into the sea of vehicles. This is it, then.

"Okay, ladies," she says, straightening her shoulders and using her firmest coaching voice. "IDs and boarding passes out. Let's get going."

I send a sidelong glance at Emma, who rolls her eyes at Pauline's impatience with any emotion that isn't grim satisfaction or controlled disappointment. The thing is, though, that mind-set works pretty well when you've got weeks of intense training and the most important competition of your life looming at the end of them. It's why Pauline is a great coach and how she turned Emma and me into great gymnasts capable of sticking landings and winning medals.

So, as she marches into the airport, commandeering a luggage cart and pretending to be oblivious as she briskly cuts in front of a large group of people to get into the security line, I smile. We fall in behind her, keeping our heads down, letting her lead the way. She's gotten us this far, and I wouldn't want to do it with anyone else.

———

"How did you do that?" Emma asks as we put our seat backs into their full upright and locked positions, like the captain asked over the intercom.

"Do what?" I ask, yawning and stretching forward with my fingers interlocked.

"Pass out the minute we took off and wake up as we're landing," she shoots back with a disgruntled wrinkle of her nose.

I shrug, relaxing back into the seat. Mostly, it was because I didn't sleep a wink last night while my back spasmed like crazy and I freaked out about heading to Olympic camp, but I can't really tell Emma that. She's never had a major injury before, and she doesn't stress. Ever. It's like she's got some kind of anxiety-repellent skin. Everything slides off her.

Deplaning at LAX is always an adventure when we're traveling to Gibby's gym, but it's rare that we're noticed among the actual celebrities coming and going all the time. Apparently, those days are over.

Photographers mob us as soon as soon as we enter baggage claim.

"Emma! Audrey! Emma! Look over here, girls!"

The reporters press forward, their flashes and shouts coming in rapid fire.

I try to imitate Emma's ease as she blithely ignores them, looking cool and composed despite it all. Security surrounds us, quickly helping us gather our bags and move through the crowd and out to a waiting car. It's one of those sleek, high-end vans with three rows of captain's chairs and a ton of legroom.

There's plenty of time to catch our breath. The ride to Gibby's gym, otherwise known as the National Gymnastics Committee Training Center, is stop-and-go all the way. LA traffic is never cooperative. I shoot a quick text to my mom and then snap a silly picture with a scrunched-up nose for Leo. He messages back almost immediately: a picture with one eye closed in an exaggerated and really freaking adorable wink.

Emma's in the seat beside me, trying to nap, and when I turn to Pauline to ask how long she thinks it's going to take, her eyes are firmly fixed on her phone and her thumbs are moving over it like mad. I know better than to talk to her when she has *that* particular look on her face—eyes narrowed, mouth set in a thin line.

Finally, the van comes to a halt beside the huge chrome-and-glass building. The air is warm around us as we climb out and smells of hot asphalt and car exhaust, a lot like home, just without the crushing humidity. Yep, we're definitely in LA.

"About time you got here!" Chelsea says, coming out of the front door with a huge smile on her face.

Emma laughs. "Some of us don't live fifteen minutes away!"

Chelsea hugs me—apparently, we're friends who casually hug

hello now—and then she pulls Emma in too. Their friendship is less new, since they bonded at worlds last year. "Is everyone else here?"

"Sierra and Jaime's plane was delayed out of Oklahoma City," Chelsea says.

We freeze and fall silent as Gibby comes out through the doors.

"Ladies, welcome," he says, nodding to us as he goes to greet Pauline at the curb.

"C'mon," Chelsea says once he passes us entirely, and we follow her into the glass atrium, dragging our suitcases behind us.

The door is barely closed before Chelsea says, "Rumor has it we're having our first internal competition tomorrow. Gibson wants to start figuring out rotation order as soon as possible."

Tomorrow morning? My heart rate launches itself into a full-fledged sprint. I was hoping he would give us a day or two to train under his eye before pitting us against one another.

It shouldn't matter, not really, where you compete relative to your teammates, but tradition is that scores build as teams compete, so the first and second gymnasts on an event tend to bring in lower scores. I need to be in the top spot on bars and at least second to last on beam to make the impression I want in qualifications and secure spots in both event finals. So, while Emma's one of my favorite people, the goal for the next few days is to come out ahead of her.

"Room assignments!" Gibby calls from behind us, making me jump. "Emma and Chelsea, you're together. Jaime and Sierra, obviously, when they arrive. Hope you don't mind a single, Audrey. You were originally supposed to bunk with Dani, but, well . . ." He raises his hands in a gesture of defeat, like he doesn't have any choice but to make me room by myself, like every single thing between now and the Games isn't his call. And like splitting up me and Emma isn't totally on purpose, making sure we stay mentally strong without each other as roommates in the next few weeks.

Sorry, Emma mouths silently as we all head inside toward the back of the facility, where the dorms are located. The training center has been a near constant in my life. Emma and I made our first junior national team when we were twelve, and since then, every few months we'd trek across the country to show Gibby and the NGC staff our skills and upgrades. It's like a second home, with Gibby serving as our overbearing father with a penchant for mind games and manipulation, passive-aggressively getting the most out of us as athletes, no matter the cost.

My name is on the door to one of the rooms, and I drag my luggage inside, lifting both suitcases onto the bed I decide not to take. Giggling and chattering plus the sound of suitcases banging against the walls of the narrow hallway float in, and my brain registers that Jaime and Sierra have arrived.

"Hey, Audrey!" they chorus together as they pass the door and move into the room across the hall.

"Hi!" I yell back. I'm actually glad I don't have to deal with their double act right now. They can be exhausting, and I don't have any mental energy to waste. All of my focus has to be on beam and bars so I can get the spots at the end of the rotation.

I have to get changed, and there's a pile of official Team USA gear sitting on the dresser. On top is a training leo, dark blue and sleeveless with a sequined star on the chest packaged with a black Team USA T-shirt and a pair of black shorts. Tucked inside the package is a note that says FIRST PRACTICE.

Okay, then: black and blue it is, because dressing in bruise colors isn't ominous at all. Visions of ice baths and cupping and heat packs swim in my mind's eye. The next few weeks are going to be the most difficult of my life, but I've been preparing for more than a decade. I know what I need to do, and I'm going to do it.

I change quickly, stretching out my back as I go. The warm-ups we run through at camp are thorough, but not nearly as focused on my core as I need them to be.

A pounding on my door is quickly followed by Emma's "Let's go!" and a few seconds later I'm out in the hallway with the rest of them, headed straight for the main gym.

"We're competing tomorrow?" Sierra whispers to Emma.

"Yep, nothing like getting tossed in the deep end, huh?" Chelsea jokes.

"For real," I agree.

It's fine. It's going to be fine. I need to kick ass. I can *totally*—

My thoughts are cut off when I literally run into Chelsea's back. "What the hell?" I ask, but looking up I immediately see why she came to such a sudden stop.

FBI agents are swarming the atrium ahead of us. Cars with cherry lights spinning wildly sit parked beyond the large glass walls of the front entrance. Two agents emerge from the crowd with someone between them. I push up on my toes to try and see past Chelsea's head, and my entire being freezes in shock.

Gibby's eyes are wild, looking around for rescue, but the agents have him by both arms, secured with handcuffs. There's no escape.

As they lead him to the door, one of the agents says, "Christopher Gibson, you're under arrest."

chapter seven

Gymnasts flipping on the beam and lining up at the vault, coaches off to the side chatting, music blaring through the speakers, the volume turned up so loud that the bass pulses through my chest with every beat. Anyone would think it was a normal day at the NGC Training Center.

Until they look outside.

The glass walls of the main training gym normally frame out a bustling LA street, cars and pedestrians racing through their day, unconcerned with the gymnasts flipping and flying inside.

Today, though, paparazzi crowd the sidewalk and news vans line the street, reporters huddling just outside the front door, waiting for someone, anyone, to come outside and comment.

But that's not the really distracting part. That's just the bullshit icing on the what-the-actual-fuck cake that this day has been.

What's really holding my attention is what's going on across the gym, beyond the metal beams in the rafters holding up banner after banner proclaiming success of the NGC and the USA gymnastics team, behind the closed door of the training center's conference room. The same room Gibby and his staff used to determine our fates during national team and world championship selection camps. The same room where he would have chosen the order we'd compete in once we arrived in Tokyo.

The FBI is using that room to question everyone: NGC staff, personal coaches, and athletes alike. Pauline's in there right now, which is the only reason why Emma and I are getting away with standing at the chalk bowl, pretending to get ready for bars.

"What do you think they're asking her?" Emma whispers. "What do you think they're going to ask us?"

With a shrug, I dig into the chalk, which will give me a decent grip on the bars when it's my turn, because a bars routine is definitely the best thing to take my mind off the fact that our coach just got led away in handcuffs.

Bam!

Thwap!

"Ugh."

The groan spills out from Jaime as she rolls over on the vault mats, her face twisted in pain after landing flat on her back. "I'm okay," she manages to say as she gingerly gets to her feet and shakes out her limbs, proving it to us and maybe herself too.

"This is ridiculous," Chelsea says, joining us at the bowl. "Someone is going to get hurt, like seriously hurt. How the hell are we supposed to focus?"

She's got her phone out, and my vision flies wildly around the gym, hoping that none of the NGC staff notices. "Are you crazy?" I ask through clenched teeth.

"Gibby's not here to tell me to put my phone away. None of these people are actually in charge, and they've told us literally nothing about what's going on, so I don't see why we . . ." she says as she continues to scroll. "Oh my God."

"What?" Emma and I ask together, moving to her shoulders to look at the screen.

BREAKING: US GYMNASTICS COACH FALSIFIED DRUG TEST RESULTS

Flicking away from the article before we can read beyond the headline, Chelsea immediately opens a text message. Dani's name is at the top, along with a bunch of unanswered texts Chelsea sent over the last week. She taps out a message at lightning speed and clicks send.

Did he mess with your drug test?!

I inhale, holding my breath when those three dots appear.

. . .

. . .

. . .

And then finally . . .

Yes.

I breathe out.

"I knew Dani wouldn't cheat. That asshole set her up," Chelsea bites out.

"That can't be true," Emma whispers to me. "Why would he do that?"

I pull up the article on my own phone, and it goes through the timeline pretty quickly: that Dani's "failed" test was from just before trials and the reporting agency had her results listed as negative, totally fine. So Gibby messed with the results.

Was that enough to get arrested by the FBI? Lying about a drug test? Sure, it's shitty, but a crime? I don't know. Fraud maybe? But that still leaves the question, why would Gibby do that? Dani wasn't doping. That definitely makes sense. But Gibby messing with the results? What would kicking his second-best gymnast off the team just weeks before the Olympics accomplish?

"Audrey!" Pauline's voice carries through the cavernous space. My head jerks up.

"I guess it's my turn." I unstrap my grips, trying to keep my hands from shaking when I release them into the chalk bowl.

I hadn't thought we'd ever have to talk with anyone official about Dani's doping—or, I guess, not doping? What the hell am I supposed to tell these people? I don't know anything.

Pauline shoots me a tight smile when I meet her at the door and reaches for my shoulder, probably to give it an encouraging squeeze, but she stops halfway and then leads me into the room.

"Audrey Lee?" the suited man asks, offering me his hand to shake. My handshake is firm, like my dad taught me, so firm a layer of chalk slides from my hand to his.

"Shit!" I cringe. "Oh, wait, sorry, I . . ."

Cursing in front of the Feds. That's a great jumping-off point for an interrogation, Audrey.

The agent chuckles and then shakes his head before using the pocket square in his suit jacket to wipe off his hands. "We've heard worse, I promise. I'm Special Agent Greg Farley, and this is my partner, Special Agent Michelle Kingston." I shake her hand as well. "We're from the FBI. If you don't mind, we have a few questions for you."

The conference room is one of the few private spots at the training center, no glass walls for everyone to see through, just drywall and paint, lined with photographs of Gibby and the gymnasts who've trained here over the years. I'm on that wall multiple times, pictures chronicling my career better than even my mom had with her newspaper clippings and memory books. My first developmental camp awards ceremony, where I won physical abilities testing, all the way through when I was named to the world championship team two years ago. Every junior and senior national team I've been on since I was twelve is up there, and so are the podiums at worlds, for the team and for my uneven bars medals.

I look back and forth between Agents Farley and Kingston, the same agents who'd led Gibby away in handcuffs. How had it come to this? Our coach, the man who was supposed to lead us to Tokyo and a gold medal, decided to screw with drug tests right before the Games, and now what? He's just gone. It doesn't make any sense.

Unless . . . what?

Unless he wanted Sierra on the team over Dani all along and couldn't get the rest of the committee to agree? But why would he want that? Dani is the stronger gymnast. If anyone would be replaced by Sierra because of gymnastics, well, it'd be me.

"Do you understand, Miss Lee?" Agent Kingston asks, breaking off my own totally amateur mental investigation for her legit one.

First cursing and now zoning out. *Oh my God, get yourself together, Audrey.*

"I'm sorry, what?"

"Your coach," Agent Kingston says, her eyes flickering over my shoulder to Pauline, "has informed us that over the years she's served as a legal guardian when your parents were unavailable. She has paperwork to that effect, but we want to make sure that's okay with you. We can call them if you want, but you're not in any trouble, Audrey. We're simply trying to get a complete picture of the current situation."

I hesitate and look back to Pauline, who smiles again, but the tension around her eyes is obvious. Nodding, I shift in my seat, sitting up straighter, folding my hands in my lap, and looking back and forth between the two agents, eyebrows raised.

Agent Kingston begins in a soft voice, "What can you tell us about the night you made the Olympic team?"

"I already told you, she doesn't know anything," Pauline cuts in, and all three of us stare at her. She's fiddling with the end of her ponytail. The last time I saw her doing that was at worlds during Emma's final rotation, but I don't think I've ever seen this particular expression on her face. Jaw set, brow furrowed, her eyes darting back and forth between the two agents like she doesn't know where she should be looking.

"Ma'am, if you're going to hinder this interview—"

"Wait." I glance back at Pauline and then look the agents in the eye, one after the other. "It's fine . . . I just . . . Do you want the whole day?"

"Just start after it was announced you made the team."

I have no idea what any of this has to do with drug tests, but they're the investigators, not me. So I tell them about my interviews and back pain, then about my drug test taking forever and about being last on the bus and going to the reception party and meeting Leo and getting that text from Emma about the party.

"Did you go to the party?"

I wrinkle my nose and have to actively stop myself from glancing back to Pauline. Pretty sure she didn't know about Emma and me partying all night in that suite. Not that it should matter at this point. I mean, I'm being questioned by FBI agents and my head coach has been arrested. Perspective and all that, right?

"Yeah, Leo walked me back to my room and we . . ." Do I have to tell them about the almost-kiss? "And we said good night," I mumble, hoping that's enough to get the point across. The agents both smile, maybe making more of it than it actually was.

I catch Pauline's reflection in one of the picture frames over the agents' heads, her mouth twisted into a frown, but I'm not about to lie. I watch the news. Lying to the FBI is a crime, and way bigger fish than me have gone to jail for it. "He had a flight to catch, so he left right after that, and then Emma and I went to the party."

"Did you see Daniela Olivero there?"

"I . . ." I start and then hesitate. I thought Dani had been there, but did I actually see her? "No, I don't think so."

"Do you remember the last time you saw her that night?"

"Um . . . maybe . . . maybe at the reception for a minute, but I . . . I was distracted."

Agent Kingston nods sympathetically, the way I'm sure she was trained to do when dealing with younger people she's interrogating, probably to make me feel safe and more willing or some bullshit. "It's okay if you don't remember, Audrey. Just do your best."

"Okay."

My palms are sweaty and sliding against each other, despite the chalk that's still caked in each line and crevice.

"Did you receive any texts that night, besides the one from Emma?"

"No, I don't . . . Oh, wait, yes, I did, from Gibby—er, Coach Gibson."

"And what did it say?"

Crap—I don't remember exactly, just the feeling it gave me. "I think it was something like that I should celebrate that night, but remember what he told me or said to me, something like that, just like a reminder."

Agent Farley's eyes light up. "A reminder of what?"

That part I know. "That I needed to work hard on my beam connections in the next few weeks. I haven't really hit them solidly all season, and that's important if I want to medal."

The agents nod and make some notes. I turn to Pauline, who smiles at me tightly and sends me an approving nod.

"Okay, I think that's it," Agent Kingston says, nodding to me.

I take that as my cue to leave.

"Emma Sadowsky is next. Would you mind sending her back here, Audrey?" Agent Farley says.

"Sure."

The tension in my shoulders releases the moment I step through the door. The other coaches are nearby, and the gymnasts are all gathered where I left Chelsea and Emma, lying on the mats.

"Em," I say, approaching the group and nodding behind me. "You're up."

"Was it bad?" she whispers when I reach her. I hold out a hand to help her up from the mat.

"Nope, not at all. Easy."

I plop down in the spot she vacated. "So, training's done?"

"Yeah," Chelsea says, barely looking up from her phone but handing mine to me.

"Thanks."

I have a bunch of notifications, and I quickly type out a message to the group chat with my mom and dad that I'm fine and I'll call them later. I skip everything else until I get to Leo.

Your coach got arrested?

Are you okay?

Read this right now!

Attached to that last message is a link, and after reassuring him that I'm okay, I open it with a swipe of my finger.

"Are you fucking kidding me?" Sierra screeches just as the article loads on my phone and . . . whoa.

BREAKING: Embattled US Gymnastics Coach Accused of Sexual Assault by Suspended Athlete

Scanning the article, it builds on the previous story, everything unfolding in a sickening timeline. *As reported earlier today, Gibson is accused of falsifying Daniela Olivero's drug test results . . . Olivero suspended under suspicious circumstances the day after Olympic trials . . . FBI alerted after she submitted to a follow-up test . . . a desperate attempt at a cover-up for his alleged yearlong sexual abuse . . .*

"Ladies!"

I force my eyes away from the utter insanity unfolding on my phone's screen.

"Line up!" an NGC official yells over the growing buzz in the gym. I think her name is Liz, but I can't be sure. I remember her from trials, though, ushering us back and forth between the locker room and the competition area and back for interviews.

Out of sheer muscle memory, we all stand and come to attention, the same way we always have in this gym whenever anyone calls out those words. My hand clutches at my phone, now hidden behind my back. I want to read that article again, even as my stomach churns at the thought of it.

"We're going to cancel training for the rest of the day," Maybe-Liz says. "We will have dinner brought to your rooms instead of gathering in the cafeteria as usual. I want everyone to get a full night's sleep. Despite our . . . circumstances, we still have an Olympic Games to prepare for, and that means tomorrow, we'll be starting our internal verifications. I expect everyone to use tonight to clear their minds of these distractions and come prepared, the way Coach Gibson would expect were he here. Do you understand?"

"Yes, ma'am," we respond in unison, and there's a weird sense of comfort in this familiar answer. It shouldn't be comfortable now, though, should it? It's should actually be terrifying.

We're ushered back to the dorms, and it's only a few minutes before Emma slips into my room. Our doors are all open, and the hallway is small enough for everyone to hear when she stops and says, "They're canceling the rest of the FBI interviews for today."

"Did you see the article?" I ask, and she nods quickly, sitting at the end of my bed while I tuck myself into the corner against the wall.

Only seconds later, Chelsea and finally Sierra and Jaime wander in. Five of us jammed into a room barely big enough for the two twin beds. Sierra and Jaime have pushed my luggage to the floor, and they take up the other bed while Chelsea paces near the door. The tension is pressing in, the silence suffocating.

"Do you guys think it's true?" Emma asks. I blink at her. Gibby was arrested right in front of her face. She has doubts? My surprise must be written on my face. "I mean, did anyone ever see him acting weird with her? Like—"

"No," Sierra gripes. "None of us saw anything because nothing was going on."

"Sierra," Jaime warns. That's a switch. Usually, Sierra is the one bossing Jaime around.

"No, I'm not going to sit here and pretend like we don't know exactly what's going on. That bitch is screwing with our gold medals."

"You mean Dani," I say.

"She failed a drug test and now she's all, *My coach raped me and everyone should feel sorry for me.*"

Seriously? How did she even come up with that?

C'mon, Audrey, you're a smart girl, think about it. Would Dani do something like that? Would she take drugs to get an edge and then accuse Gibby of raping her when she got caught? That makes even *less* sense than what the article claimed. Way less sense. So that's it, then. Gibby was abusing Dani and . . . maybe she told him no? Maybe she threatened to come forward? Whatever it was doesn't matter—he freaked out and tried to discredit her and take her dreams away in one fell swoop.

My stomach twists in revulsion thinking about this so coldly, so analytically, but I don't know if I can really let myself think about it any other way. It's too hard.

"Look, it says it right here." Sierra holds out her phone, showing an article from one of those news sites my dad rants about for the crap they publish. The headline makes me cringe.

BREAKING: Gymnast Alleges Affair with Coach after Positive Drug Test

Dani's picture is below it—not the official NGC picture that the other article used, but one she posted earlier in the summer of her in a bikini at the beach. It's so gross. Not the picture, but what they're trying to say about Dani with it. They're trying to act like she's the kind of person who'd do something like what Sierra is saying.

Chelsea is nearly shaking when she knocks Sierra's outstretched arm away and steps closer to her. "You're just pissed because she's going to take her spot back."

Now, that—that I can believe. If Dani didn't cheat, she's probably going to come back, and that means Sierra becomes an alternate again, right?

Sierra points her finger straight into Chelsea's face. "I'm pissed because that bitch cheated, and I *earned* that spot."

No, she didn't.

"You earned shit," Chelsea says, echoing my thoughts, her eyes blazing and her fist clenching at her side.

They move even closer, just inches apart.

"Oh my God, get out, everyone," I snap, standing up. They turn and stare at me, but I'm not going to back down. "You will not throw down in here. You're going to get hurt or hurt someone else. Get. Out."

Chelsea nods and steps away, but Sierra holds her ground, still breathing hard, staring at Chelsea's back as she leaves. Then after a moment, Jaime drags Sierra away, and it's just me and Emma.

"Do you want me to sleep in here?" Emma asks, eyeing the other bed. I feel like maybe she's asking for the both of us.

"Yeah."

Barely a minute later, she's dragging her suitcase across the hall and then sliding into the bed opposite me.

"We just need to sleep," she says. "We'll take a nap and eat dinner and then just sleep. A good night's sleep and we'll be ready to go tomorrow."

"Yeah," I agree. "We'll be ready to go."

———

I am *so* not ready to go. For once my body is okay—at least the parts of me that do gymnastics—but my head is pounding. Maybe it's the stress or maybe it's a side effect of the cortisone or maybe it's both. We took a nap, ate dinner, and got a good night's sleep, but I still woke up feeling like I landed a vault on my head.

Now I stand in the lineup, my eyes watering at the bright lights from the training gym's ceiling. I keep my eyes half-closed against the intense lighting and try to focus my attention on Maybe-Liz, whose name I still haven't confirmed.

"We all have to stick together and present a united front to the world in the face of the accusations that have been leveled at Coach Gibson and this team," she says with her hands behind her back and us at attention like she's a general addressing a squad of soldiers. Our coaches are lined up behind her.

Wait, the team? What does the team have to do with it? We didn't do anything wrong. I risk a glance over at Emma beside me and her eyes have narrowed and next to her, so have Chelsea's. It feels like last night our coaches came to some kind of agreement to, what, just carry on like nothing happened? How do they think that's possible?

C'mon, Audrey. Stop it. Focus. If that's what they decided, then that's what you have to do.

"We're going to keep training hard and make Coach Gibson proud and the first step to that is the internal competition he scheduled for today. We'll be doing a full all-around competition to develop baseline scores for our lineups in Tokyo."

My heartrate thunders to a new beat, pounding in my temples, setting my back teeth grinding together. Nothing else matters right now, not Gibby, not whatever the hell our coaches decided or why they decided it, nothing except my next four routines.

"Uneven bars first, just like we've all been practicing," Maybe-Liz says. I really should find out her name if she's going to be in charge. "Okay, ladies, warm up."

"Ugh, bars," Chelsea grumbles as we hustle to the chalk bowl, pulling on our bars grips as we go. Chelsea's great at a lot of things, especially vault, but bars were never her strength.

"Yay, bars," I shoot back, forcing a cheeky smile onto my face.

"Shut up," she says, nudging me softly with her elbow, but I manage to make her grin a little bit. This isn't so bad. This is normal. Chatting around the chalk bowl. It might help to just focus on gymnastics for a little while. Maybe-Liz is right about at least one thing: we still have an Olympics to train for.

"Rotation order: Jaime, Chelsea, Sierra, Emma, and then Audrey," Maybe-Liz calls out our alternate and then the worst bars worker to the best . . . me. At least I'm starting from a position of power. Of course, that means when we head to vault for the last rotation, my final impression will be my one and a half while everyone else is busting out doubles and two and a halves.

No time to think about that, though. First, I need to hit this routine like I have in training and give myself enough cushion to make it through the other three rotations. Bars should be no problem, vault and floor are what they are, and beam? We'll see.

We warm up quickly, like we will at the Games, and bars goes exactly the way I imagined. We all hit, and the scores from the NGC members acting as our judges hold from trials, building with each routine. I smile at the three-tenths margin I have on Emma.

1.	Audrey Lee	15.4
2.	Emma Sadowsky	15.1
3.	Sierra Montgomery	14.9
4.	Jaime Pederson	14.7
5.	Chelsea Cameron	13.1

It's so rare to see my name above hers in any capacity that I let myself enjoy it for maybe a moment longer than I should. I smile at her and nod at the scores, and she rolls her eyes, but her smile matches mine. That's good. That feels normal. It can only last a moment, though, because we're headed to beam, and that needs all my attention.

"Okay, ladies: beam order is Jaime, Chelsea, Audrey, Sierra, and Emma."

I grimace, unwrapping my grips and stretching out my wrists. I have work to do. Emma is fantastic on beam, and Sierra is good, but I can beat both of them if I hit my damn connections. My mount, a back handspring layout step-out onto the beam, connected in a series to two more layout step-outs, is a huge test right at the start of my routine. When I hit it, it's one of the hardest combinations performed in the history of the sport; when I don't, it's a total mess.

Jaime and Chelsea hit their routines without a hitch, and Pauline's setting up the springboard for me. I stand at the edge of the mats and push up onto my toes to prepare for my beam mount.

Inhale, then exhale before three strides forward into a round-off onto the springboard and then a layout step-out, landing one foot and then another onto the four-inch platform we're expected to spin and tumble upon like it's the floor.

My concentration on the event is usually unbroken until I've dismounted, but even through my laser focus I see the door to the gym swing open and a group of people pour through the entrance. Leading them is a woman in stiletto pumps with a perfectly shaped Afro. I recognize her immediately. It's Tamara Jackson, the head of the United States Olympic Federation.

"That was lovely, Audrey," she says as everyone stands still, gaping at her, "but please come down from the beam. This competition is over."

chapter eight

Tamara Jackson, dressed in a white suit jacket and matching pencil skirt, is simultaneously more intimidating and confidence-inspiring than anyone I've ever seen in my entire life.

With a quiet *snick*, the door to the gym closes behind our coaches and the rest of the NGC staff after she smoothly, and with minimal protest, ejects them from the room. The cavernous training gym is almost empty now. Standing in front of the beam, my eyes swing from that door back to the head of the USOF and wait for her to begin.

"Ladies," Mrs. Jackson says, smiling widely at us, her teeth bright and shiny against her deep purple lipstick. "First, I want to thank you. Your years of hard work and dedication have brought you to this point. Hundreds of thousands of young girls dream of getting to where you are right now, but only a few ever make it to the Olympic team."

My head is buzzing with her words. She means well, I'm sure, trying to take the sting out of whatever is coming next, but what could it be? So far, we've got a fake doping scandal and sexual assault. What's next? Murder? Emma's hand creeps into mine and squeezes tight.

"You've all worked so hard over the years and bonded with your coaches in a way that most people will never understand, spending more time with them than perhaps even your families, and that's why this next part is so difficult. The USOF has been made aware of some concerning information regarding the NGC's response to Coach Gibson's behavior and subsequent arrest. That also extends to the conduct of your personal coaches."

My breath catches, and, panicked, I look back to the door where Pauline and the other coaches left just a minute ago. Then my eyes meet Emma's. They've gone wide, and her mouth has actually dropped open in shock.

"What do you mean?" Chelsea asks.

"Obviously, it's an ongoing investigation, but what I can tell you is when the athlete in question's—"

"Dani," Chelsea cuts in, and Mrs. Jackson raises her eyebrows but nods.

"Yes. When Ms. Olivero's tests were delivered to Mr. Gibson, despite there being no positive results for any banned substances, he followed the doping protocol we have in place. He called a committee meeting to review the results. Your coaches and the NGC officials present here were all a part of the committee that signed off on Ms. Olivero's suspension from the team despite there being no credible evidence to support a failed drug test."

My knees start to weaken as Mrs. Jackson speaks, and bile rises in my throat, burning as I swallow it back.

Our coaches lied.

Pauline lied.

I don't want to believe it, but it all rings so very true. From back at trials and Gibby's speech about keeping NGC business within the NGC to Pauline's nerves during my interview with the FBI, even to the show of unity this morning before we got started.

Mrs. Jackson has more to say, and I refocus on her.

"The USOF has made the unprecedented decision to immediately suspend the NGC as a national governing body until at least after the Olympic Games. Going forward, I will be supervising your training along with a new USOF-appointed coach. I have all the confidence in the world in you as athletes, and though it will be difficult, I know you can get through this as a team. It's unfortunate that we have to go to these extreme measures, but please understand we cannot allow the complicity of those whose sole focus should have been your well-being to go unpunished."

Maybe I'm in shock. Maybe it's all finally become too much, and my brain can't deal with the rest of it, but I blurt out, "Can we talk to them? Our coaches, I mean." She pins me in place with her eyes. "Sorry," I whisper.

At that, her expression softens a touch.

"I'm sorry, Audrey. We've been advised by the FBI not to allow any further contact with your coaches at this time."

Chelsea clears her throat beside me. "Who is going to coach us, then?"

"You'll be introduced to your coach when we arrive at your new training facility. Rest assured, she will not only be able to prepare you for your Olympic journey, but she's uniquely qualified to handle the trauma you all have been through the last few days. Pack your things, ladies; we leave in fifteen minutes."

I'm still tossing my stuff into my bags when my door flies open. Emma slips inside and closes it behind her. For a moment, the only sound in the room is our breathing, but then our eyes meet.

Something in my chest cracks, and the tears spring into my eyes completely unbidden. I let out a choked sob. Every ounce of tension

I've been shoving down in the past few days, maybe even since back at trials, bubbles to the surface and spills out in tears.

My legs give out, and I sit down on the bed, Emma falling in beside me a moment later. She pulls me straight into a hug, and we hang on tight. She's the only one I'd ever let see me like this. We've been through so much together and we still have so far to go.

After a long, sniffly moment and a few hiccoughing, awkward laughs, I pull away.

"What are we gonna do?" I ask, wiping at the tears and trying to bring myself back under control with slow breathing.

"We're gonna do whatever Tamara Jackson says," she immediately answers, looking as unruffled as usual. "Liz"—so her name *is* Liz—"might be in charge of the NGC with Gibby gone, but the head of the USOF definitely outranks her. We need to follow Mrs. Jackson's lead, and everything will be okay."

"Oh, will it?" I ask with a laugh. We thought that after Dani's suspension and then Gibby's arrest and now . . . now what is happening exactly? Is the USOF disbanding the NGC? That's what it feels like. There's a certainty in Emma's voice, though—she sounds so sure of herself. Maybe if she believes that's the right thing to do, I can let her believe it for the both of us.

——

"I told you, Mom. Pauline's not with us."

It takes everything in me not to choke on those words and burst into tears again, as the betrayal and confusion and disbelief wind their way through my veins. *No time to cry about this anymore,*

Audrey; there's way too much at stake. Don't think about how your coach, the woman you trusted with your entire life, betrayed you and your dreams. Don't think about how maybe it wasn't just the one lie. Don't think about every single moment when she pushed you a little too hard or let you do one more rep despite the agonizing pain. Don't think about how maybe with a different coach, how maybe your back wouldn't be this screwed up, about how maybe the person who was supposed to do what was best for you did what was best for herself instead.

Emma is sitting across from me. There were two of us and our coach pushed us both just as hard. My body broke down. Emma's didn't. And I'd never really thought about how maybe . . . maybe that didn't have to happen. It still doesn't feel possible that she could have done this, but obviously I didn't know her as well as I thought.

"Where is she?" Mom asks, her voice getting a little high-pitched. Pauline called her after Gibby was arrested, and the last she heard we'd be competing today, not taking a van tour of Southern California. It took a while to get ahold of her since she was at work when everything went down. By the time she called me back, we were two and a half hours into a drive down the Pacific Coast Highway, and her freak-out level had hit maximum.

"I don't know. On a flight back to New York, maybe? I'm with Mrs. Jackson from the United States Olympic Federation. Do you want to talk to her? She's going to tell you the same thing I did."

I shift in the captain's chair. This is a luxury van, and I'm buckled into what feels like a first-class airplane seat. The air-conditioning is pumping, fighting and winning a battle against the heat outside, but it's also making the leather seats almost slippery, and it's been pretty hellish on my back. I twist back and forth, trying to loosen up the tightness.

"No," Mom says, her voice resigned. It's been a long time since she's dealt with anything to do with my gymnastics. I started traveling without her and Dad when I was twelve. "Make sure you check in with me when you get settled."

"I will. I promise."

"I love you," she says.

"I love you too." My voice cracks as I end the call, but I swallow back the emotion again. No more. From here on out, I'm just going to focus on getting to the Olympics and winning gold and deal with everything else later. *Sure, Audrey, a couple of decades in therapy should do the trick.*

"Audrey couldn't even tell her mom where we're going. This is ridiculous," Sierra says, not exactly *to* Mrs. Jackson, but more at her—just the latest in the running commentary she's provided for most of the ride. "I feel like we've been kidnapped."

"Don't you ever get tired of hearing yourself talk?" Chelsea says, clearly fed up.

"Sorry, Chels, I didn't realize you were the only one around here allowed to have an opinion."

"We all know your opinion. You've been stating it pretty clearly for the whole ride. Enough."

I lean forward in my chair, stretching out my back, but also bringing me a little closer to Mrs. Jackson, whose seat is in front of mine. "Are we almost there?" I whisper, trying not to feed into the bitch fest behind me.

We drove past San Diego a few minutes ago and went over a bridge. Unless we're on a border run to Tijuana, I'm pretty sure we have to be close to wherever we're going.

"Nearly," Mrs. Jackson says, and I sit back, concentrating on drowning out Jaime, who of course had to chime in to back up Sierra's crap.

A few minutes later, the van pulls to a stop. Mrs. Jackson wasn't kidding.

The driver slides the van door open for us, and we're met by the bright sunshine and the roar of the ocean. The air is salty and warm as I inhale and then exhale, glad to be out of the muscle-tightening AC. The wind whips strands of my hair loose from the bun I'd meticulously put together that morning, and I brush them away, squinting against the sun. *Where the hell are we?*

"Audrey?" a voice I didn't expect in a million years calls from behind me. "What the hell are you doing here?"

I whip around and there's Leo Adams clad in board shorts—and nothing else—a surfboard under his arm, smiling widely.

We're in Coronado.

That building behind me? That's Janet Dorsey-Adams's gym.

"Leo Adams, I presume?" Mrs. Jackson asks, looking between the two of us with something suspiciously resembling a smirk on her usually cool features. "Is your mother inside? I need to speak with her."

"Er—sure," he says, giving me a questioning look, but I gape at him. I cannot believe he's here or we're here or whatever. "Is she expecting you?"

"We spoke on the phone this morning," Mrs. Jackson says, and my eyebrows shoot up toward the clear blue sky. That wasn't exactly a *yes*. Are we *crashing* Janet Dorsey-Adams's gym? I've only met the woman a couple of times and never beyond a quick hello, but by reputation, that doesn't really seem like a thing she'd be cool with.

When she comes out of the front door, my instincts are confirmed. A white woman, no more than forty and about my height, she looks fit enough to bust out an Olympic-medal-worthy floor routine. Except now, with her arms crossed over her chest and one eyebrow lifted in challenge, I'm not in awe so much as terrified.

"Tamara?" she asks, but she's looking at us and not Mrs. Jackson. "What's going on?"

"I presume you know who these young ladies are?" Mrs. Jackson says, striding forward with her hand extended.

"Obviously," Coach Dorsey-Adams says, her mouth curving into a frown, ignoring the hand, "but I thought I made it clear this morning . . . Oh, I see, you thought you'd corner me into this."

"I . . ." Mrs. Jackson begins, but then wavers. The coach's frown deepens during the hesitation. "Is there somewhere we can speak privately?"

"Not really," Coach Dorsey-Adams says, turning away and signaling to Leo, who's still beside me, to follow her. He doesn't move, and something in that gesture—his split second of solidarity—spurs me on.

"Wait, please," I say before I can even think about it. "We don't . . . we don't have anywhere else to go . . ." I trail off, losing my nerve.

"We need a coach," Chelsea finishes for me, stepping up to my other side.

Coach Dorsey-Adams looks between us and then beyond at Emma, Sierra, and Jaime, who've been silent until now. "And what about you three? Do you need a coach too?"

"Yes, ma'am," Sierra and Jaime say together. The urge to roll my eyes loses out against the fear of making a bad impression, but it was a close race.

"Please," Emma finishes for them, an urgency in her voice I'm not sure I've ever heard before.

"Hmm," she says, seemingly unimpressed with our efforts. "Tamara, come inside and let's talk."

They disappear into the building. What the hell? Mrs. Jackson already asked her to coach us and she said no. How is this happening? How are we even here right now instead of back at the training center competing?

"Hey," Leo says, reaching for my hand and then catching himself, leaning back a bit. "Are you okay? I heard about Gibson and . . . I know you said you were okay, but . . ."

I rock back on my heels and fold my arms over my chest, not sure what to do with my hands. "Yeah, I'm fine. At least, I think I am."

He rubs anxiously at the back of his neck with his free hand. "I . . . I'm really sorry about . . . everything, and I can't believe you're here right now."

"Yeah, me neither," I agree, but bite my lip and then look away. This is so surreal that he's here in front of me, and I want to, I don't know, hug him or something, but instead my feet are rooted to the pavement.

"I still don't get why we have to be here," Sierra says under her breath. "We don't even know what happened."

Apparently, she's still on that crusade to prove Gibby's innocence or at least Dani's guilt, like that even matters anymore. Gibby's gone. Our coaches are gone. All we have left is one another.

Leo ignores her. "Listen, I don't know how much luck that lady is going to have with my mom. I'm gonna go see if I can help." He turns to leave but hesitates. He leans in, his hand gently cupping my elbow, and whispers, "I'm really glad you're here."

A shiver passes through me, but I try to play it cool.

"Me too," I say with a small smile, and I feel the tension slide away as he grins back.

With that, he jogs to the gym, propping his surfboard against the wall before disappearing through the doors.

"Well, thank God Leo has a thing for Audrey. We might actually have a place to train," Sierra says, and her voice feels like a foghorn, breaking the small trance Leo put me in with his smile.

"God, do you *ever* stop?" I bite back at her, but mostly because the words hit their mark.

Sierra whirls on me, but Emma cuts her off. "We're screwed anyway. Janet Dorsey-Adams has never even coached an elite. She's not going to be able to help us."

"She's an Olympic medalist, a coach, and a sports psychologist," Chelsea points out. "And yeah, she doesn't have any elite gymnasts, but can you think of an elite coach whose head wasn't shoved up Gibby's ass to the shoulders? Even Sarah's and Brooke's coaches worked closely with him during their individual qualifying process. The USOF isn't going to let us train with anyone remotely associated with him."

Red blossoms over Sierra's cheeks and she spits, "Then we should be allowed the choice to work with *our* coaches, no matter what they did. It's ridiculous that weeks before the Olympics, the people we've trained with our entire lives aren't allowed to help us. We need our coaches. I don't care what happened with Gibby and Dani. I don't give one shit. It's not about that."

That's definitely a lie. She definitely cares, but I don't think it has anything to do with our coaches. She's scared that Dani is going to come back and take her spot. Dani deserves to be here with us, that is . . . if we're even staying.

It's more than twenty minutes later before Mrs. Jackson walks out of the gym, replacing her sunglasses over her eyes.

"Okay, ladies, back in the van."

"So, did she say yes?" I ask, climbing in behind Emma.

"She's thinking about it," she says with a tight smile from the front seat. "Either way, you all need a place to rest up, so the USOF has rented a house nearby."

———

"I feel like I'm on one of those home-decorating shows or something. This place is amazing," Chelsea says, and a smile blooms on Mrs. Jackson's face. At least someone is happy right now.

The house is gorgeous—that's totally undeniable. It's right on the San Diego Bay. The three-story building is a warm sand color with a red Spanish tile roof. Inside, it's totally California chic, with gigantic windows overlooking the water and lots of whites and blues in the decor. There's a massive outdoor deck with lounge chairs and a dock with kayaks and Jet Skis for guests who don't have to train for the Olympics.

"C'mon," Emma says as we drag out suitcases up the stairway set off to the side of the large open living space with vaulted ceilings. The luggage clangs against the open metal stairs as we climb, but that's the least of my worries right now.

What are we going to do if Leo's mom decides against coaching us?

Was this really the USOF's only option?

There has to be another coach somewhere. Pauline's face appears in my mind, and I glance at Emma, but I tamp down the slow, crawling sense of resentment that's taken up a corner of my mind. There's no time for that, not when it feels like the world has turned upside down on me in the middle of a handstand and I'm digging my fingernails into the earth itself, just barely hanging on.

I follow Emma into one of the rooms. It has two queen-size beds, and the light blue walls and white fluffy duvets are soothing. My eyes start to droop. Emma drops her luggage next to one bed and then leaps into it with a bounce, settling up against the pillows.

"I need a nap." I let go of my suitcases near the door, not even bothering to drag them all the way into the room before heading straight for the empty bed and falling on it with a heavy sigh. The clock on the table between us reads barely noon, but it feels like we've crammed a month into the last five hours.

"Do you think the beds at the Olympic Village will be this nice?" Emma asks.

"At this point I'd take a sleeping bag on the floor as long as we actually get to the Olympic Village," I say, keeping my eyes firmly shut.

"You think we won't?"

"It feels like the Olympics are years away. None of this feels real."

"Not even Leo Adams?" she asks, but her words are starting to fade.

"Especially not him," I murmur, not even sure if I really said it out loud before the world goes black.

———

"Rey, wake up," Emma's voice cuts straight through into my deep sleep, her hands shaking me awake.

"What?" I whine back at her, but shrieking from downstairs wakes me up fully.

There are curse combinations being thrown around that I've never heard before, and I leap up off the bed and follow Emma, who's already hit a dead sprint ahead of me toward the stairs.

"You stupid bitch! How dare you show your face here after what you did!" Sierra screams as we reach the stairs. Mrs. Jackson stands behind her, holding her at the waist and keeping her from literally launching herself at Dani.

Holy crap.

It's Dani. She's near the doorway, like she'd barely gotten more than a few steps into the house before Sierra tried to attack her.

Emma and I finally make it down the stairs as Mrs. Jackson drags Sierra out of the room and outside onto the deck. We can still see them, but at least there's a wall of thick plate glass between us.

A wan smile plays across Dani's face as she says, "Hey, guys. I'm back."

Emma hesitates, and so do I, but Chelsea doesn't. She takes one step and then another toward her, and my stomach sinks when Dani flinches away, but then Chelsea finally closes the distance and envelops our teammate into a hug.

"I'm so glad you're back, and I am so sorry about what he did to you," Chelsea says.

There's a moment when Dani is stiff, staring at me and Emma over Chelsea's shoulder, and then the tension dissolves and she's hugging back, her eyes screwing shut.

I don't know what to do. Emma still hasn't moved.

Dani's back, and that feels right. We know she didn't dope—despite Sierra's delusions—and she's back now, so maybe that means it's all going to be okay. Maybe our team is finally whole again.

Then, as Chelsea pulls away, I look past them, out to where Sierra is still ranting, with both Jaime and Mrs. Jackson trying unsuccessfully to calm her down.

Then again, maybe not.

———

The hot July sun warms my skin as I stretch out on a lounge chair looking out at the San Diego Bay. *Audrey Lee, when was the last time you were this lazy? Back when you were recovering from surgery maybe, but that was a forced laziness. You couldn't physically train.*

This? This feels wrong. Except I don't really have a choice. We don't have access to a gym right now. We might not ever have access to it, and by the end of the day we could be on another bus or airplane looking for a new home leading up to the Games.

We're the best group of gymnasts in the world. It shouldn't be this hard to find a place to train, and yet here we are. We deserve better than this. We need better than this if we're going to succeed in Tokyo.

"So, do you think Sierra's burst a blood vessel yet?" I ask Emma from my lounge chair. We've pulled our chairs into the shade under the patio awning. The last thing either of us needs is a sunburn. Gymnastics and fried skin are not a good combination.

"She'll get over it," Emma says, slathering on another layer of sunscreen. "She's pissed that Dani's back. I mean, I get it, but Dani's been ahead of her all year. Sierra's a pro; she'll come around."

"Maybe."

Or maybe she'll stay pissed and drag Jaime along with her like she always does and make the next few weeks miserable. Not that I'm going to say that out loud. Ever.

"Do you think she'll tell us what actually happened?" I ask, nodding toward where Dani and Chelsea are sitting, their legs dangling into the water off the dock.

"I don't want to know," she says, and I glance back at her. I'm never going to ask Dani about it. If she wants to share, she will, but I can't believe Emma's not even the least bit curious. I guess that's just how she is, though. Stuff never bothers her once she decides it's not going to.

My headache from the morning is nearly gone. Was that really just this morning? Maybe all I needed was a little rest and some sun. Vitamin D can do wonders, or so I'm told.

I shield my eyes against the glare off the water when Chelsea and Dani stand and wander toward us, smiles on their faces. Dani looks exactly like I remember from Olympic trials. Not that I thought she'd look different, but it's somehow weird that she looks the same? I don't even know.

"Look who's back," Chelsea says, her gaze focused behind me.

Leo—this time with a shirt on, the addition not diminishing his good looks at all—is walking up the driveway. The plain white T-shirt sets off his brown skin in the sunshine of the afternoon.

I leap from the chair, singeing my bare feet a bit as I move from the wood planks of the dock onto the stone patio on the side of the house. Emma, Dani, and Chelsea are right behind me.

"So?" I ask, bouncing up on my toes impatiently when he reaches us.

"So, you're in," he says, smiling sheepishly. "She's going to pawn off our junior girls to other gyms for a few weeks. You'll have the facility all to yourselves."

I shriek straight from the back of my throat and leap at him. His arms circle around me, and his chest vibrates against mine in a deep chuckle.

"Thank you so much. I don't know what you said to her, but thank you!"

"You're welcome," he says, setting me down, but not letting go. There's something in his eyes, though—something not quite right. I don't know him well enough to be sure, but it looks like it could be regret.

"Is everything okay?" I ask, tilting my head in confusion.

He smiles, any trace of that odd emotion disappearing. "I mean, I wouldn't turn down another hug."

That I can do. Hugging him is nice, and it's something I could definitely get used to.

I pull him close again, breathing in the scent of salt water and a hint of chalk from the gym we'll be training in until we leave for Tokyo.

Maybe now, *finally*, our Olympic journey can begin.

chapter nine

I have to choke back a sob of joy when I swing up onto the bars the next morning, my grips and palms scraping lightly against the cylindrical fiberglass. Or it could be just the chalk dust getting caught in my throat. Either way, it feels amazing to actually be training.

Aside from the single routine we managed to get through yesterday before the world imploded again, I feel like I haven't done gymnastics in months. My arms ache pleasantly as they hold my weight in a handstand on the high bar. I change my grips through a full pirouette, then release into my dismount, my body straight and tight while I spin into a triple twist.

"You know, when I saw you debut that move on TV, I actually started applauding from my couch," Janet says from beside the landing mat. "Creative, difficult, and it stands out from the crowd. Plus, you twist like a top."

I smile, rubbing the leather of my grips together and moving away from the uneven bars so Emma can swing up onto them.

"You're a half a second late on that full, though, and it's costing you at least a tenth."

"I've had problems with it in the last couple of months. I'd rather be a split second late finishing the pirouette than not quite make it to the handstand and not connect it to the dismount, you know?"

"You're capable of it doing it all, though. It was smart of your coach to give you that cover during the trials process, but despite it not feeling that way, we do have time to fine-tune some of the details between now and Tokyo. It's costing you a tenth at least, and a tenth will mean the difference between silver and gold on the event," she says as Emma dismounts with her double layout, sticking it cold. She wasn't late on her pirouette. One-tenth.

"Got it." I move away to chalk my hands. Digging into the bowl, I let my eyes wander the quiet gym. Normally, there must be dozens of kids around, Junior Olympic and recreation classes buzzing in and out all day long, but true to her word, Janet has sent her kids—almost all of whom are in their competitive off-season anyway—to other gyms so she can help us prepare for Tokyo.

It's a nice facility, but not exactly state of the art. It's way smaller than our gym at home and isn't filled with banners proclaiming the club's success. Instead, there are murals painted on the walls, brightly colored silhouettes of gymnasts leaping in the air, toes pointed, legs fully extended, perfect form. The far wall is like a garage door, and right now it's open to let in the breeze off the ocean.

The six of us are paired off: Emma and me on bars, Chelsea and Dani on beam, and Jaime and Sierra on vault, both back to being alternates again. Once we finish our assignments, we'll come together to work on floor. This is how it's supposed to be. We might not be at the training center, and we might not have our own coaches, but when it's all said and done, gymnastics is still gymnastics.

Leo is over in the corner of the gym, working out on a leg machine. It's kind of amazing that he's here. It's also super tempting. Maybe way too tempting, considering that his mom is now my coach.

Now is not the time, Audrey. Right now, the most important thing in your life has to be nailing that postpirouette handstand on the high bar, sticking your vaults and tumbling passes, and making sure your beam connections are super smooth and in rhythm. Nothing else matters. Not even Leo Adams.

One more bars routine, this time—according to Janet's approving nod—a much more acceptable handstand prior to dismount, and we're moving to beam. It's not Gibby's decision to make anymore, but beam is still where I need to improve my results from nationals and trials.

First step, solidifying my mount series, a roundoff, layout step-out onto the beam, and then two layout step-outs connected to it. A lightning-fast combination that to the naked eye will look as easy as if I'm flipping across the floor.

Emma goes first, her beam routine solid as usual. Everything about Emma's gymnastics is solid and always has been. When we were younger, people kind of gave her crap for it. She was never the gymnast who would catch your eye, but she hits her routines, which, if you've ever watched elite gymnastics, you know is a rarity. Then last year she sort of steamrolled everyone with her solid gymnastics and the addition of some carefully placed, super-difficult elements. So, at the tail end of her routine, as she lines up about three-quarters of the way down the beam and laser-focuses on the end, I'm not the least bit surprised when the Arabian double front she launches herself into is stuck cold.

"Nice!" I cheer her on, and we high-five after she salutes.

I move toward the beam with a chunk of chalk to mark some of my placements.

Janet's critique rings out in the nearly silent gym. "Your skills are solid, but watch your tempo. Olympic judges want to see flow on the beam, and as world champion, they're not going to go easy on you. Difficulty can only go so far, Emma." And then louder, to me, "Okay, Audrey, show me what you've got."

Her words register, but they're mostly buzz at this point. I set up the springboard and test it, falling forward toward the beam to make sure it's the correct distance away. Then I take a few steps back to the end of the beam mat.

One breath and then two, and I'm running forward into a round-off, layout step-out. My first foot hits the beam, and the rest of my body follows before my back foot lands. My balance is solid, and I don't even think before connecting it backward to another layout step-out and then another.

Good.

Another breath and a couple of leaps move me to the opposite end of the beam, and it's time for my second series.

It's supposed to be a triple turn connecting straight into a single L-turn—which is super hard because my leg is held out in front of me while I spin—and then from there a full illusion, where I kick my leg up and around, my whole body following it while I spin one full rotation. Each skill separately is tough, but together they make one of the hardest beam combinations in the world.

I release a slow breath and then go into the triple turn, which becomes a double when my shoulders come out of alignment into the L-turn, but I have to stop—my momentum isn't controlled enough to connect it to the full illusion, and it's either break the connection or fall.

Keeping the disappointment off my face is instinct at this point, trained into me as a kid, but that was definitely not what I wanted to do. I pause for a second to regain my balance fully and then complete the full illusion without a hitch.

"C'mon, Rey, you got it," Emma's voice breaks through, which forces me to refocus. Another huge combination is next, and after missing that previous connection, I need this one.

An aerial cartwheel, and I'm off balance again. I correct myself with a grimace, leaping into a switch split, changing legs in the air, and then a gainer back layout down to straddle the beam.

Damn it.

Everything needs to be seamless.

My final skill before the dismount is one that almost no one else does anymore: a one and a quarter turn on my back. It looks like a move out of a break-dancer's repertoire, and it usually gets the crowd pumped up, but there's no crowd right now. Just my new coach, who I definitely wanted to impress. So much for that.

I'm ready to dismount. I set myself, arms lifted above my head, and then I'm counting out my contact with the beam, one-two, one-two, hands-feet, hands-feet, into a triple twist, and I'm landing with a small step to the side.

Saluting, I look up through a stray hair that came loose from my ponytail. Janet's face is stern but not unkind.

"Go on, Emma," she says to my best friend, who shoots me a tight smile as she passes. When I finally reach her, Janet nods, crossing her arms over her chest. "It's okay, Audrey. We have time."

I nod, but I'm mostly ignoring her, running through my routine in my head, trying to figure out where I went wrong.

Janet's voice yanks me out of it. "Shake it off," she says, "literally. Whenever you're unhappy with a routine or a skill, just shake your head a bit. Acknowledge it and then move on so you can refocus and improve next time out."

My brow furrows deeper with every word. She's my coach, and I have to do what she says, but honestly, it sounds like a load of crap. I shake my head.

"Good, now don't stress. Like I said, we have time."

Don't stress? I blink at her in disbelief.

I'm not sure a coach has ever said that to me before and meant it. Stress is just sort of part of the gig, and I kind of like that I've been able to survive in the midst of its constant onslaught. Like back during worlds training camp a couple of years ago when Gibby's final test before naming the team was to have us compete until a fall. He never said it out loud, but we knew the first person who broke was going to lose her spot on the team. I felt strong back then, for outlasting the other girls, but now it just seems incredibly fucked up.

We finish up on beam, my connections a little bit better in my second routine than in the first, but it still isn't good enough.

"It's fine," Emma says as we grab some water. Easy for her to say; she hit her routine.

"Okay, everyone, meet on the floor," Janet calls out, moving toward the floor herself. We line up in front of her, all six of us at attention. She snorts. "At ease, ladies," she says, sticky sarcasm dripping from each word. "This morning's session was successful. From what I've seen, you're all extremely well prepared physically, but my concern is about your mental and emotional well-being.

What I'd like now is for you all to spend the remainder of the day in meditation and visualization."

"What?" Sierra and I say at the same time and simultaneously cringe at our lack of self-control.

"You heard me. Meditation and routine visualization for at least an hour. Put some music on if you need to, but I want you all resting your bodies and working your minds. Picture the Olympic arena and imagine yourself becoming comfortable with it as an environment. Make it a safe place for you mentally, and once you're there physically, you'll be fine."

"But you said you'd train us." I look to the other girls for support, but there's none to be found. Emma's eyes are wide, and she shakes her head once, obviously trying to get me to stop. "This isn't training."

Janet smirks. "Yes, it is."

No, it's not. It's an entire afternoon wasted lying on the carpeted floor, feeling the springs beneath me but not being able to use them to do any gymnastics. This is probably why Janet doesn't have any elites in her gym. She's a coach, yes, but she's clearly a sports psychologist first, and while I'm all about prioritizing mental health, this is just ridiculous.

It's not like visualization isn't a valuable tool. I've been visualizing my routines since before I turned elite, but that was in *addition* to training, not in place of it.

My last real work session was the day before we came to California, and that was more than two days ago now. You don't just take off two days in a row in the lead-up to the Olympic Games. And it's not just that. My body is wired and craving activity. I'd go

115

for a run, but we're under strict orders not to do anything physical now that practice is over, and while my need to train is strong, my well-developed instinct for obeying someone with the title *Coach* in front of their name is even more ingrained.

We trained for two hours. Two hours. Warm-up, two events, and then a lecture on improving our mental game, which definitely put me in the perfect mood for an afternoon of reflection and meditation.

I do dozens of circuits in my head with my noise-canceling headphones, blocking out everything around me, but there are only so many times I can imagine my routines before my brain shorts out. I know what it's all supposed to look like. I have to do it.

Someone nudges me with their foot. I open my eyes. It's Emma. I can't hear what she's saying through the music blaring in my ears, but it's easy enough to lip-read "Let's go."

She's been visualizing too, but her foot is bouncing up and down in agitation. She's as restless as I am. I sit up and narrow my eyes at the empty gym.

I shift my headphones off my ears. "Where did everyone go?"

"Lunch. Janet saw how in the zone you were and didn't want to disturb you. She told me to set my timer for another twenty minutes. Time's up and I'm starving—come on."

Jumping to my feet, I glance around to make sure we're alone. There's no one else in the gym, so I take a jogging start and do a quick roundoff, back handspring into a double back, sticking it cold and saluting. It's a dumb way to rebel, but it's something.

"Good thing Janet didn't see you."

"Yeah, because it makes sense that our gymnastics coach wouldn't want us to do gymnastics."

"At least we have a coach."

Maybe it's easier for her, to just listen to what our new coach says and do it without question. She listened to Pauline, and now she's the favorite to win the all-around. I listened to Pauline and . . . *What, Audrey? You made the Olympic team? Poor you. Don't be ungrateful for that, even if the rest of it is fucked up.*

"She's not coaching, she's psychoanalyzing."

Emma laughs. "Well, we probably need more of that anyway. C'mon, let's go."

The gym isn't far from the house—only a few blocks away. The walk back is nice and refreshing with a soft breeze coming off the ocean. I bet it would be even more refreshing if we were hot and sweaty from training. The air would feel incredible against overheated skin and sweat-soaked hair.

As soon as we walk through the door, my mouth waters. Someone is grilling steak, I think, or maybe fajitas? I think I smell peppers and onions cooking too.

"What?" I manage to stutter out when Chelsea walks down the stairs.

"Right?" she says, grinning widely. "Leo brought steak. Beats plain chicken and steamed vegetables, right?"

Two sides of me instantly go to battle at the idea. The food smells amazing, but this wasn't a good day. It wasn't even an okay day. It was a shitty day, and steak isn't going to make it better. Plus, if we aren't going to be doing two-a-day training sessions, then I have to be super careful what I eat. The NGC had a nutritionist that took care of our meal planning before major meets, and while chicken and fish were constant staples, steak definitely wasn't ever on the menu.

Emma and I follow Chelsea out onto the patio, where Dani is setting the table. Leo is at the grill, an apron tied around his neck and waist.

"If that thing says 'Kiss the Cook,' I'm taking a picture and never letting you live it down," I say.

He turns toward me for a moment and opens his mouth to respond, but instead he just shakes his head and sends me a tight smile.

I stop in my tracks and blink at him, but he's already turned back to the grill. "Can someone call Jaime and Sierra?" he asks over his shoulder. "These things are perfect."

For a moment we all hesitate.

Sierra hasn't exactly been a joy to be around, and Jaime tends to mirror her moods.

"I'll get them," Emma says finally. Dani and Chelsea are sitting at the opposite end of the table, whispering to each other, and that leaves me and Leo and this suddenly awkward tension that's making my skin itch.

The urge to fill the silence wars with a sudden desire to flee. Literally. I want to sprint away, maybe get rid of some of this excess energy and block out this weird vibe I'm getting off of the first guy I've ever let myself really like.

He finally turns from the steaks that he's been carefully transferring over to a serving dish, and his eyes flicker behind me, back to the house. "Listen, Audrey—"

"It's fine," I cut him off and turn away. His words and tone are clear enough, and I don't need to be let down easy.

Emma returns with Sierra and Jaime, saving me from whatever he was going to say next. They all grab seats, and I snag one next to Emma, and Leo slides in beside me. That entire side of my body comes alive as he settles just inches from me, but I try to ignore it as the tension in the room expands way beyond us, radiating through everyone at the table. The brief respite we got from it at training has somehow made it exponentially worse now that we're all sitting around a table together.

Sierra's stony silence is almost as obnoxious as her ravings from yesterday. Jaime won't engage at all because when Sierra's not talking, she has no one to echo. Chelsea and Dani are still whispering together at the other end of the table, but not loud enough for anyone to join in, and Leo, Emma, and I are caught in the middle, none of us with anything to say.

"Who wants peppers and onions for their steak?" Janet says, stepping through the sliding doors. I didn't even realize she was in the house. She breaks through the awkwardness, but only slightly.

"I'll have some," Leo says, holding his plate up for his mother.

"Thanks, me too," I say, and she scoops them onto my plate. Everyone politely accepts some from her, but there's still no conversation beyond the quiet murmurs from Chelsea and Dani.

Janet seats herself beside her son and looks around the table. "You all know you're allowed to talk during meals, right? The NGC didn't ban conversation at that training center, did they?"

"No," Chelsea says. "I . . . uh . . . I think there's . . . we're all still a little . . ." She trails off, gesturing around us.

"Don't worry. Plenty of time to get comfortable in the next few weeks. I know this isn't what you expected, and some of you didn't expect to be here at all, but I promise we'll get everything figured out before the Games."

The table falls into silence.

Janet tries again. "I'm looking forward to seeing your floor routines tomorrow, ladies. Audrey, what's the inspiration behind yours? Leo has been talking about it nonstop since we got back from trials."

The entire table is silent, not even the click of forks and knives filling up the quiet of the moment as everyone looks at me and then Leo and then back to me.

"Careful, Leo," Sierra snarks under her breath, but loud enough for everyone to hear, "next thing you know she might accuse you of rape and we'll all be back to square one."

Nearly everyone at the table explodes in protest, except me and Dani. I'm too in shock to say anything, and she just stares in silence before standing, her face ashen but her mouth firm. Then she walks away, through the sliding doors and back into the house.

Chelsea stops midshriek in Sierra's direction and follows her, catching up as they make it to the stairs.

That's good, because I've had it. My whole body is almost vibrating from how much I want to punch Sierra in the throat. I need to be away from the ridiculousness of this whole situation.

"Audrey," Emma calls softly when I slip out from between her and Leo, but I ignore her, walking and then jogging and then sprinting across the patio, through the living room, and out the front door into the Coronado night.

chapter ten

The gym door is unlocked.

Whoops.

Emma and I were probably supposed to lock it when we left. I flick the lights on, and with a rattle and hiss, the fluorescent bulbs come to life. The clear, salty air in my lungs from outside gives way to the familiar, comforting scent of chalk dust, mat cleaner, and sweat.

Janet told us not to train any more today, but Janet doesn't have to compete in Tokyo in three weeks. And Janet doesn't have a back held together with cortisone and a prayer, so Janet will have to get over it.

I lift my arms, swinging them around, trying to get warm. My back feels almost absurdly good as I stretch out, but it's a false positive. If I felt like this without the cortisone, life would be sweet.

I'd go to the Olympics and then maybe to college, where the routines wouldn't have nearly the same kind of physical impact on my body. I'd get four years to compete with a team, win national championships, go to parties, get a degree, and keep doing what I love. Instead, there's a countdown clock, not only on my Olympic dreams, but on gymnastics, the thing I love the most in this world. As soon as these last moments tick away, that's it, it's over—Olympic gold medal or not. And right now, it feels more and more like not.

Jogging back and forth across the floor, I accelerate to sprints until my legs are warm and ready, then make a beeline for the balance beam.

I keep it simple at first, pushing up to a handstand, swinging down to straddle the beam and then back to the handstand before lowering my legs into a split and holding. I stand and bend into a back walkover before using my momentum to kick a leg out and flip into a back layout step-out, landing solidly on the beam, one foot then the other. Behind me the door squeaks open and then clicks shut again, but I ignore it. It's probably just Emma anyway.

I'm not really warmed up enough for a full dismount, but a roundoff into a double twist feels sweet and easy as I land.

"That was nice."

Okay, not Emma, then.

Leo is off to the side, hands in the pockets of his shorts, rocking back and forth from his heels to his toes. He might look cool and casual, but his eyes are telling a different story, burning into mine even from yards away. That strange aloofness from back at the house is gone. This is the boy I remember from the hotel and the day I arrived in Coronado.

He steps closer slowly, too slowly. I take a step toward him and then another, closing the gap.

"You're an incredible gymnast, you know that?"

"Hmm." I hope he understands that compliments aren't what I want right now, not when he's so close and I feel his heart thundering in his chest and his breath is warm against my cheek as he leans down.

He brushes his lips along my jawline, his arms gathering me close. He leans in but stops short of a kiss, his breath ghosting against my lips. He doesn't close the distance. I'm about to turn my head to meet his mouth with mine when his voice rumbles out softly, "Audrey, we . . . can't."

My stomach drops and then twists in on itself, and raging insecurity comes flying to the surface. Maybe I'd gotten it all wrong. Maybe I'd misinterpreted it all. I pull away. "But I thought . . . wait, is that why you were acting weird before at the house? Do you not want—"

"No!" he nearly yells, his eyes wide with panic. "I mean, yes. I do want. Obviously. I don't know if you get just how much I want, but when my mom agreed to coach you, she pointed out that maybe it wouldn't be such a great idea if we were . . . if we did this." He motions at the space between us, at the invisible but palpable something that sets my skin aflame whenever he's near me.

Duh, Audrey. Of course this can't be a thing. It's a massive conflict of interest. You're such a dumbass. And that Janet thought of it before you, well, that's just super embarrassing too.

"I feel like such an idiot. God, and your mom had to point it out like . . . she *knew*."

"I wasn't exactly subtle about it," he confesses. "She wasn't lying before. I really haven't shut up about you since we got back."

"That's not helping."

Leo lets out a shaky laugh. "Yeah, sorry. It's . . . This really sucks. I don't want to stay away from you, but I'm pretty sure that's what I have to do."

"You're right."

We stand in silence, letting time tick away like it might solve the problem for us. Eventually, it will, I guess, but as close as the Olympics felt just a few minutes ago, now they seem like eons away.

"She likes you, you know," he says finally.

"Your mom?" I hadn't gotten a feeling one way or another from her, but I'm pretty sure contradicting her during training and then walking out on the meal she'd planned for us didn't endear me to her at all.

"She thinks you're a throwback, old-school."

"In gymnastics speak, that means maybe I'd have been good enough twenty years ago, but not now."

"Nah," he says, his eyes sparkling with amusement. "You don't know my mom. It's a compliment. She likes you."

"Yeah?" I may not agree with her coaching methods, but having an Olympic medalist like me is pretty cool.

"Uh, could you not do that?" He suddenly looks super uncomfortable, fidgeting back and forth on his feet.

"Do what?"

"Look totally turned on by the idea that my mom likes you," he says, his nose wrinkling.

"Wow, are you jealous?" I ask, laughing. He rolls his eyes, and I laugh harder.

"Jealous?" he asks. "Of my mom, no, but of your dreams, maybe a little? Right now they're way more important than me, and I'd never forgive myself if I stood in your way."

I fall forward, resting my head against his shoulder. He still smells like the steaks he grilled for lunch, but I don't want the reminder of that right now, of what we left back at that house.

"Dreams are overrated. You work and work and work, and then they end."

"Endings are beginnings too."

"Wow," I say, lifting my head, "is that from an inspirational poster in here with a picture of someone crossing a finish line?"

"Someone on top of a mountain, actually. C'mon, Rey"—he scoffs playfully—"races and finish lines are so *pedestrian*."

A laugh bubbles out of my chest completely unbidden except by his awful joke. "Oh my God, you didn't. Seriously? That was the worst." I try to pull my hand away as punishment for the pun, but he doesn't let go.

"I don't know what you're talking about. Mountaintops are the *peak* of inspirational art."

"Stop it," I protest, laughing harder.

"You don't like puns?" he asks in mock horror. "That's it. I'm calling it. This was brief and beautiful, but the race is over, the mountain has been scaled, and it's not worth it if you can't handle my puns, Audrey Lee."

"I hate puns, and I hate that we can't be together right now, but maybe after the Olympics, we can have a very serious conversation about that."

"Yeah?" He smirks. "I like the sound of that."

"You should." I move away as my brain flits back to the total team meltdown I walked away from back at the house. "We should probably head back."

"Probably. My mom banished your teammates to their rooms for the rest of the day and then sent me to get you."

"And you let us stay here this long? She probably thinks we're in here hooking up or something. She's my coach. I can't let her think that I—"

"Too late," he says with a casual shrug that makes me narrow my eyes in real annoyance.

"Leo!"

"Let's go back, then," he says, and I feel the eye roll in his words even though he's smiling down at me.

"Snowboarders: you're all so fucking chill about everything." I disentangle our fingers and march out of the gym, making sure he can't see the smile blooming on my face.

"I didn't know gymnasts swore," he calls from behind me, laughing.

I reach the door but stop and look back over my shoulder at him, still standing near the beam. "There's a lot you don't know about me."

In a few strides, he's caught up, reaching around me to hold the door open. "And I can't wait to find out."

On the way back to the house is when things shift. We go from walking side by side, our hands brushing over and over again, to a foot away from each other. It feels wrong, almost dangerous, like we have our backs to a tornado and ignoring it will somehow stop it from plowing into us.

He stops at the end of the driveway. "So, this is it."

"Yeah," I agree, but I don't look up into his eyes because I'm pretty sure I'll renege on that instantly, and I can't risk that. I can't risk jeopardizing everything I've worked for my entire life—not for Leo, not for anything.

With a deep breath, I walk away from him, up to the front door and into the house, refusing to let myself look over my shoulder to check if he's still there.

"Welcome back," Janet says as I walk through the door. She and Mrs. Jackson are sitting on the couch. "You went to the gym."

"I did. Can I?" I motion upstairs.

"Not yet," Mrs. Jackson says, motioning to one of the armchairs. I hesitate to sit on the white linen—I'm still covered in chalk from the morning's workout—but I perch gingerly on the edge of the chair and fold my hands in my lap.

"Audrey," Janet begins, looking to Mrs. Jackson and then back to me, "I know this might be awkward, but we have to discuss you and my son . . ."

"No, it's okay." I gather my courage. "Leo and I spoke, and we decided that . . . to not . . . you know, be together, since you're my coach now and . . ." This is almost as embarrassing as what happened earlier, but I tamp down the urge to flee again.

"I think that's wise," Mrs. Jackson says. "We don't want any appearance of impropriety or favoritism. We can't afford even the slightest hint of a scandal after *everything*."

Janet picks it up from there. "I want to impress upon you the importance of staying away from each other while you're training in my gym."

"I understand."

"I'm not sure that you do," Mrs. Jackson cuts in. "We are running short of time, and quite honestly, we're out of options, Audrey. While none of that is your fault, Coach Dorsey-Adams must be seen by the entire world as an impartial judge of your abilities. So, that being said, if you don't stay away from Leo while you're here, I'm afraid the consequences could be extreme."

"Extreme?" I repeat.

"Should complaints arise about bias and the like," Mrs. Jackson says, "we may have little choice in how we deal with them."

"You'd kick me off?" I ask, looking back and forth between them. "For liking a boy?"

"It's not quite that simple. This team is already fractured, and I'm concerned that any additional discord could be the straw that breaks the camel's back. So if any athlete is found to be contributing to a negative environment, they will be removed from the team posthaste. Your teammates, particularly those who have already expressed discontent at our current circumstances, have been warned of these consequences as well."

She means Sierra and her piss-poor attitude. Well, that's something at least.

"If it makes you feel any better, understand that you're not the only one making a sacrifice here. Ms. Olivero's coach has agreed to stay away from this process. She didn't have anything to do with the activities leading up to Dani's suspension, but she's choosing to help us avoid even the perception of a conflict of interest or partiality."

Well, that sucks. I mean, it's actually fair that we all get to train with the same coach now, but Dani's coach stepping aside so no one can say she got an unfair advantage? That's intense and way more of a sacrifice than just staying away from a guy I like until after the Olympics.

"Audrey," Janet says. "I've already discussed this with Leo, but I want to make sure you understand. No private conversations, no sneaking off to the gym after hours, nothing"—she hesitates— "nothing physical."

"I understand," I say quickly, needing this conversation to be over right now. "Can I go?"

They nod, and I book it up the stairs.

"Hey," Emma says when I slip through the door. "Please tell me you and Leo hooked up, because it would be great if something good came of today's bullshit."

"Nothing happened," I say dully, hoping she doesn't push. I'm not in the mood to rehash every embarrassing detail of what just went down.

"Wow, way to take advantage of the alone time, Rey."

I ignore her sarcasm and start to gather my shower kit. All I want right now is to stand under a long, hot stream of water until the whole day is washed away.

"Sierra went off after you left," she says, carrying on the conversation without me. "She thinks Dani faked her second drug test and should still be suspended."

"Wait, what?" I ask, dropping my stuff onto my bed. "The USOF retested Dani. How does she think Dani fudged those results?"

"I don't know, but, like, it's not impossible. There are drugs that won't show up after a certain amount of time."

"Please." My simmering annoyance from everything that went down earlier rekindles. "Sierra is totally deluded. She just wants her spot on the team back, and I get that, but she basically attacked Dani when she got here. That's insane."

"That was a bit much," Emma concedes, sitting on the edge of her bed, "but I don't think she's totally off base about that whole situation."

I blink at her in disbelief. "You don't believe Dani?" I snap. *What the hell? Does she think the FBI arrests people for fun?*

"That's not what I said."

"You haven't said *anything*," I shoot back, "but that's what you always do, isn't it? Just sit there and pretend like there's nothing you can do about the shitstorm around you, right? Dani gets suspended? No big deal; bring in the alternate! Gibby's arrested for sexual assault? It's fine, just gotta focus up! Pauline betrays us? Whatever, we'll get a new coach. Sierra spews lies and conspiracy theories about Dani and me, your best friend, over lunch and you're like, maybe she has a point? Do you give a shit about anything?"

Emma's blue eyes flash at me. "What was I supposed to say? *Sierra, don't be mean to Audrey*? That's pretty awkward, and as for the other stuff, Dani hasn't even told us her side of the story, so how the hell am I supposed to defend her? Maybe she and Gibby *were* hooking up. Maybe it wasn't that big a deal for her."

"You don't mean that."

"Well, according to you, I don't care one way or the other," she says, shaking her head so hard her red hair starts to fall free from its bun.

And suddenly it feels like a chasm has opened up, splitting the room right down the middle—me on one side, Emma on the other.

"Emma—"

"No. Fuck you!"

She's out the door before I can respond, slamming it behind her, but I have no idea what I would have said and no idea what just happened, really.

We've never fought like that.

Not ever.

It's at least partly my fault. I can own that. I took out my frustrations about Leo and about, well, everything, on her, but I'm not totally to blame. Some of what I said was legit, especially the stuff about Dani.

Footsteps in the hallway draw me out of my thoughts. Dani and Chelsea are headed to their room at the end of the hallway, their voices are low. I can't make out what they're saying, but their heads are together, and they're both laughing softly.

"Hey, Rey," Dani says, and Chelsea smiles.

"Hey," I call back as they disappear into their room.

My anger at Emma fades as it all clicks into place for me. That's the first word I've actually said *to* Dani in the day she's been back. Even with everything that's happened, I haven't really thought a ton about that night after trials. And then it hits me—Dani hasn't told me her side of the story, like Emma said, but I haven't told her I believe her or that I support her or anything like that.

I'm gonna make sure I talk to her tomorrow.

It's seriously, literally, the least I can do.

chapter eleven

I hate vault. I hate it with every fiber of my being. I hate that less than a second of gymnastics determines a quarter of my all-around score. I hate that my back can't handle more than a one and a half twist. I hate that the most difficult skill I'm physically capable of has a blind landing and thus is so much harder to stick than the doubles other girls seem to crank out with ease.

I especially hate that when Emma does her two and a half vault, her difficulty level is so far ahead of mine that I don't stand a chance.

"I hate vault," I grumble, and Chelsea snorts beside me, catching her breath after she executed a near perfect two and a half.

"I hate bars," she says, but it's not the same thing. Her skills on bars four years ago were good enough to keep her in the all-around running. She even made an uneven bars final a few years before that at worlds.

Her weakness on bars was a speed bump.

My weakness on vault is a roadblock.

And Emma's strength on vault is annoying as all hell.

She flies past us and launches into a near-perfect two and a half, sticking and saluting before moving off to the side with Sierra and Jaime.

"Here we go, Dani, let's see it!" Janet calls with a clap of her hands from beside the vault as Dani sets herself down at the end of the run.

"Yeah, Dani, don't fuck up," Jaime sings under her breath. Sierra smirks, and Jaime practically glows at her leader's approval.

Janet's too far away to hear it, but Dani definitely did. She takes a hesitant step before stuttering a bit. Then, shaking her head, she resets and goes. Twelve strides take her to the vault and into a roundoff, back handspring, then a high and tight two and a half twist off, nearly stuck with just a shuffle of her feet on landing. She salutes straight ahead and then turns toward Emma, Jaime, and Sierra and salutes in their direction too. If Janet notices that Dani's middle fingers, and no others, are raised, she doesn't say anything about it.

My regret at not defending her prickles a little sharper.

"Nice vault." I hold out a fist for her to bump as she walks over to me and Chelsea. She hesitates and glances to Chelsea in clear surprise, but then knocks her chalky fist against mine.

"Thanks," Dani says, like she's not sure of my sincerity. I don't blame her.

"I especially liked the salute," I say. Chelsea covers her laugh with a cough.

Dani grins at that, but it fades just as fast. "I wasn't sure if you would."

"I do," I cut in. I've been a crappy teammate and I don't want to make it even worse by making her think that's her fault. "Listen, I believe you, and I'm sorry for not saying that sooner."

Chelsea reaches out, slings her arm over Dani's shoulders, and squeezes. "See? You're not alone."

Dani sniffles a bit and looks away, her eyes shining. Damn it, I didn't mean to make her cry.

Emma, Jaime, and Sierra are still on the other side of the vault run, talking too softly to be heard, but it's suddenly super obvious a battle line has been drawn, and I've aligned myself against Emma.

Janet walks over and frowns at the tears swimming in Dani's eyes. "Dani, why don't you take a quick bathroom break?" she whispers, with her back to the other girls, ensuring they don't hear her. I was not expecting that. It kind of makes me want to hug her. It was genuinely kind and had nothing to do with our training or the Olympics or anything except making sure Dani was okay. My mind spins as I try to figure out the last time I saw a coach act like that, and the only answer I come up with is *never*. Never. Not even Pauline. Crying happens in training, frustration overflows, exhaustion takes over, but even Pauline would just walk away, ignoring us until we got ourselves together.

Dani nods, wiping at her cheeks quickly and walking away. "Audrey, I want one clean one and a half twist, and Chelsea, let's see both your vaults." Janet turns to the other girls. "Ladies, warm up."

They move off to the floor, Sierra leading them with a smug smile on her face and Jaime smirking. It's so weird to see Emma falling in line behind them. How is she siding with them? I hate that we're divided, and I hate that I don't see a way to fix any of it.

"Come on," Chelsea says, pulling me out of my own head. "You're really close to sticking that one and a half. Get your hands down a little quicker onto the horse and you've got it."

Right. Vault. C'mon, Audrey, concentrate on vault and not the drama. With a quick inhale and exhale and then a head shake, the drama slides away.

Huh, I guess Janet's shake-it-off thing actually works.

"Let's go, Rey!" Janet shouts from the vault, where she's adjusted the springboard for me. She claps her hands together sharply, and I can't help but notice that we have the other trio's full attention, even though they should be warming up.

Janet follows the path of my eyes. "Girls, let's go!" she calls out and that jolts them into action.

"Remember, quicker into your block," Chelsea says from behind me, pulling my attention back to the task at hand.

I take off at a run into a roundoff back handspring, hands quick to the vault and off, twisting one and a half times around, open up and land, stick. That was a good one, and my back didn't even twinge.

"Excellent," Janet says with a firm, approving nod. "Go on and get some water before joining the others in warming up for floor."

I move away and flash Chelsea a thumbs-up for the advice. It really was the best vault I've done in a long time.

"Audrey," Janet calls out. "Why don't you go check on Dani first?"

Spinning in the opposite direction, I head for the bathroom, pulling at my wrist guards. I use them for vault, but I don't need them on floor. I'm only about halfway there when someone falls into step beside me and my heart gives a soft lurch at his proximity.

"Nice vault," Leo says, his voice low and a little rumbly.

"Thanks," I whisper back.

He doesn't break stride as he leans slightly into me, the back of his hand gently ghosting over mine, sending a wave of shivers through my entire body, and then he's gone, his longer stride pulling him ahead, his vision focused solely on the exercise bike in the far corner.

It was no more than a spilt second, but my heart rate doesn't slow as I continue on toward the bathroom, trying to subtly glance around the gym to see if anyone noticed. As nice as that felt, we just cannot do things like that on the regular if I'm going to keep my sanity or my spot on the team.

I slip through the bathroom door and find Dani with her hands on the edge of the sink, staring into the mirror, and any fears I have about Leo are gone. This is way more important. There are tears running down her cheeks and tissues on the ledge in front of her full of smudged black eyeliner and tan concealer. Her reflection gives me a watery smile.

"Janet wants us out for floor, and if you could make sure Emma feels you breathing down her neck for that all-around gold, that'd be great."

Dani snorts. "Yeah, that'll happen."

"What? You finished, like, two-tenths of a point behind her at trials, and you actually beat her on day two. It's possible."

"Please, the judges were handing out points like candy that night, Rey. I just can't believe you guys are fighting. It, like, defies the laws of the universe."

"I guess so. She's . . . I don't know. I've never really seen her like this. It's gotta be the pressure." It feels like the problem is working itself out as I speak. "Personally, I think she's terrified of you."

The thought hadn't even really occurred to me until I said it. The whole world expects Emma to win the all-around, maybe most especially Emma herself. Her only rival was supposed to be Irina

Kareva, but Dani's rise over the last year has been meteoric and took literally everyone by surprise. Maybe, despite the media attention at trials, even Dani doesn't understand how close it is between them.

"Whatever it is, she's pretty dumb to fight with her best friend right before the Olympics." There's something in her voice, like maybe she feels guilty. "I'm sorry if I—"

"No way," I cut her off. "I believe you. If Emma thinks that siding with those girls is going to get her any closer to the gold medal podium, then that's her choice, but I know you're telling the truth."

"Damn it, Rey," Dani says, laughing through a new set of tears. "You're good people."

I smile, feeling my own tears building but forcing them down. We need to get back out there. "You're good people too."

"Come on—your boyfriend is probably dying to see your floor routine up close and personal again." She's deflecting, but I'm cool with it, especially because of the dark half-moons under her eyes.

I haven't gotten much sleep in the last few days, but she's probably barely slept since trials, and she's dealing with all of it and still doing awesome gymnastics.

If she can do it, then so can I.

"He's not my boyfriend," I shoot back as I follow her out of the bathroom. "We can't, you know, be together now."

"Well, that sucks," she says, eyeing me with sympathy as we walk back toward the floor. The other girls are warming up their tumbling, and we join Chelsea in one of the corners as she waits for Sierra to finish her run. I deliberately keep my back to where Leo is working out across the gym.

"Yeah, it does."

I push up onto my toes and run into the pass, a roundoff, a back handspring into a two and a half twist immediately into a front full. It's my hardest tumbling run, and I stick it perfectly enough to lift my leg in arabesque at the end as a flourish. I finish with a salute and smile in satisfaction. That was a—

"Nice one," Emma says when I pass her. Maybe there's a hint of contrition in the softness of her voice, but to be honest I'm really not in the mood at all, not after seeing Dani as upset as she was.

"Thanks," I mumble and stand behind her, bouncing up and down on my toes as she takes off toward the other corner, executing a perfect triple twist.

"Okay, ladies," Janet calls, clapping her hands together. "We'll be rotating through in the order that we'll likely compete in Tokyo, but alternates first. Jaime?"

With the press of a button, Jaime's music blasts through the gym's speakers. It's "Zorba's Dance," retooled to begin at lightning speed for her to get her most difficult tumbling in with the music at crescendo, before slowing down in the middle of the routine for her dance sequences and some choreography that sort of resembles the actual Zorba's Dance.

I've always thought it was a weird choice for Jaime, who is decidedly not Greek, but she does manage to make the routine work well despite some pretty big lunges and hops on her tumbling landings. Then she falls out of her double turn too, which will drop her difficulty, not to mention her execution score.

She finishes off her routine with a double back and then salutes. It's actually pretty obnoxious how loudly Sierra and Emma applaud for what's a painfully average routine. Not that I can judge—mine is pretty much on par with it in difficulty, but Chelsea and I look to each other meaningfully before applauding as politely as we can.

Janet waves Jaime over to her. "Good job. Excellent height on your tumbling. Okay, Sierra, up next."

I blink at the lack of correction. There were a bunch of things wrong with Jaime's routine—her landings, not finishing her turns completely. Oh, that must be another one of Janet's sport psych things: positive reinforcement. I guess Jaime knows what she did wrong. We always know what we did wrong.

Sierra's music blares to life: a theme from *The Magnificent Seven*. Her family owns a ranch, and her music has been some kind of tribute to the Wild West since we were little. It definitely has an epic quality to it, but I'm not in the mood to be generous. I smirk when her heel drops during her double L-turn and when she doesn't hit a full split on not one but two of her leaps. Dance elements aren't her strength. Tumbling, however, definitely is, and she lands a routine packed full with a double layout, a triple twist, a one and a half through to double Arabian, and a full-in to end.

"Yeah, Sierra! Kill it!" Jaime cheers when Sierra lands the full-in with a hop back.

"Good job, Sierra," Janet says, applauding as well. "We'll work on the turns tomorrow, but way to sell that routine. Your emotional connection really came through."

Sierra nods but jogs back to Emma and Jaime with a huge smile on her face.

I move out onto the floor and nod to let Janet know I'm ready to go.

"Audrey," Janet says, before she presses play. "I only want a dance-through. No tumbling."

"But, Coach . . ." I stop at the word. Coach. She's my coach now, and I've never called anyone that, except Pauline. As the silence stretches, Janet walks over to my corner of the floor.

"Just a dance-through, Audrey, please," she repeats softly, and I nod, swallowing back another protest.

She cues up "Moon River" and I do my best to focus on my choreography, a waltz over the floor with an imaginary partner leading into balletic turns and spins that don't just add in difficulty but link the choreography to the gymnastics skills. Where most gymnasts do the most difficult move they can execute without falling, Pauline and I worked really hard at finding creative and rare elements that would highlight my dancing while still helping out my difficulty. Something Janet seems to appreciate, by the way she's nodding along with my routine.

I push away thoughts of both coaches, old and new, and line up for a fake tumbling run, jogging across the mat and jumping up slightly to imitate a landing before moving back into my choreography. This time a leap series across the floor, linking them together with the dance and then finally into my last turn, before finishing with my arms raised and my head tilted back.

Applause breaks out, and it rattles up into the high ceilings of the gym. It was a good run-through, but without the actual tumbling, it's meaningless. I smile at Chelsea and Dani, who are waiting for me in our corner. Dani offers me a bottle of water for when I catch my breath. Chelsea's up next, and she runs through her routine to Otis Redding's "Down in the Valley," with Otis's voice edited out thanks to the stupid rules against songs with vocals. According to her, it was her grandad's favorite song, but it melds perfectly with her playful style on the floor. My gaze flies across the room to Leo, and the urge to take him by the hand, pull him off the stationary bike he's riding, and dance to this is nearly overwhelming, so I look away and concentrate on Chelsea's powerful—if a little out of control—tumbling.

"Easy, Chelsea," Janet corrects as she overdoes a double layout and nearly bounces out of bounds from the ricochet. She reins herself in and keeps the routine going.

Chelsea finishes with a flourish of her arms in the air and a sassy twist of her body on the piano's chords. Anyone who watches that routine without smiling isn't human. It's the total opposite of traditional gymnastics wisdom, but Chelsea owns it, and who exactly is going to argue with the defending Olympic champion over her floor music choice?

Emma is up next, and her routine to Copland's "Hoedown" has a similar tone to Sierra's, but Emma's gymnastics is head and shoulders above hers. Her tumbling is high and clean, with stellar landings, and her dance is impeccable. I can practically hear the Olympic crowd clapping along as she wraps up the routine in the all-around final, cheering her on to gold as she finishes dancing across the floor, playing an imaginary fiddle, before collapsing to the mat with feigned exhaustion. It really is a spectacular routine, and I've never allowed myself to hate her for it, but watching her run back to Sierra and Jaime for high fives and congrats makes that feeling super easy to let in.

"Dani, you're up," Janet instructs for the final time that day. I have no illusions now. We've had a morning workout on vault and floor, and I fully expect that we'll be visualizing for the remainder of the day once Dani has landed her final pass.

She's one of the best floor workers in the world, and it shows. Even before she was a top all-around contender, she'd always been incredible on floor. Her charisma, tumbling, and dance training seep into every step of the routine, and she expresses every note of the music, even with her tumbling. An instrumental remix of songs from *The Greatest Showman* has been her floor music for two years now, but even after all this time, it's still awesome up close.

As she finishes up her routine, Mrs. Jackson comes in through the doors, dressed more for a business lunch than a gym as usual, and applauds with the rest of us when Dani sticks her triple twist to end the routine.

She runs to us, and Chelsea and I give her hugs and fist bumps. Over Dani's shoulder, Emma glares, but I roll my eyes. She treats Dani like a leper and sides with Sierra and Jaime, and I'm supposed to feel bad about it? No way.

"Lovely, Dani," Mrs. Jackson says, moving toward the edge of the floor. "I'm sorry to interrupt your training session, but if you girls could gather around, I have an announcement."

I want to tell her not to worry about it, that Janet was probably about to declare us finished for the day anyway, but I figure it's probably not a great idea to mouth off to the head of the USOF.

We stand in a semicircle around her, but the divide is clear: three on one side, three on the other. Her mouth twists into an unhappy pout, but she shakes her head and says, "I had been hoping to avoid this, but after consultation with the board of directors at the USOF, they've raised concerns that I think we all share about the decisions made prior to our arrival here and any potential conflicts of interest in our current situation. As such, they've made the unanimous decision to host another competition to determine which girls shall represent the United States in Tokyo."

"We trained for months to peak at trials," Chelsea says, her voice firm but respectful. "I could have qualified individually, you know? I could have done what Sarah and Brooke did, but I wanted to help this team win gold, and now I might lose my spot entirely because of something that isn't any of our faults?"

Mrs. Jackson holds up her hands in supplication. "I know, and I understand your frustration, Ms. Cameron, but the decision has already been made. I suggest you focus your energies on the competition ahead instead."

Chelsea nods but keeps her arms crossed over her chest. It's clear what she really thinks of that suggestion.

Mrs. Jackson raises an eyebrow. "The team will be determined by a group of judges who were not at trials, and their scores will be the final word. The combination of girls that will bring in the best scores across all four events for the team will be chosen, not necessarily the top all-around gymnasts. Obviously, we know that regardless of the outcome, you girls will represent the United States with honor and dignity. Do you understand, ladies?"

"Yes, ma'am," we all say as one, a leftover instinctive response from Gibby's tenure.

She leaves us as quickly as she appeared.

"We got this," I say, and both Chelsea and Dani nod quickly. A few feet away, the other girls are practically in a huddle, maybe saying the same thing.

Janet clears her throat, and we all snap to attention. "Okay, girls. Good workout. I want you mentally prepared for training tomorrow, so please take the rest of the session to visualize or meditate. Go over your weaknesses in training from today and yesterday. Tomorrow we'll be working on those particular issues."

We all start to disperse, but then she calls us back. *What now? A new meditation technique? An announcement that we'll only be training one event a day from here on out?*

"Also, ladies. If you six can't get your heads out of your asses long enough to see that dividing up this way is never going to win you gold, then please let me know so I can resign. I have no interest in watching a civil war play out in the next few weeks. Get over yourselves or get the hell out of my gym."

chapter twelve

There's been almost a full week of peace.

Training is smooth as silk. We've started working together to set up every apparatus the way each of us likes, chalking the bars, moving mats, placing springboards, and working through our rotations like clockwork. It's exactly what we'll have to do in Tokyo with just Janet on the floor instead of a cadre of coaches like we've always had at international competitions. If nothing else, figuring out the logistics of who does what and when has been a welcome distraction.

They should send Janet Dorsey-Adams to every war-torn corner of the world to broker cease-fires with a few pointed words and a raised eyebrow.

When I roll out of bed on the morning of our second Olympic trials, I immediately sit on the floor and begin my stretches, making sure my back is loose after stiffening up overnight.

As my range of motion starts to improve, my split fully extended and my arms finding the space well beyond my toes, Emma rolls over with a groan and then slides out of bed, careful to avoid tripping over me, or worse, making eye contact and actually having to exchange a word.

She heads for the bathroom first and is done with her shower by the time I'm finished stretching out.

Then we swap so she can get ready and leave for breakfast by the time I'm back.

The routine doesn't leave much room for talking things out, but it's also kept the awkward silences to a minimum here and in the gym. It's actually kind of sad. I doubt we'd have come to such a perfectly in-tune pattern of avoiding each other if we weren't so close in the first place.

I take a little extra time with my makeup. Our leos are a bright metallic red, and I want my lips to match, with winged eyeliner to play up the drama. I'm blotting my lipstick just as Dani leans against my doorjamb.

"Ready?" she asks.

"Who cares?" Chelsea grumbles behind her. "I need caffeine, and it can't wait for Rey's smoky eye to be perfect."

"All done, smart ass." I cap the lipstick and toss it into the front pocket of my competition backpack. "And have I made you wait at all this week?"

"No, that's the annoying part," Chelsea says, slinging an arm around my shoulders. "Your makeup skills are dark magic."

"You are so doing my look in Tokyo," Dani says.

I stop in my tracks. "If I go."

"You're going," Chelsea says with a snort. "I've run those numbers from nationals and trials a million times. Gibby might have been an abusive asshole who deserves to have his testicles eaten by mountain lions—"

"Crows," Dani cuts in, and she shrugs when we stare at her. "It'd be slower."

"Crows, then," Chelsea says. "But you, me, Dani, and Emma— our scores made the best combination for the team competition, and nothing is going to change that."

Unless I fall, I say in my head but don't voice it. "You're right. I know you're right."

"Good, now, please, caffeine soon, before I pass out."

We're about halfway down the stairs when I see them: Agents Farley and Kingston in their black suits talking to Mrs. Jackson.

Agent Kingston is speaking in her soft voice. "Mrs. Jackson, we're just trying to find out the truth. I think you can appreciate that."

"Of course I can, and we have been more than cooperative throughout this investigation, but now is *not* the time. Forgive me if I don't want to put them through the emotional wringer of an FBI interrogation before the most important competition of their lives."

"What's going on?" Dani asks, taking the last few steps in one leap.

Agent Farley turns to her. "Dani, I'm so glad to see you here."

"Thanks," she says, but she isn't about to be deterred. "What's going on?"

"We need to speak to you and your teammates again," Agent Kingston says.

Dani takes a step back away from them, almost leaning into me and Chelsea as we reach the bottom of the steps. "But I told you. I told you everything, and you said you believed me."

Agent Kingston flinches like Dani's words slapped her across the face. "We do, Dani, but . . ."

Dani doesn't even wait for her to finish before a sob rips out of her throat. She's off, running out of the house toward the dock. She flashes by the glass windows overlooking the bay at full speed and then disappears from view.

Chelsea is on her heels, calling after her. "Dani! Dani, wait!"

I'm right behind her, but as I drop my bag by the door, I hear Mrs. Jackson say, "You can speak to them, but *after* the competition. You've done enough damage this morning."

Passing through the door, I follow the path Dani and then Chelsea took out into the early morning haze. The dock is still damp from the night before, and there's a slight chill in the air. I shiver despite the tracksuit I layered on top of my competition leo. They're at the end of the dock, rolling up the legs of their pants and sitting down, letting their feet dangle into the water.

I hesitate for a second, rocking back on my heels. Do I belong here? Before the last two weeks I barely knew Dani, but . . .

"Don't just stand there, Rey, get in here," Chelsea says over her shoulder and tilts her head toward Dani's other side.

Kicking off my sneakers and pulling my pant legs up to my knees, I sit down on the edge of the dock. The water is cool against my ankles, and Dani's hand is warm when I take it in mine, mirroring Chelsea's grip on her other hand.

"Apparently, my word isn't good enough," she manages to croak out. Her grip on my hand tightens. "I told them everything. I told them how . . . how he's been doing this to me for a whole year. He'd tell me he needed more from me, that what I was giving him wasn't good enough, but that he was rooting for me to come out on top, to prove to him that I was good enough. He'd text me just so I'd know he was watching. I just . . . I wanted to make this team so badly. I swear, the first time he came to my room . . . I thought he wanted to talk to me about my gymnastics. I didn't even think it was weird. How stupid is that?"

"It wasn't stupid," Chelsea whispers. "I would have thought that too."

"We all would have," I add. "He was . . . he was in charge of everything. When we ate, trained, slept. Everything."

Dani laughs, and it's a hollow sound that chills me far more than the air. "Sleeping, yeah. Do you know he gave me my own room at worlds last year? I knew why and I didn't say anything. Didn't ask anyone to share. I just stayed there and waited like an idiot."

"You're not," Chelsea and I say at the same time, and when Dani laughs at us, it sounds a little stronger than before.

"Do you know what happened at trials? I was so stupid. I thought, *I'm on the team now. He can't touch me anymore. What's he going to do, kick me off?* and then he just *did*." She stops and takes a rattling breath. "I guess I should be grateful for that, that he fucked up enough to get caught, but now half the world thinks I cheated. Shit, half this team thinks I cheated, test results be damned, and that I'm making this up just to get back at him."

"They're idiots," I say.

Dani laughs.

Chelsea nods. "She's right. They are, and you're an amazing gymnast, and you're going to go to the Olympics and dominate."

"Ladies?" Mrs. Jackson calls from back at the house. The click of her ever-present stiletto heels is the tick of a countdown as she approaches. "I know it's difficult," she says, stopping behind us, "but the others have left for the gym, and we have a schedule to keep."

Dani sniffs and pulls her hands free from ours, wiping at the tears I hadn't noticed streaming down her cheeks. "We're ready to go."

"Are you sure?" I mumble as we stand. The nylon fabric of my track pants slides down to my ankles, sticking against my damp skin.

Straightening her shoulders, Dani nods, her eyes flashing in determination. "Yes."

———

Janet is already at the gym with the judges who will be evaluating us during the competition this morning. Emma, Sierra, and Jaime are stretching out on the floor and laughing together like they don't have a care in the world, like Dani hasn't just had an emotional punch to the gut, like this is another practice and not the competition that will determine the rest of our lives. A trip to Tokyo as a member of the best team in the world, the runaway favorites to win the team gold medal, or as an alternate, doomed to watch someone else achieve your dreams. My annoyance with Emma flares to life again. It must be nice to be able to ignore all that.

Cameras are mounted near each of the events, lights hung from the ceiling, and cameramen dressed in all black milling around too. Everything needs to be on the up-and-up, as Mrs. Jackson has said over and over again this week. All of our performances need to be out there for the world to see. The girls who perform the best today will make the team. Nothing more, nothing less.

Chelsea, Dani, and I move onto the floor and jog around it quickly, circling our arms and warming up. As we come to a stop a few feet away from the other girls, Leo edges over, stopping to bend down and tie his shoelace. With the cameras around, he's not taking any chances.

"She okay?" he whispers, not looking up from his sneaker.

"Yes."

His eyes flicker toward Emma and the others before looking up to me. "Are *you* okay?"

"Yes."

"Good."

He stands and immediately moves off back toward the small set of bleachers against the wall, and we run through team warm-ups led by Chelsea and Emma—we haven't named a team captain yet, but if we had to vote today, I have a pretty decent feeling the vote would be split down the middle.

Finally, Janet claps her hands together and we jog to her. "Okay, ladies, Olympic order today: vault, bars, beam, floor. But before we begin, I just want to say that you have all worked tremendously hard these last few weeks under perhaps the worst circumstances I can imagine. Don't let the results of today, no matter what they may be, change what you know to be true about yourself. You deserve to be here. All of you."

There's a softness in her voice, a warmth that I've never felt directed at me before a competition, and it's . . . wonderful, but then she straightens her shoulders and the moment passes.

"Okay, hands in. USA on three. One, two, three . . ."

"USA!" we all shout together.

"Now let's get started." Janet nods to the judges, who take their seats beside the vault.

I recognize them from competitions over the years, but none of them were at nationals or trials. A fresh set of eyes might be a good thing, but who knows? These people could be the Sierra Montgomery Official Fan Club, for all I know. I just have to go out and prove I'm better than her.

We sprint down the carpet to the end of the vault run. This feels good, familiar, even if it is the first competition I've been to without Gibby in charge or Pauline coaching me or Emma rooting for me.

Ugh, Audrey, don't do this.

I shake my head, literally. I hate to admit it, but Janet was right. Physically shaking negative thinking out has actually worked. I can't think about all the things that have gone wrong up until now. I can't think about anything other than the four routines that will decide the rest of my gymnastics career—or lack thereof.

"Welcome, ladies and gentlemen, to something that has never happened before!"

My head snaps around. There's an announcers' booth nestled into the corner of the gym, and I cannot believe I didn't see it. The network logo is stamped across the front, and two reporters I recognize from our major competitions are seated behind it with headsets and microphones. The gym is practically empty. Every word is loud and clear as we run through our warm-up vaults.

The announcer continues his opening monologue, "We're coming to you live from Olympic training camp, where after days of seclusion following the arrest of the team's head coach, Christopher Gibson, these young athletes will be competing for the right to represent the United States of America at the Olympic Games."

Yeah, that's not going to be distracting at all.

Loud arenas are one thing; all the noises blend together and then fade to the background. A constant narration over what's supposed to be a small, closed competition? That's another thing entirely.

"They'll start on vault, an apparatus where Chelsea Cameron, the defending all-around champion from Rio, will be able to set herself apart, right, Cindy?"

"Yes, Jim, but this is an evenly matched group of athletes. I'm telling you right now, we're going to see the leaderboard shuffle over and over again before the competition is over."

A timer rings out in the gym, and I guess that's the sound for the end of warm-ups. As the weakest vaulter, I'm up first.

The gym is silent, so the mock-whispers from the broadcast booth ring out loud and clear. "Audrey Lee isn't the strongest vaulter on the team, so she'll have to maximize every tenth of a point in the one and a half twist she performs. The other girls will all be doing doubles or two and a half twists—the Amanar."

I close my eyes for a moment and visualize a perfect vault, and then I'm running, a dozen steps, a hurdle into the roundoff, back handspring onto the vault, block fast and a one and a half twist with a small step to the side. I overrotated it a touch.

"A slight overrotation, but overall a good vault," Cindy says, and I grimace before pulling at the tape on my wrists. I tape them differently for bars, where I need more support.

The judges are using an old-school flip board for the scores, and I nod to myself as a 14.2 pops up and is shown throughout the gym. That feels about right. That's where Gibby always wanted my vault, especially if I couldn't manage the double. He always used to say it like it was some kind of character flaw that my body would break apart if I added that extra half twist. My mind flickers back to trials in the trainers' room and his words ringing in my ears: that he needed more from me to get on the team. Like I wasn't trying hard enough.

I shake my head. *Focus, Audrey, focus.* I peek at the scoreboard set up in the corner beside the broadcasters, and it's nice to see my name at the top.

"A good start for Audrey Lee, but if everyone else hits, that will be our lowest vault score of the day," Jim chimes in.

Ugh. Really?

The problem is he's right. For a few moments, my name is beside the number one, until Jaime and Sierra fittingly put up identical vault scores for their double twists, a 14.5 each, pushing me down into third.

Now the big guns come out. Our team has three Amanar vaults— it's one of the reasons we're the best team in the world. No one can match the kind of lead we'll take if we hit three good Amanars in the first rotation.

Bam. Bam. Bam. Three vaults, three fantastic scores, and the leaderboard is right around where I thought it would be after the first rotation.

1.	Chelsea Cameron	15.0
2.	Emma Sadowsky	14.9
3.	Dani Olivero	14.8
4.	Sierra Montgomery	14.5
4.	Jaime Pederson	14.5
6.	Audrey Lee	14.2

I have some ground to make up, but bars are next, and this is where I should pop up past Jaime and Sierra. That is, if I hit. Nothing is guaranteed in gymnastics, not even on your strongest apparatus.

Jim the broadcaster's voice cuts through the air as we march to bars. "Our first competitor will be Chelsea Cameron, who has significantly deteriorated on this event since her run to the all-around gold four years ago."

"They were never really her strength before," Cindy interjects.

"Nothing like a confidence boost before going up there," Chelsea says as we all gather around the chalk and work it into our grips while Janet adjusts the bars for us to our specifications.

"Chelsea Cameron, Olympic champion, rattled by two dumb reporters? I doubt it," Dani says. Chelsea gives her a smile before they bump chalk-covered fists.

I don't think she was rattled, not really, but her bars are never great, and this time is no exception. A fall, a massive break in form on her transition from the high bar down to the low, and then at least three extra empty swings during the routine to get herself back on track.

Dani draws Chelsea into a hug once she makes her way back to us, and I wait my turn before hugging her tight. It's one thing to understand intellectually that you aren't the gymnast you once were. I can personally attest to that. It's another thing for your performance to show it.

The scorecard flips up—a 12.5—and I cringe. It's not unfair, but it is awful.

"Vault and floor. You'll make it up there," Dani whispers to her before heading up to bars herself.

Her bars routine is super solid. It's one of the major reasons she's been able to close the gap between her and Emma in the last year. She's so strong, being able to tune out everything that went down before the competition started. I tighten my grips and swing my arms around as she dismounts.

"Nice!" I say.

"Get it," she replies before Chelsea pulls her into a hug.

"That was amazing," Chelsea squeals to her roommate, and the judges agree, posting a 14.8.

Her roommate. That word triggers something inside my head. Dani has a roommate now. Not like last year at worlds, when Gibby made her room by herself. I can't even imagine what that must feel like, sitting in a room alone, knowing there would be no one to stop him, knowing that if you say anything, it could cost you your lifelong dreams. My stomach lurches, and I can actually feel bile burning up my throat at the thought.

No, not now, Audrey. Focus on what you have to do.

"And that's a great routine from Emma Sadowsky!" Jim's voice pulls me out of my head, and I'm grateful for it. If Emma's done on bars, it means I zoned out for Jaime's routine. While I have no idea how she did, I need to prepare for my own set. If I'm going to have any chance at all, I need to hit the crap out of bars and take a lead on Jaime that she can't overcome on beam and floor.

A quick look at the scoreboard tells me Jaime's routine was decent, and then Emma's 14.6 slides into place and propels her into the overall lead.

Now Sierra's up, and she's my main competition here. She might be a total bitch, but she's a total bitch who can swing bars.

"And that's a nice transition between low and high, legs glued together and toes pointed, and now into her dismount, a full-in, and a step on the landing," Jim says from the booth.

It was a good routine. A very good routine. I'm going to have to step it up. I need to separate myself here.

I'm saved from having to clap politely for her routine because I'm prepping the bars for my own, but I glance out of the corner of my eye and see a 15.0 on the scorecard. Damn it, I wanted to be the only one who hit fifteen on bars today, but I guess I'll have to settle for being the top worker.

I smile before turning to the judges and saluting. I hope they're watching closely, because I'm about to own this routine.

Thirty seconds later, after sticking my triple twisting layout to finish, it takes everything in me not to actually scream in celebration when I raise my hands in salute.

That's why I love this sport: the feeling of my toes digging into the mats and my arms up in the air after I dare the judges to find one mistake in that routine. I mean, they will, but I made it a lot harder than usual.

Jim says it better than I ever could as I pass the booth, undoing my grips as I go. "That was one of the best bars routines you will *ever* see from Audrey Lee! Incredible form in the air, full extension, pointed toes, and she just flies on her transitions and release moves. A lot of people counted her out when she couldn't compete at worlds last year, but she's worked her way into top form, and look at those standings, Cindy!"

"Audrey Lee rates a 15.3 on uneven bars, and while Dani Olivero has a one-tenth lead on the field, we have a three-way tie for second place halfway through this competition!"

"We knew it would be close, but right now it feels like this is anyone's game!"

1.	Daniela Olivero	29.6
2.	Audrey Lee	29.5
2.	Sierra Montgomery	29.5
2.	Emma Sadowsky	29.5
5.	Jaime Pederson	29.0
6.	Chelsea Cameron	27.5

"That was ridiculous," Chelsea says. We fist bump, chalk flying out into the air on contact. Then Dani holds both her hands out as well.

"That was sick, Rey."

"Good job," Emma says, patting me awkwardly on the shoulder, while Jaime and Sierra smile tightly. The act is getting harder to fake now that it comes down to the results from two events. One slipup and our dreams are dead.

And, of course, we're headed for balance beam.

chapter thirteen

I pop off the beam, finishing my warm-up so Emma can get in a few skills before it's time to compete.

"Patience up there, Audrey," Janet says as I pass her on my way off the mats. "Let the skills flow. Don't force it."

Nodding, I accept her correction and then grab my water bottle. I have some cushion now, thanks to that bars routine, but I need to hit beam.

Jim picks up his commentary after we finish warm-ups. "Here's where we'll see Emma Sadowsky and Dani Olivero pull away from everyone else and maybe see Jaime Pederson make a move into the top four."

I'm half annoyed that he doesn't even mention me, but honestly, it's probably better. I'd love to make his voice crack again the way it did when he freaked over my bars score.

Poor Chelsea has to lead off. There's no shame in being more of a specialist, especially since she already won Olympic gold. She shouldn't have to prove anything, but there she is, up on the beam and struggling to put together combinations that will keep her difficulty level competitive. She dismounts with a double back and then salutes with a chagrined shake of her head.

Jim and Cathy's voices buzz in my head, but I zone them out as Dani begins her routine. Closing my eyes, I visualize my skills like I've done dozens of times in the past week. I let my arms travel around me, imitating the motions I'll make once it's my turn, trying to activate as much of my muscle memory as possible. The more familiar it becomes on the ground, the easier it'll be once I've only got four inches of space to work with up there. Groans from the small crowd break through my trance, but without an accompanying *thwack* of feet—or body—hitting the mat, I assume Dani's had a small hiccup but not a fall. I open my eyes in time to see her dismounting with a roundoff into a double Arabian. She sticks it defiantly, clearly pissed at herself for whatever mistake she made.

It's a 14.3.

Not a terrible score, but definitely not her best.

"You'll get it back on floor," Chelsea says to her, still offering her a fist bump. I put mine out too for what's quickly becoming a tradition for us.

"Let's go, Sierra!" Jaime yells as her best friend salutes the judges. I close my eyes again and run through it all one more time, slowly and then again at the pace the judges will be looking for in a great routine. Skills are important, but so is rhythm. By the time I open my eyes, Sierra's routine is over, and Emma is on the beam, working through her connections easily enough. I glance at the scoreboard. Sierra got a 14.6. Not bad.

I'm up next, so I move toward the beam. "Come on, Emma, you got this." I say it more out of habit than anything else as she launches for her dismount: two back handsprings into an Arabian double front. She takes a big hop forward after giving the skill a little too much juice, but better too much than too little on that particular dismount.

"All you, Rey," Emma says as we pass each other. She must have heard me cheer her on while she was up there, the tiniest peace offering breaking through the awkwardness and animosity of the last few days.

Janet sets the springboard for me, and I test it out, making sure it's the perfect distance from the beam. I wait for Emma's score, rocking back and forth from toe to heel and keeping my breathing steady and even. Then the judges flip their scoreboard around. It's a 14.7, right around where she's been scoring all year.

Okay. My turn.

Narrowing my vision, focusing on the springboard, I picture hitting it at just the right speed to land lightly on the beam, then I exhale and go.

I bounce off the springboard, up and over then onto the beam. My feet are steady, so I immediately connect it back into the two layout step-outs. I salute to show control and move into the rest of my choreo to prepare for the next section. I don't hesitate before moving into the triple turn—which again turns into a double, and then I lose my center and I'm folding at the waist, trying to keep my balance. One of my hands instinctively goes down toward the beam to stop my momentum, but I'm able to pull it away in time and find my center of gravity, holding myself still for a beat and then another, but that was a major mistake.

At least I didn't fall.

I exhale and lift my chin in the smallest acknowledgment of the little victory. The rest of the routine flies by with only a few wobbles, and before I know it, I'm setting myself for the dismount, and I count it out in my head as I launch into the double back handspring and tuck my arms in to my body for the triple twist. It's slightly under-rotated, and I twist into the ground a bit, but it's a good landing, almost a stick.

I move off the mat, trying to clear my head, and that's when I feel it.

A flicker in my back.

Fuck.

It was there, but now it's gone. It hasn't been that long since my last cortisone shot. It can't be wearing off yet. It was the landing. The landing was a little short, so it hurt, and I'm just not used to it after feeling so good since the medicine kicked in.

That's it.

I'm fine.

It's going to be fine.

"Way to save it," Dani says, pulling me in for a hug when I move off the mat to wait for my score. There's still Jaime's routine left in the rotation, so I have a chance to gather myself a bit before we move to floor, the last event of the day and the minute and a half of gymnastics that will decide my fate. I have to clear my head. No distractions, no pain. Just me and my floor routine.

"Jeez, this is going to be close," Chelsea says as my score comes up: a 14.3.

It makes sense. I probably took about a half a point in deductions on that almost fall. A 14.8 would have solidified my spot. Now? Now I have no idea how this is going to play out.

My back twinges while I dig through my bag for some tape. I sit down and gingerly wind the tape over my ankles, careful not to pull my skin too tightly as Jaime goes up to perform.

"Let's go, Jaime!" Sierra calls out, and we all applaud as she salutes and begins.

I probably shouldn't watch, but I can't help it.

The pressure is on her now to hit.

She does. At least, she does for the most part. Kind of. There's a bobble here and there, but nothing major. On beam, a lot of little nothing-majors can quickly turn into a crap score.

We wait.

"That wasn't great," Chelsea says between gritted teeth, sitting down beside me to wrap her own ankles.

"I know," I say, standing up and testing the tape by flexing my feet and moving up and down onto my toes.

"Wow!" Jim, the announcer yells in shock, his voice carrying far enough to reach us from across the gym. "Only a 14.6 for Jaime Pederson on beam, and while that's a good score for anyone else, that's not what she was looking for on her strongest event."

1.	Emma Sadowsky	44.3
2.	Sierra Montgomery	44.1
3.	Daniela Olivero	43.9
4.	Audrey Lee	43.8
5.	Jaime Pederson	43.6
6.	Chelsea Cameron	40.5

There isn't enough time to think about what this all means. I'm in fourth going into the last rotation, but floor is a strength for literally everyone else and a major weakness for me.

I'm up first, and "Moon River" pumps through the gym's sound system, but in my head it's the London Philharmonic playing their hearts out, and I'm a dancer onstage captivating the entire audience as I waltz through my routine. After days spent steaming about dance-through after dance-through, my muscles are singing at the opportunity to not only dance but tumble through this set. There's more power than I remember having a few weeks ago in each of my tumbling lines, so much so that I bounce out a bit from almost every landing. It costs me precious tenths, but part of me doesn't care. I know this routine is beautiful, and the judges know it too. That'll help as they put their pencils to paper.

I'm at my final tumbling run, a simple double back, and I land perfectly, chest up, knees cushioning but not too bent, and I raise my arms in the air to salute quickly—too quickly—and my back spasms.

The music is wrapping up, and I manage to perform my ending pose despite the tremor of pain. It wasn't intense—the same as the last one—but it was there. It's gone, but that wasn't a fluke. The cortisone is wearing off.

I try to reel in my breathing as the other girls surround me for high fives, fist bumps, and an awkward side-hug with Sierra where she turns her head completely in the other direction, like she can't even stand to look at me. The feeling's pretty mutual, actually. I used to envy Sierra for her creamy skin, blue eyes, and blond hair that wouldn't be out of place on some perfectly boring teen soap, but now? Her face makes me want to punch it. Hard.

The score takes longer than the other events—there's more to look at in a floor routine than any other apparatus—but after a minute, with my breath finally coming at a normal rate, a 14.0 is posted, followed by my total all-around score.

57.8

Right around where I was at trials.

It was good enough to get me on the team last time, but now? Who knows.

I fall into one of the chairs and cringe at the jolt the abrupt contact sends through my back.

Careful, Audrey.

"Hey," I call to the USOF trainer, "can I get some ice?"

"You okay?" Dani asks, sitting down beside me. She has some time to kill. She'll be up last in this rotation.

"Yep," I say, not really able to manage any more than that.

Dani reaches out and holds my hand as the trainer arrives to help me wrap the ice around my torso, and I'm back on the dock this morning, holding her hand while she talks about Gibby and what he did to her, what he put her through. There's no reason to push it aside now.

Chelsea does a nice routine and scores a 13.9, putting her at a 54.4, nearly four total points below me. I inhale and exhale deeply as she sits on my other side, helping me hold the ice pack in place while the trainer runs for a wrap. I'm sitting between these girls, them sheltering me the way Chelsea and I did for Dani, and the whirring in my mind finally slows.

It feels like I'm missing something, like my mind is trying to weave the threads of something together, but I can't focus on it. Not when everything I've worked for my entire life is on the line. Right now, I have to worry about this. Whatever else is happening in the world, it can wait a few minutes.

Jaime goes up and scores a 14.1, putting her at a 57.1 total. Not even close to my score. I'm going to finish fourth. I start doing math in my head because it doesn't matter if I finish fourth if my bars and beam scores combine with the others to bring in the best overall team score.

"You're going to explode," Chelsea says as Dani leaves us to start warming up. "I can, like, see actual steam coming out of your ears. Stop doing math and watch."

I take her advice. She's an Olympic champion, after all. She knows best. Sierra takes the floor, and for a minute and a half we're transported back to the Wild West. Her landings are a little rough, and her smile seems pasted on, the connecting fiber between the routine and the music off. She let the pressure get to her.

What a shame . . . really. Okay, not really.

We're all going through the same thing, and if she can't handle the pressure here and now, she won't be able to handle it in Tokyo. The judges are scratching away at their papers, taking deductions, and when Sierra's finished, her score posts exactly even with mine.

My mind goes as numb as my back with the monstrosity of an ice pack attached to it. Emma and Dani perform, and my eyes watch, but I don't actually see either routine. I'm vaguely aware that they both outscore me, and when I look up at the final scores, I still really don't know what any of it means.

1. Daniela Olivero	58.5
1. Emma Sadowsky	58.5
3. Sierra Montgomery	58.3
4. Audrey Lee	57.8
5. Jaime Pederson	57.1
6. Chelsea Cameron	54.4

Dani and Chelsea have enveloped me into a group hug but release me pretty quickly. They both did what they needed to do today, while I managed to screw up just enough to have no idea whether this is the best or worst day of my life.

Emma comes over and hugs me tight. It's probably just for the cameras. She's going to make the team, obviously, but it's clear from just how tense she is in the embrace she didn't expect Dani to close the gap, not really. There they are, though, at the top of the standings together with exactly the same score.

Jaime and Sierra don't come over at all. Jaime's head is buried in her hands, and she's sobbing uncontrollably. Sierra stares into space. I don't blame her. She beat me in the all-around, but that's not really what matters.

Mrs. Jackson and Janet still have to do the math behind finding the four gymnasts who will combine for the best score in a team final, and that's going to take more than a minute.

The wait is excruciating, but probably not nearly as long as it feels, and then finally Mrs. Jackson is at a microphone.

"This competition was fierce and a testament to the talented young women we have here with us today. I want to thank each of them for their efforts in such trying circumstances. Now, the scores were tight. So tight, in fact, that three different combinations of girls produced the exact same score. Thus, we moved to a tiebreaker that was unanimously agreed upon by our judges, myself, and Coach Dorsey-Adams."

A murmur goes up in the gym. A tiebreaker? What the hell? Had it really been that close?

Mrs. Jackson is still talking. ". . . it was determined that priority should be given to the athletes with a longer history at high-pressure international competitions and the best chance to compete for multiple individual medals. Therefore, the four athletes who will represent the United States in the team competition are Daniela Olivero, Emma Sadowsky, Audrey Lee, and Chelsea Cameron. Jaime Pederson and Sierra Montgomery will remain our alternates, prepared to substitute should the need arise, making us equally proud, I'm sure. Thank you, ladies, for a truly inspiring and well-fought competition in the face of much adversity, and congratulations."

I made it.

I'm going to the Olympics.

chapter fourteen

There's no party this time, no parents and sponsors and coaches giving a champagne toast, just the kitchen table in the rental house and two FBI agents asking us questions with Mrs. Jackson off to the side, observing.

"So, this is one way to celebrate making the Olympic team, I guess?"

I sit down in the chair across from Agents Farley and Kingston.

"Congratulations," Agent Kingston says, her voice soft. "And we are sorry we have to put you through this again."

"No, it's fine," I assure them. "I want to help. I just . . . I already told you everything."

Agent Farley nods. "I'm not sure we were asking you the right questions back then, Audrey."

"On the night of Olympic trials, did Christopher Gibson send you this text message?" Agent Kingston asks, and then reads from a piece of paper. *"Celebrate tonight, but remember what I said."*

"He did."

"Now, please think back, Audrey. What was that in reference to—his exact words, if you can recall them?"

I replay that night in my mind and start talking. "I was in the trainers' room, and he came over and wouldn't look at me. Then he said something about how Emma and I wanted to be on the team together and that . . . that she was holding up her end of the bargain, but that he needed more from me than I'd given him so far."

"And you took that to mean?"

"That he wanted me to do better on balance beam."

"Did he explicitly say that?"

I hesitate and try to remember. "No, he . . . I don't think he did."

"Is there anything else?"

"Just that he was rooting for me to do well."

"Is that the last time you spoke to him?"

"No, he came over to talk to me and my parents the next day to congratulate us."

Agent Kingston glances sharply at her partner and then turns back to me. "Your parents were present for the conversation?"

"Yeah, he congratulated them and then said something about training camp, that he was excited to get started—wait, why are you asking me this?" I ask, but as I do, the awful truth begins to settle around me, everything becoming crystal clear in an instant, but somehow also the most confusing thing I've ever tried to wrap my brain around.

Agent Farley says, "We're attempting to establish a pattern, Audrey, with how he handled his victims, how he groomed them. That's what we call the behavior leading up to the abuse. Usually, it's the perpetrator attempting to gain their target's trust or, in Gibson's case, leveraging a position of authority over his gymnasts."

For years, Christopher Gibson had been one thing: a coach, a man to be respected and feared and obeyed without question because the only road to Olympic gold was through his approval and good graces. In the last few weeks, I understood, at least in theory, that all of that was a façade, a cover for the sick abuse he inflicted on my teammate. And now I know the awful truth.

He was going to abuse me too.

"Can you confirm that he assigned you a single room at the training center when you girls arrived?" Agent Kingston asks softly, breaking through my thoughts.

"He did. I thought it was weird because usually Emma and I . . . Wait, Dani said that he did that to her at worlds last year, gave her a single room, so he could . . . was he . . . was he going to . . ."

"Perhaps. It matches up with some of his earlier behavior, and had the opportunity presented itself, then yes, I'm afraid it was a possibility. I'm sorry."

I sniffle and wipe away a ridiculous tear that's escaped from the corner from my eye. "No, it's okay . . . It didn't happen and that's what matters. Is that how he always groomed girls?"

"Several other young women have confirmed these and other behaviors prior to being abused."

"Several? Then it wasn't just Dani?"

The agents don't respond, but I know it's true.

"How long has he been doing this?"

"As far as we can tell, a little over two decades."

My heart feels like it weighs a ton, every beat a physical effort at the truth of what happened to my friend and who knows how many others.

"Twenty years? Are you kidding?"

"Unfortunately not," Agent Farley says. "Will you be willing to testify to all of this at trial, Audrey?"

"Yes, of course, whatever you need. I want to make sure he rots in prison."

Agent Kingston smiles sadly. "Thank you, Audrey, then that's everything for now."

The scrape of the chair on the tile floor is jarring as I push back and stand up, wiping at my eyes one more time. Why the hell am I crying? Nothing even happened to me. *Jesus, Audrey, get it together.*

The living room is empty when I leave the kitchen with Mrs. Jackson. She reaches out and touches my shoulder softly. "I'm sorry," she whispers, but before I can answer, she's already walked past me and up the stairs, probably to find Emma, who is scheduled to go next.

Chelsea and Dani are upstairs too, but I'm not sure I'm ready to face Dani yet. I don't know if I'll be able to look at her and not start sobbing. She doesn't even know it, but she saved me from what she went through, and I don't know how to feel about that. Am I supposed to be grateful that she was abused, that he chose her before he chose me?

My feet keep moving, taking me from the living room and out the front door, into the warm beach air. The nights here are perfect, a salty breeze, a bright moon, the soft crashing of waves just a few streets over. But I'm numb to all of it. How is this the same world I existed in just a few minutes ago? Everything feels completely different.

My phone buzzes once, and then again, messages from Sarah and Brooke in our brand-new group chat:

CONGRATS!!

SEE YOU IN TOKYO!!

I shudder and pocket my phone. Congratulations don't feel right. Nothing feels right.

The tips of my fingers start to tingle, and my heart rate ticks up, my breathing coming short as the world closes in around me. I've only ever felt like this one other time: when Dr. Gupta first diagnosed my back pain as chronic and said I might have to give up gymnastics entirely.

Everything is catching up to me all at once, and I need to just not be here, to not have to go back in that house and face Dani or Emma or anyone. I take off, across the front yard and onto the sidewalk, sprinting as fast as I can down the street. I run like something is chasing me, but it's nothing I can outpace, no matter how long my stride or how quick my feet.

I have no idea where I'm going. The only thing I'm familiar with is the walk from the house to the gym, and I flew past the gym without thinking, but I hear the roar of the waves in the distance and head in that direction. I run until the pounding in my temples and the burning in my chest are too much to take, and I skid to a halt at the edge of the beach, the sun just beginning to set in the distance.

Bending over at the waist, I try to catch my breath, but it's impossible. My throat tightens, the bile rising out of my stomach, and I can't control the spams pushing the vomit up and out onto the sidewalk.

There's barely anything in my stomach, so it doesn't last long, but I stay bent over, trying to even out my breathing like Janet taught me.

"Audrey?" a voice asks, laced with concern and a whole lot of questions.

It's Leo.

It's super embarrassing, but there's nothing I can do. I hold up a hand, keeping him at a distance for a second while I shakily wipe the involuntary tears that leaked out of my eyes and then run my forearm over my mouth. I stand up gingerly, inhaling and then exhaling, letting out the breath with deliberate slowness.

When I turn to face him, he's in his board shorts and a T-shirt, an old backpack slung over one shoulder and a surfboard under his other arm. His hair is still wet, tiny rivulets running down his neck and soaking the collar of his shirt.

"Hey," I say finally, knowing there's no sense in playing it cool.

He digs into his bag and comes away with a water bottle. I take it without a word, swishing the water around in my mouth then spitting it out. Another sip, and this time I swallow it down, soothing my burning throat.

"Are you okay?" he asks when I hand it back.

"I think . . . I think maybe I'm not," I say, feeling my heart rate tick up again.

He studies me carefully for a moment and then another. "C'mon," he says, nodding over his shoulder toward the beach.

I don't even hesitate. I just follow. When he reaches for my hand, I take it and let myself lean into him, our shoulders brushing, and he shifts his palm against mine, the pads of his fingers catching against my hard-earned calluses before he twines them together and squeezes gently, pulling me just a little bit closer as we walk.

I've missed him, which is dumb because I never actually had him to begin with, but that's what it feels like: like I've found something I lost.

There's a gate up ahead, and when we reach it, Leo nods to the guy beside it, who opens it up for us. They slap hands quickly, snapping them apart the way boys do sometimes, and then he closes it behind us, turning to face the street again.

"Smooth," I whisper, half giggling, and that feels normal. Like I didn't just find out that I might have been the next victim of a serial sexual abuser, like I'm just hanging out at the beach with a guy. Like it's all good.

Good enough to risk your spot on the team, Audrey?

I push away that thought. No one knows we're here; my hair is down, and I'm not in a leotard. I'm virtually unrecognizable. Besides, what good is having a spot on the team if I'm an emotional wreck? I need to breathe, even for just a little while, and being around Leo helps.

"It's the Del's beach," he says, nodding toward the huge white building, the Hotel del Coronado, looming next to us, the spires of its red roof blending in with the early evening sky, outlined by white lights, twinkling in the distance.

There are a few people milling around, mostly couples wandering near the shore, and there's a family a few yards away with a fire going making s'mores, but when Leo sets down his surfboard and then lays out the towel from around his shoulders onto the sand, it feels entirely private, like the little patch of beach is ours alone.

Kicking off my sandals, I sit, looking out onto the water, the waves rolling in seemingly from nowhere.

"You want to talk about it?" he asks, settling beside me.

"They asked me to testify at the trial, I guess, eventually. I told them I would."

"Okay," he says, clearly not sure what that means, but he doesn't push. I could kiss him for it.

"They think maybe . . . that maybe he was grooming me as his next victim or something. They said that his behavior matched what he's done before."

That's met with silence, and the tears are back, slowly blurring my vision before spilling out onto my cheeks, one by one. I try to blink them away, but all it does is make more come.

Leo shifts around, looking me in the eye, holding that contact for a second and then another. "Can I?" he asks, lifting his arm out, and I nod, practically falling into his shoulder, letting that arm tighten around me before it's joined by the other. I bury my head in the warmth of his neck, inhaling the scent of his skin—a hint of salt and soap and gym chalk from the competition earlier—and then he pulls me in closer.

I'm not even crying anymore, but I don't ever want to leave his arms, and that's kind of terrifying in its own way. The good kind of terrifying. Like jumping out of an airplane or cliff diving or chucking a triple twist off the end of the beam—the kind of heady, dangerous rush that I've craved my entire life. And it is dangerous, way more dangerous than just sitting with a boy should ever be, but right now it's the only thing I need.

My stomach twists at that thought, and I pull away. He lets me go. I haven't processed it all, not yet. I'm not sure I'll be able to until after the Olympics, until after I know how it all ends. And it will end. One day, all of this will just be a memory.

And what do you want to remember about it, Audrey? Tears and awkward hugs and pulling away when you didn't want to?

"Promise me something?" he says as we stand up, dusting the sand off. "Don't let that asshole ruin this for you. You're going to the Olympics, Rey. Your dreams are coming true, and that's something most people won't ever get to do. Enjoy it."

Nodding, I reach out and lightly grasp the cotton of his T-shirt. "Maybe I should start now?"

He raises his eyebrows, asking how I plan to do that without uttering a word, but I just smile and spin away from him, sprinting to the water. The ocean air whips my hair into my face, but I don't let that stop me, pulling my T-shirt over my head and tossing it into the sand, stopping at the edge of the water for a second before I slide out of my cotton shorts. The thumps of his feet racing over the sand sound behind me, but I'm already thigh-deep into the chilly water by the time he reaches me, his arms immediately going around my waist before dunking us both into the surf.

We emerge together, laughing. My hair is plastered over my eyes and mouth, and he chuckles softly, wiping it away so I can see him again. His shirt is gone, abandoned on the shore like my clothes.

"You're amazing, you know that?" he whispers.

"So are you."

I brush a kiss on his jaw, the highest part of him I can reach without his help. I can feel him shiver at the contact, and I'm smiling even before I pull away.

"Cold?" he asks, running his hands up and down my arms, his fingers briefly catching against my bra strap, but the shivers suddenly wracking through me are only half because of that.

"Oh my God, yes," I confess, my teeth beginning to chatter.

"You East Coast girls with your warm ocean currents thinking you can just dive into the Pacific at night." He laughs before taking my hand and leading me back out of the water.

When we've finally reached dry ground, I blink up at him, drops of salt water still dotting his shoulders and chest. His smile is warm and true, maybe even a little bashful, when he leads me back to the towel and lifts it from the ground, wrapping it tightly around my shoulders.

I clutch my shirt and shorts in one hand, and he takes the other before we walk back toward reality, but I'm not quite ready yet.

"Wait!" I tug at his hand to stop him. He halts immediately and looks down at me, concern flashing through his green eyes. "Thank you. This was . . . this was perfect."

He doesn't say anything, not with words. He just looks at me, his eyes holding mine, and there's something in them, something that's the same kind of terrifying as before. Finally, he looks away and clears his throat. "C'mon, let's get you back."

The walk back feels way shorter than my desperate flight from the house, and it's not long before it looms in the distance. I hesitate as we get closer. I'm glad I ran into Leo tonight, but reality is setting in, and that caution I threw to the wind not so long ago comes back with a vengeance. I need to get inside without anyone seeing me, and he needs to go.

I drop the towel that's still wrapped around me and pull on my shorts and shirt before turning back to Leo, whose eyes fly up toward mine quickly. Way too quickly. I smirk at him but let it go.

"You should probably . . ." I trail off.

"Yeah," he says, hesitating for a second. I watch his gaze flicker to my lips ever so briefly, but then he leans away, taking a step back and then another before he disappears around the edge of the property.

I slink up against the side of the house, around to the back, where the dock lines up against the rocky shore of the bay.

There are two lumps at the other end of the dock. In the low light from the outdoor sconces, I can barely make them out, but then screechy giggles burst into the night, and I'd know that sound anywhere. Sierra and Jaime.

Sighing, I step forward, and as I get closer I have to tiptoe around the cans of cheap beer and a half-empty bottle of vodka. The urge to roll my eyes at them is nearly overwhelming, but I'm not sure I would have reacted differently if I were in their shoes. Missing out on the Olympics, not once, but twice. A dream dead with no idea what comes next.

I should help them into the house before they hurt themselves.

"Audrey?" Sierra slurs. "Is that Audrey Lee, Olympian? Oh my God, can I have your autograph?"

Jaime just giggles as I reach for her, slinging her arm around my shoulders. I turn to Sierra, now leaning heavily against the house, keeping herself upright, but barely. I shift Jaime against my side, and she spits out some of my hair from her mouth.

"Ugh, why is your hair wet?" she asks, but her alcohol-soaked mind doesn't wait for an answer as we walk through the sliding glass doors into the—thankfully—dark living room and up the stairs.

Sierra is still muttering to herself. "Audrey Lee, she's going to the 'lympics!"

"Shh!" Jaime says as I struggle to get her up the stairs, Sierra hopefully following behind. "Don't wanna get caught."

"Why not?" Sierra shoots back, her voice rising with every word. "What're they gonna do? Kick us off the team? Not even on the team."

The light is on upstairs, but there aren't any sounds from the other rooms. Sierra and Jaime are at the end of the hallway. I haven't been in their room yet, but it looks a whole lot like mine and

Emma's—white fluffy bedding and a nautical theme, except seafoam green paint adorns the walls.

I carefully unwind Jaime's arm from around my shoulder and sit her down on the bed.

Sierra stumbles into the room. "See, Jaime, Audrey's perfect—that's why they picked her instead of me. She hates us, and she helped us anyway."

I want to correct her, tell her I don't hate them, but right now that's not exactly true.

Jaime just giggles again, flopping back on the mattress as I unlace her sneakers for her.

"It's not funny, bitch," Sierra bites out but curls up into her bed. "Should have just said something last year. None of this would have happened."

"Last year?" I ask, moving to undo the straps of Sierra's sandals.

"Yeah, when we saw Gibby and that slut at worlds," Sierra says, her words still slurring but coming through crystal clear.

"Gibby and Dani?" I ask sharply, my voice rising, but I bring it back down to a whisper. "You saw Gibby and Dani last year at worlds?"

"Yep, in the trainers' room, down on her knees making sure he wouldn't tell about her doping. I know it."

The last part's BS. Dani wasn't doping; the USOF and FBI already proved that. That's how Gibby got arrested in the first place—forging the results—but my brain is trying to catch up with what Sierra just revealed.

"You saw Dani and Gibby together at worlds last year, and you didn't say anything? You didn't tell the FBI?"

Sierra rolls her eyes and then groans. I imagine it made the world spin. "What do you care? Fuck you, Audrey Lee," she croaks out, not making any sense, and I want to shake her, wake her up, dump black coffee down her throat until she sobers up and tells me everything she knows, but instead I watch her fall back onto the pillow.

Jaime is softly snoring behind me, but I stare hard at Sierra. Her mouth is open, but her breathing is starting to come slow and easy. She's falling asleep.

What the hell am I supposed to do?

I don't sleep. Back in my room, I drift in and out of consciousness, but *sleep* is not the word I'd use to describe it. All I keep thinking about is Gibby and Dani and how there are two eyewitnesses to the abuse he put her through. I'm going to tell the FBI and Mrs. Jackson and Janet. First thing in the morning, I'm going to tell them what Sierra told me last night, and they're going to make it right. They have to.

Bam!

My eyes fly open at the noise, and I sit up in bed. My heart is ricocheting against my ribs as the room comes into focus. Sunlight trickles through the window. It's morning.

The door slammed. That was the noise.

Glancing over, Emma's bed is empty except for a pile of covers, and Sierra is at the foot of my bed, eyes bloodshot, skin pallid and tinged with green, but clearly sober.

"How much did I tell you?" she asks, her arms folded over her stomach like she's holding back her vomit.

My eyes narrow at her. "Everything."

181

She considers me for a long moment, her breathing slow and even. "Then I'll tell them everything," she says finally.

A wave of relief washes through me. She's going to do the right thing.

"On one condition."

Or maybe not.

"God forbid you just do the right thing."

"Shut up. I did the math. Our scores were one of the ties. You and me, we're interchangeable parts, and let's be real, the only reason they picked you was because you're screwing Leo."

"I'm *not* screwing Leo, and they picked me because I'm going to win gold on bars," I say between clenched teeth.

"Whatever." She brushes it off. "You want me to do the right thing, right? Tell them what I saw?"

"Yes."

"If you want it that badly, then you'll give up your spot."

"You want me to what?" I ask, already knowing that I will never, ever do what she's suggesting. I've worked my whole life for this; why would I give it up because Sierra's a lying bitch?

Sierra shrugs. "Think about it. It's an easy swap, you for me. You say your back is acting up and you just can't stand the pain anymore."

"I'll tell them what you saw."

"And I'll just tell them the opposite. It'll never hold up in court, but an eyewitness who saw it a year ago, way before she accused him? He'll go away for a long time. You can guarantee it."

And suddenly, hearing that out loud, knowing that this will clinch the case against Gibby, it's all very simple.

Dani saved me, and now I'm going to save her.

"Okay," I hear myself saying. "Okay, I'll do it."

Sierra brightens immediately, a smile blooming across her face. "I thought you would. The agents are here right now. You should go tell Mrs. Jackson that you're withdrawing, and when you do, I'll go tell them what I've been *so afraid* to reveal up until now."

I swallow roughly and nod. If I'm going to do this, I have to do it now, like ripping off a bandage, before I can change my mind. This is the right thing. I'm going to do the right thing, and it's going to cost me everything.

Numbly, I follow Sierra out of the room and down the stairs.

I'm only a few steps behind her, staring at my feet to make sure I don't lose my footing. My hands are shaking, so I grip the handrail, but I nearly trip anyway when Sierra shrieks, "What did you do, you stupid bitch?"

My head flies up, and I brace myself for her to come flying back at me, but instead her eyes are focused ahead of her, in the living room. Emma, Chelsea, and Dani are all sitting on the couch with Janet and Mrs. Jackson beside them.

Jaime, however, is near the foot of the stairs with Agents Farley and Kingston, a greenish tint to her skin from the night before, her eyes red-rimmed and full of fire.

"I've had enough!" she bellows. "You think you're so smart, cutting a deal with Audrey, her spot for your testimony. So what? You get to go to Tokyo, and I get to sit there and watch? I saw them together too, and you said we should keep it to ourselves. You said there wasn't anything we could do, that it would just get us in trouble or make him turn on us next. This is all your fault. I never should have listened to you. I should have told the truth back then, and now I did, and guess what, Sierra? You lose!"

"Enough!" Agent Farley finally says, taking control of the room. "Mrs. Jackson, we're going to need you, Sierra, and Jaime to come with us."

They disappear into the kitchen, and that's when what happened hits me like a kick to the chest.

Jaime rolled on Gibby and, in a way, Sierra. She told the agents what they saw at worlds. The FBI has the information they need, corroborating Dani's story. Gibby's going to go to jail, and me? I get to compete for Team USA at the Olympic Games.

I manage to make it all the way down the stairs to sit with the rest of them and look around, taking in everyone's faces, but Dani's bright smile is what sends me over the edge. The sobs come hard and fast. I'm probably freaking everyone out, but I can't stop, my chest heaving as my body forces me to take a decent breath.

"Hey, hey, it's okay. Breathe," Chelsea says, suddenly right there. Her arms slide around my shoulders and pull me into a hug. She's so much smaller than me, but I cling to her because if I don't, I think I might fall. "It's okay."

"I don't have to do it," I manage to choke out between shallow breaths.

"It's okay," she says again and holds me tighter.

And it is. It's okay. Finally, it's okay.

chapter fifteen

"We're so proud of you, kiddo," Dad says, his face pixelating on the screen, especially as Mom squeezes in beside him.

She beams at me, her smile taking up most of her face, but then she's completely blocked by the magazine she's holding up. After the team was officially announced a week ago, again, we had a day with the media plus a bunch of photo shoots for publicity leading up to the Games. The crown jewel of those long hours in front of the camera is the *Sports Illustrated* Olympics special edition with the four of us on the front cover, the faces of American gymnastics, as diverse as the country we represent—finally. When I was little, most gymnasts did not look like us. Now, here we are, three women of color front and center, and I'm super proud of that.

"Your first magazine cover. I bought every copy they had at the store and gave my students extra credit if they found me more."

"I'm sure your dean is thrilled with that." I try to smother the embarrassment of college kids clearing out all the newsstands for points on their English essays.

"Actually," she says, lowering the magazine, a smirk replacing her smile, "he asked for an autographed copy."

"You're a star," Dad says, "and speaking of stars, Emma's agent called yesterday. He's been fielding calls about you all week."

"Ugh, it isn't anything dumb, is it? Like, I don't want my face on—"

"I don't know," Dad cuts in, "is Adidas still cool? I feel like it's probably still cool . . ."

"Are you kidding me?" I shriek. Aaron Judge is with Adidas. I could be with the same sponsor as Aaron Judge and, like, a million other superstars. What is even happening?

"Hey, Emma!" Dad says. I see her waving at them in the reflection of my laptop screen.

"Hi, Mr. and Mrs. Lee!"

"Hi, sweetheart!" Mom says. "We had dinner with your parents just last night. Can't wait to see both of you in Tokyo."

"You too," Emma says.

"We'll let you go, Rey. You have a long flight ahead of you."

Twelve hours. On a plane. With Emma.

Yep, definitely going to be a long flight.

"Night, guys. Love you!"

Their image freezes, and I close the laptop.

"So, our parents are having playdates in our absence." She laughs, but it's high-pitched and totally fake.

"Yeah."

We haven't spoken since Sierra and Jaime got shipped back home to Oklahoma. Mrs. Jackson sent in our official Olympic roster, and as alternates, they don't get to travel with the team since Brooke and Sarah will be in Tokyo to fill in if necessary. "Emma, I—"

"Mrs. Jackson said to bring our suitcases downstairs." She keeps her eyes directly on her own luggage while she says it.

"Em—"

"Five minutes," she says, wheeling her bags out of the room and not looking back.

I don't even know what I was going to say to her. I just miss my best friend, but even if we can't get that back, I still want to know why she sided with Sierra and Jaime, why she didn't believe Dani.

I glance down at the bed, where my own copy of the magazine stares back at me. Chelsea and I are on the ends, with Dani and Emma in the middle. They're standing back-to-back with their arms crossed over their chests, steely expressions in their eyes. Could it really just have been about their rivalry? Was that enough to keep Emma from believing Dani?

"Audrey! C'mon," Chelsea calls from downstairs. "We need you for this!"

I tuck the magazine into my carry-on bag and then drag my two massive suitcases out of the room and down the stairs carefully.

Dani and Chelsea are waiting expectantly. Emma's beside them, but she still won't look at me, not even when I make it down the stairs and stand with them.

"Ladies, it's been an experience for sure, but we still have one more thing to address before we head to the airport," Mrs. Jackson says, walking into the room with Janet. She's holding four pieces of paper and four pens in her hand. "We need a team captain. Secret ballot, write a name down, place it in . . ." She looks around and then snatches the knit cap Leo was wearing off his head, his curls bouncing out as soon as they're released. ". . . here."

My eyes fly to Chelsea. She's the easy choice for this. She's been to the Games before, and she knows exactly what we're about to go through.

Mrs. Jackson hands out little sheets of paper to us, and I carefully write out Chelsea's name and then smile at her when I hand it in. She's already our captain in practice; might as well make it official.

Mrs. Jackson digs into the cap, flips through the four pieces of paper, and then looks up. "It's a three-to-one vote. Audrey, congratulations."

What, seriously?

Chelsea and Dani squeeze me into a hug from either side, and I embrace them back, too stunned to do anything else. Emma smiles at me and then makes a show of grabbing her luggage and taking it outside for the driver to load into the van.

I turn away from her only to see Mrs. Jackson studying me carefully with one eyebrow lifted in interest, like I'm a specimen she finds surprisingly fascinating.

The girls finally release me, and I turn to Chelsea. "It should be you. You've done all of this before. You deserve it."

Dani rolls her eyes at me. "Chelsea voted for you."

"That's because you can't vote for yourself."

"Do you think this one would have any problem voting for herself if she thought she was the best person for the job?"

Chelsea shrugs, patting down a sprig of hair that's come loose from her bun. "Sometimes being a leader is about knowing when it's not about you, doing the right thing for the team."

"I just did what anyone would have done," I protest.

Dani snorts. "No, *anyone* would have just pretended like they never heard it."

"I couldn't do that."

"Exactly," Chelsea says. "That's our point. *You* couldn't do that."

I want to argue more, but then I'd have to reveal everything. I'd have to talk about how Gibby might have been grooming me too and how Dani coming forward probably saved me from him and how a wild mix of guilt, fear, gratitude, and friendship crystallized into a willingness to give up my lifelong dream to ensure that man would rot in prison for the rest of his life. And I'm not ready to do that. Leo knows, and for now that's enough. So instead I just shrug my shoulders and give up.

Dani laughs. "See? We're right."

"C'mon, Cap," Chelsea says over her shoulder as she pulls her luggage through the front door. "Tokyo is calling!"

The ride out of Coronado is bittersweet, especially with the sun rising in the distance, giving the world a golden hue as we speed over the bridge back into San Diego. When we arrived here, it was with shock and sadness, and more than a little bit of terror. My newly minted captaincy aside, the shock is gone—there is very little in the world that could shock me anymore. The sadness? That's still there, but it's different, muted, like background noise. And the terror? Well, that's taken on a new form entirely. From the fear of my Olympic dreams being dead to the fear that now I'm the only one who can control their outcome . . . I'm not sure which is scarier, really.

I swallow back the panic at that thought, just like I've pushed away the pain in my back. This is what I want. It's what I've worked for my entire life, and nothing, not even the enormity of it, is going to keep me from doing what I've set out to do.

The van pulls up to the curb at departures, and we're led through the throngs of people toward security.

"Ladies," Mrs. Jackson says as she hands us our boarding passes, "I will see you in a few days." She stops, and for a moment it looks like she wants to say more, but she doesn't. Reaching out, she shakes Janet's hand and then gives us each a quick squeeze of the shoulders and a peck on the cheek. I'm last, and when she pulls away, Leo is releasing his mom from a hug.

Janet looks back and forth between us, her mouth pressed in a firm line, the same expression she makes whenever I cheat a little on the connection before my bars dismount.

"Just one minute, Mom," Leo says, his eyes pleading with her. "We did what you asked, and I think we've earned a goodbye."

"Audrey, we'll be in line. Meet us there," she says before sending Leo a significant look and walking away, Chelsea, Dani, and Emma behind her.

"So . . ." he says, rocking back on his heels. "This is it."

"Yeah," I agree. I have no idea what to say to him. He was there for me during one of the worst times in my life, and I don't know how you thank someone for that.

"Audrey," he says, his voice making that incredible rumbling sound it does whenever he's actually taking something seriously, "thank you."

"What?" I manage to choke out. "I'm the one who should be—"

"No," he says, "I mean that I want to try and come back, after watching you these last weeks, seeing how much you want it, how hard you work. You inspire me, Audrey Lee, more than anyone I've ever met before."

I still don't know what to say, but I definitely know what I want to do. I want to push up on my toes, grab a fistful of the hoodie he's wearing, and pull him down to me. But I can't do that, so instead I step forward and wrap my arms around his waist in a fierce hug. For a few precious seconds, I rest my head against his chest, and then he returns the embrace, his arms squeezing gently. If I don't pull away soon, what's supposed to be nothing more than an extra-friendly goodbye will turn into something else entirely, so I do, loosening my grip and then stepping away.

The understanding in his eyes is clear, and I smile tightly.

"When I get home from Tokyo, we're going to have that conversation."

"The very serious one?"

"Mm-hmm."

He swallows roughly at that, stepping back a bit farther, plastering his arms against his sides, like he's keeping them from reaching for me again.

"I should go." I'm trying to avoid his eyes. This is way harder than I thought it would be.

"Go be great," he rasps.

I walk away and don't look back. Finding the others in the security line is easy enough.

"That is some serious tension," Dani says, nudging me with her shoulder.

Chelsea looks like she's about to burst, but I shake my head at her, then turn to Janet instead. "Thank you," I whisper quietly.

She nods and then busies herself with her luggage. Emma's ahead of us, scrolling through her phone like it's the most fascinating thing she's ever seen in her life.

Someone at the USOF—probably Mrs. Jackson—sensing another opportunity for positive publicity must have let it slip that we were on the flight, because when we arrive, the gate is completely decked out in USA gear, with our pictures plastered up near the door. A sign hangs below them with GOOD LUCK, EMMA, DANI, CHELSEA, AND AUDREY scrawled in gold paint across it.

The gate's speakers are also blaring out patriotic music on a loop while we wait for our flight. It feels like every single song that mentions our country, from Miley's "Party in the U.S.A." to Simon and Garfunkel's "America," is cycled through at least twice before they call us for boarding.

We're the last ones on, at Janet's request. The less time we have sitting on the plane, the better, even if it's an extra fifteen or twenty minutes, especially for me and my back. Getting through the flight is almost a part of our training—if we don't do it quite right, it could have a major impact on our performance.

The key is to sleep for most of it. If we can do that, we'll arrive around the middle of the afternoon feeling like we're starting our day, albeit a little bit later than usual. We've got to trick our bodies into thinking that a twelve-hour flight with a seventeen-hour time difference is, you know, perfectly normal.

The USOF has spared no expense. We're ushered into the front of the plane, to the sleeping pods that fully recline. I've flown first class before, but not like this.

Emma is in the pod across from mine, and I have to smile. We always sit next to each other on flights to big international competitions, and it'll be nice to do it one last time.

Maybe it's the sheer nostalgia of it all, but as we're about to sit, I turn to her and say, "Thanks, Em."

She turns to me, eyes wide, clearly startled. "For what?"

"You voted for me for captain. That was . . . really nice."

"You deserve it," she says, shrugging and running a hand through her red hair. And then she smiles, a familiar, mischievous one that I haven't seen in way too long. "Besides, you'll need something to console yourself with after you win silver on bars."

I bark out a laugh and get an unimpressed glare from a woman a few rows ahead of us who looks way too dressed up just to sit on a plane for twelve hours.

"Ladies," Janet calls from the other side of the aisle. "Settle in and try to get some sleep."

———

I do manage to sleep, I always can on flights, but it's one of those weird states in between rest and restlessness rather than a total conk-out, and it doesn't last long.

The journey passes in a slow-motion blur of drink orders, food being left and then taken away, and a few trips to the bathroom. By the time I reach the conclusion that I probably should have taken a sleeping pill, like Emma, it's way too late in the flight. I'm exhausted, my back is starting to stiffen up, and every one of her soft snores makes my eye twitch.

Twelve hours on the plane, an hour on line at customs, and then nearly an hour in traffic to the athletes' village, and I'm feeling every single second of it. The soreness that can crop up a day or so after a cortisone shot—especially if you don't move around enough—is rearing its ugly head at the injection spot. It feels like someone's taken a hammer to the small of my back, and the rest of me doesn't seem to understand that it's the afternoon today and not the middle of the night yesterday. My eyes feel heavy enough to drag my whole body to the floor. And even though we've only been here for a few hours, the sheer amount of time that I've spent explaining that I'm not, in fact, Japanese, and that I only speak English has been a super-fun way to kick off the Games.

"Drop your luggage. You have some time to rest," Janet says as we're led by an Olympic official to a suite opposite the men's gymnastics team, where the bass from their music is already pounding through the walls, "but remember, we have a training session in a couple of hours."

I follow Emma into the room we're sharing. It's not quite as glamorous as the bedroom back at the rental house in Coronado, but since it's the actual Olympic Village, I'm willing to let that slide. There are two twin beds with brightly colored duvets emblazoned with the Olympic logo and two soft-looking pillows. Oh, what I wouldn't give for a nap right now, but there isn't enough time, and it would throw off my body clock even worse.

The only issue is that the AC is blaring against the heat outside, and it's freezing in the suite. The building is a high-rise on the water, and our room happens to overlook several other buildings and the wide expanse of Tokyo Bay, blue in the distance. We're over five thousand miles from the San Diego Bay we said goodbye to this morning, but it really reminds me more of New York, where the bridges connect Queens and Brooklyn to the city. The water is murky, but that makes me feel even more at home.

Thinking of home makes me think of my parents. I'd call them, but they're actually on their own flight right now.

"It looks like home," Emma says, coming up behind me.

"Right?" I agree, and this is good, talking to her again. "Listen, Em, I'm sorry for—"

She cuts me off. "No, I'm sorry. You were right. I should have defended you and Dani, and I shouldn't have—"

"No, but we all deal with things differently, and I shouldn't have made you feel bad for how you were dealing with it. I was taking out my frustrations about some other stuff on you, and that wasn't fair."

"Like having to stay away from Leo Adams?"

I blink at her. "How did you know?"

"God, Rey, we might have been fighting, but I still know you better than anyone else in the world."

"It wasn't just that, though."

"I know," she says. "Me too."

I don't know what she means, but I don't get a chance to ask.

"We're here!" two voices ring out from the common area. Together, we leap up and nearly collide at the door before laughingly spilling through it. Sarah and Brooke are here, the final two pieces of the USA women's gymnastics team, dragging their suitcases behind them. They're already hugging Dani and Chels, and then they turn to us.

"So, what did we miss?" Sarah asks, pulling me into a hug.

Emma looks at me, and then I look over to Dani and Chelsea. Then Dani breaks into giggles followed by a serious laughing fit. It's contagious, and we're all laughing our heads off, with our two new arrivals staring at us like we've lost our minds.

This is it.

We're all together, finally, and now the Olympics can start.

chapter sixteen

The opening ceremonies were tonight, but we weren't able to make it.

Instead of marching into the Olympic stadium with our fellow athletes, we marched into the Ariake Gymnastics Centre, with its old-school cedar roof and wood bench seating. After almost a week practicing in a training gym, it was time for the real thing. It's not the biggest venue I've ever been in, but definitely the most important, and my pulse thumped just a little bit harder as we rotated through all four events. The twelve thousand seats were mostly empty today, just the media and a few of the other teams there to observe our podium training rotations.

That might sound like we practiced standing on the medal podium, waving to the crowd, but it actually means we performed on the raised podiums where the vault, bars, beam, and floor have been set up to make the competition easier to see from the stands. It's something we're pretty used to. All our main competitions in the US are done on podiums, and every world championship has them too, but it's always nice to have a chance to practice in the arena and get a feel for the equipment, especially since being on a podium can make everything a little bouncier, and thus that much more difficult to control.

To be honest, I would trade a million opening ceremonies for the podium training we had. It was perfection. We're a well-oiled machine at this point, and we have Janet to thank for it. For all the one-session-per-day practices that I rebelled against when we first got to Coronado, I'm here at the Games, I'm healthy—relatively speaking—and that's what matters.

We're led out of the arena by an Olympic volunteer holding a sign with USA scrawled across it, through a poorly lit tunnel, back toward the training gym and locker rooms.

"Excellent job, ladies," a voice echoes against the concrete walls of the tunnel. Stepping out of the shadows, Mrs. Jackson smiles at us, a chic white tracksuit with USA on her lapel and matching white sneakers taking the place of her usual skirt suit and stilettos. That she's here now is yet another sign that the last week of practice has been just that: practice. Things are about to get very real.

"Can I steal Dani and Audrey for a moment?" she asks.

"We have a press conference in ten," Janet reminds her.

"They'll be right behind you," Mrs. Jackson promises.

"What's up?" I ask, stepping out of the line as the other girls follow Janet out of the tunnel for our first meeting with the media since arriving in Tokyo.

"I wanted to warn you both. I can't control the international media the way I would be able to back home, and I've heard rumblings that our alternates have been talking to the press. Dani, we've asked them to be delicate about your circumstances, but there isn't much we can do beyond asking."

"It's okay," Dani says, but her answering smile is a little shaky. I reach out and take her hand, squeezing it gently.

"I've got your back."

"Thanks, Cap."

Mrs. Jackson raises her eyebrows at us and then focuses her attention on me.

"Audrey, remember when I told you to stay away from Leo Adams?"

I crinkle my nose, bracing myself for whatever she's about to say next. "Yes."

Shaking her head, Mrs. Jackson sighs. "Is there any reason to believe media reports to the contrary?"

My grip on Dani's hand tightens, and she squeezes back.

"I hugged him goodbye at the airport?" I try, already knowing that's not what she means.

My mind flashes back to that night out on the beach, huddling close together on the sand, racing to the water after stripping off my clothes. I am such an idiot.

"Any other reason?" she prods, pursing her lips as if she's daring me to deny it.

I don't.

"It was just after our second trials, after I talked to the FBI, I was freaking out and needed to talk to someone . . . and he was there, you know?" My voice rises in pitch and speed as sheer panic descends. "And besides, I don't think it's right that anyone gets to tell me who I spend time with, especially after what happened with the last people who were in charge. We have a right to make our own decisions. I have that right."

Mrs. Jackson raises an eyebrow but then says, "I agree. I may have been a touch precipitous in asking you to refrain from any contact with Leo."

"Crap, that worked?"

If I didn't know any better, I'd say the noise she just made was a snort, but I'm pretty sure Tamara Jackson would never do anything so undignified.

"Just keep your answers to the press simple and to the point," she says and dismisses us.

Chelsea and Emma chuck our tracksuits at our heads as soon as we rush through the door to the locker room. I'm still zipping up the jacket as we march back out to the media room just a minute later.

There's a long dais and rows upon rows of reporters in front of it, video cameras lining the back of the press area, their red lights on, ready to record the entire session. The chairs at the dais have our names taped to the backs, along with cards on the table to let the world know who we are.

Their questions start off slowly, mostly asking us about how we felt during podium training, how we like the Olympic Village, how we feel about the upcoming competition, and then finally one that lands like dead weight on our chests.

"How does it feel coming to the Olympic Games without your personal coaches?"

Pauline's face flashes through my mind, her long blond pony-tail, her stony blue eyes, and the last time I saw her, disappearing behind a closing door back at Gibby's training center. My eyes meet Emma's for a moment. She's a little paler than usual. She's probably wondering the same thing I am: How much did Pauline know about Gibby, about the drug tests, about what he did to Dani?

Chelsea is the first to recover. "Working with Janet Dorsey-Adams has been an incredible experience, and we're so grateful that she stepped up when we needed her."

"And, Audrey, what of the speculation that Coach Dorsey-Adams had a conflict of interest considering your relationship with her son?"

I straighten in my seat and do my best to channel every boring nonanswer I've ever heard an athlete give a reporter. "Everyone watched the selection live on television. Mrs. Jackson and Coach Dorsey-Adams explained why they chose the team sitting here, and their selection criteria were no different from what has been used in the past: performance, experience, and potential for success as a team and individually. Beyond that, I have no comment."

A disgruntled hum passes through the crowd of reporters and then one follows up. "Dani"—we all tense at her name—"what do you say to the skeptics out there who believe your accusations against Coach Gibson were used to cover up a history of using performance-enhancing drugs?"

An uncomfortable silence settles in the room as Dani blinks and then shifts forward in her seat, reaching out to adjust her microphone. But before she can speak, Emma leans forward and clears her throat.

"I'll take this one," she says, and our heads swivel to her. She's right next to me, and as she starts to talk, her hand grabs mine underneath the table, invisible to the crowd in front of us. "Dani would . . ." She falters and I give her hand a squeeze. "Dani would never cheat. She's never tested positive, and she's been cleared by the USOF, just like the rest of us. The actual FBI arrested the man who claimed that she failed. And if that's somehow not enough for you, I can say, as the person who has the most to lose from her competing, I believe her."

I don't know if she means it or if it's just for show. Emma has always been great with the press, knowing how to say just the right thing to have them eating out of her hand, but it feels genuine, or at least I want to believe it does. She's my best friend, and I want her back.

"So do I," I say.

"Me too," Sarah says.

"I believe Dani," Brooke chimes in.

And then finally Chelsea says, "We believe Dani. And you?" She nods at the reporter. "You can go fuck yourself."

I stand up, pulling Emma with me and the others follow as I lead them off the dais, effectively declaring our press conference over. The reporters shout over one another as we leave, but their calls die with the slamming of the door behind us.

"Really, Chelsea?" Janet says, shaking her head at the group of us in exasperation. When none of us look even the least apologetic, she laughs.

Chelsea shrugs and flicks her hand dismissively over her shoulder. "That prick deserved it."

She looks over us as a group, standing together.

"Yes, he did."

———

My alarm is set for seven, but it's no surprise when I wake up before it goes off. Emma is already awake and looking back at me. In all the years we've roomed together at competitions, she never fails to wake up before me.

I wrinkle my nose at her. "Were you watching me sleep, creeper?"

"I was staring at you until your survival instincts kicked in and woke you up," she says, laughing.

We throw our covers back at the same time, and then I turn to her. "Hey, Em?"

"Yeah?" she asks.

"Today, we're gonna be Olympians."

She lets out a high-pitched shriek of joy from the back of her throat, throwing her covers off, and leaps up onto the bed, bouncing up and down. I haven't seen her this excited in a long time, and it's contagious. Goose bumps fly over my skin, and I throw my head back and giggle.

My phone buzzes underneath my pillow.

Kick ass today!

Leo's text is short and to the point. I send a quick heart emoji back, but that's all I have time for this morning.

It's qualifications day. The day when our fates will be decided, one way or another.

An extra hop on that tumbling pass? Kiss floor finals goodbye.

Hesitate between connections on beam? Sorry, try again in four years for that beam medal.

Score a thousandth of a point lower than two of your own teammates in any given discipline—even if you're better than the rest of the world on that event? Too bad, because only the top two athletes from a country can compete in a final, which means your two-per-countried ass will be sitting in the stands.

Our leos are bright metallic white with crystals covering both arms from shoulder to wrist, and after quick showers, we take extra care with our hair and makeup. Everything needs to be perfect today.

I stare at my makeup kit, trying to pick out the right eyeshadow, my personal battle armor for big competitions.

"Hey," I say, turning to Emma, who's blow-drying her hair into a shiny red curtain. "What if we all wear teal eyeshadow?"

"Teal?" she asks, after a moment, wrinkling her nose.

"It represents sexual assault awareness. I could give everyone an awesome cat eye too to make it really pop."

Emma stares at me for a second. Finally, a slow smile appears on her face. "That's actually a really good idea."

"I have to run it by Dani first." I leap up from the floor, about to cross the hallway, but Chelsea is already leading Dani into our room, with Brooke and Sarah on their heels.

"We heard what you said, and it's perfect," Chelsea says, and Dani nods, suspiciously wiping quickly at her eyes.

"Here," Emma says, holding out a box of tissues from her nightstand.

We all freeze. It feels like . . . I don't know, it's a box of tissues, but suddenly it feels like something more, like a peace offering. So much more so than what she said at the press conference yesterday because it's just us, no cameras, no reporters, just her teammates.

Dani is stock-still for a moment, and then she reaches out and takes them.

Emma cringes with a small shrug, like she knows how awkward this is. "I'm, uhh . . . sorry they're the cheap kind, not the kind with lotion."

Dani's smile is wobbly for a moment again, but she takes a tissue and wipes at her eyes. "Thanks, Em."

Emma looks away, focusing way too hard on putting the tissue box back on the nightstand, her own eyes suspiciously glassy.

"So, if we're all gonna cry, let's do it now, before I make masterpieces of your faces."

I wave my favorite eye kit, the one with the perfect teal eyeshadow, and a jet-black eyeliner at them.

"What are you talking about?" Chelsea says, sitting down on my bed, motioning to her own face. "This is already a masterpiece."

We all laugh, and I sit beside Chelsea to start on her eyes. This is how it was supposed to be all along.

———

"The United States of America!" the announcer calls, and the sound reverberates through the entire arena with an answering roar from the crowd. Goose bumps explode over my skin as the six of us, together, raise our left arms into the air and wave to the crowd.

It's super early in the morning, but the arena is full. We're in the same subdivision as the Japanese team, and the crowd is divided pretty evenly between the two fan bases. I'm sure my parents are up there, somewhere, but finding them would be impossible, even if I wanted to. Seeing their faces in person, after everything that happened, after so long apart, might be too much. They texted me earlier, and that'll have to be enough. My energy needs to be totally focused on one thing and one thing only: hitting my routines.

"Japan!" the announcer says next, and the fans explode again, supporting their home team.

This is going to be fun.

A cameraman follows us all the way to the bars podium, where we're led up the stairs by a volunteer. As a group, we turn to face the panel of judges. The Olympic judges. I ball my hands into fists, my fingers digging into the grips already strapped onto my wrists for my first Olympic routine. Music is blaring through the speakers, and the crowd is clapping along with thundersticks, the thumps matching my ever-increasing heart rate.

I inhale and then exhale slowly.

A Klaxon clangs over the music—our signal to warm up. We salute the judges and then turn as one to the bars, where Janet and Brooke's coach are rubbing chalk over the fiberglass cylinders we'll be swinging on in just a minute or two.

We've practiced this over and over again, running through sections of our routine before jumping down and letting the next girl go in competition order, and then, as the warm-up time expires, Brooke is left up on the podium by herself, waiting to start her bars routine to get us going.

She's a bars specialist, so it's her only routine of the day.

"Come on, Brooke!" I shout, clapping my hands together, sending up a small cloud of chalk as she bounces up off the springboard and onto the high bar.

It happens right at the start of her routine, just a half turn for a grip change before her first release, but her hand slips instead of grasping the bar and then slides off entirely, and she's down below the high bar on her knees, blinking over and over again—not even winded yet. She'd barely begun, and now it's over. She fell. No final. No medal. Olympics finished.

She stands up and moves to the chalk bowl, adjusting her grips.

I look around at the other girls, but they're all staring in silence, just like me. What is there even to say? Do we encourage her to keep going? To finish her routine strong? Do we say nothing?

What do you say to someone whose dream just died right in front of your eyes?

Brooke remounts the bars and starts her routine from the beginning. The simple grip change is executed as easy as breathing, before she flawlessly works through the remainder of her routine. She lands her double layout dismount with authority, in defiance of what her score will inevitably be, a point deducted for the fall and more tenths for the form break and lack of control just before her body hit the mat.

She leaps down from the podium and runs straight for her coach, who also happens to be her dad. He hugs her tightly and neither of them look up when the score flashes a few minutes later, a 14.0. Without the fall, it would have been over fifteen. She probably would have made the final, probably would have knocked out me or Emma, but that's not going to happen now. For the rest of the Games, she's nothing but a spectator.

"Now on uneven bars for the United States of America, Chelsea Cameron!" the announcer says, and this time I stay quiet as Chelsea takes a small leap and swings up onto the low bar.

Chelsea's a pro, and she fights like hell to get through the routine. She's winding up for the dismount, one giant, another, and then another when her feet thwack against the low bar. She releases and twists once in her double back and lands with her chest down

206

at her knees, but her feet solidly on the mat. How the hell she managed to pull it around, I have no idea. It's a major error, but it's not like we were resting our gold medal hopes on Chelsea's bars performance.

She helps Janet chalk the bars for Dani's routine and then leaps down, bumping her fist against mine.

"You okay?" I ask while she shifts her weight back and forth, pointing and flexing her toes.

"Yeah," she assures me, "just a dumb mental lapse."

Her score lights up on the board, a 13, which definitely feels about right, considering.

Janet leaps down beside us, checking in with Chelsea too. She repeats that she's fine as our eyes fix on Dani.

"On uneven bars for the United States of America, Daniela Olivero!"

The sound that explodes from the crowd is like nothing I've ever heard before, a wall of noise that just keeps building. Dani starts, her eyes briefly flickering up into the stands, before she focuses on the judges, waiting for their signal to begin.

The light switches from red to green and with a deep breath, she salutes and begins.

The steadily increasing wave of vocal support fades almost instantly to a reverent hush, just ambient music in the background, but even that seems to dissipate, the squeak of the bars overpowering it.

Dani releases the high bar and then catches again, a Tkatchev, and then flips between the bars, but when she catches the low bar, her momentum just stops. She caught it too close. It's not a fall, but it's . . . it's bad. She adjusts her grip briefly and then creates her own momentum again, pushing off the low bar and swinging down below it. Moments later, she's flying back up to the high bar and swinging around for her dismount, one, two, three, into a perfect double layout. A decent save, but damage done.

She salutes the judges and jogs down from the podium to us, ripping at her grips as she goes. I want to go to her, but I can't. I still have to compete. Chelsea sits with her on the chairs lining the arena's walls, and I flinch when I turn away and catch her score.

13.7.

Ouch.

This is starting to feel like a pattern. Dumb fluke errors happen sometimes, but three in a row, first Brooke, then Chelsea, and now Dani? Swallowing back the slowly building panic in my chest, I look up at Emma, who's at the bars now.

A green light, a salute, and she's swinging back and forth, up and down, around and over the bars. It's a perfectly choreographed dance, not a toe out of a place, not a flicker in her elbows or knees.

She lands her double layout, sticking with ease, her arms flying up to salute. Then she turns and claps at the hit routine before jumping down from the podium and heading right for me.

"You got this, Rey! C'mon!" she practically screeches, and we high-five, sending out a small cloud of chalk.

That's what we needed: our best gymnast to get us going in the right direction. And now I'm going to be even better.

I lift my arms up over my head and rotate them around once, twice, three times before swinging them back and forth as I approach the bars.

Janet and Emma chalk them just the way I like, a fine layer, just enough to grip without it clumping up and bugging me while I swing.

"Let's go, Audrey," Janet says quietly when Emma's score is posted, a 15.1. And then I'm alone.

"On uneven bars for the United States of America, Audrey Lee!"

I don't hear the crowd. I don't hear anything. My eyes are focused on one thing only, the light at the corner of the podium. It blinks from red to green. Facing the judges, I salute, one arm up, the other out to the side with a flourish, and then I begin.

Each skill flows into the next: low bar up to high, back down to low, grips scraping over the fiberglass, catching and releasing with precision, my core holding strong on the handstands, knees, toes, and elbows perfectly aligned. I reach and grasp and catch, then swing up and around, a pirouette, landing right in handstand and then down again, releasing and rising up in the air, one, two, three twists and I land, my knees bending just slightly, but that's it. I rise up, arms in the air, and the sound erupts around me, pulling me back into reality.

I salute the judges and then race off the podium. The girls are waiting for me at the bottom of the stairs with high fives and fist bumps.

"Let's go!" I yell, and I get five answering nods before we break away, grabbing our bags as we prepare to rotate.

Balance beam is next, and we're gonna own it.

The Klaxon sounds and we march to the beam. I pull at my grips and as I do, my eye catches one of the scoreboards.

ALL-AROUND QUALIFICATIONS

1.	Audrey Lee	15.3
2.	Emma Sadowsky	15.1
3.	Daniela Olivero	13.7

I want to pull out my phone and take a picture. I'm leading the all-around competition at the Olympic Games—if only for a few more minutes. It feels like something I should commemorate.

Okay, Audrey, that's enough. It's time to focus on beam.

We salute the judges and then warm up briefly. The beam is wobbly, just like it always is on a podium, but training on it yesterday helped a bit.

The Klaxon sounds again, signaling the end of warm-up, and Chelsea's beside the beam, leading us off. Just like bars, it isn't her strength, but this time she gets through the routine cleanly, with just a few wobbles here and there.

It's something I can build upon.

I bump fists with Chelsea on the stairs as she comes down and I go up. Janet is straightening the springboard for me, and when she steps away, I bounce on it and then lean forward to make sure it's exactly the right distance away. It's perfect.

I shift back and forth on my feet, the seconds ticking by as we wait for Chelsea's score. Across the arena one of the Japanese girls is finishing her floor routine, the crowd clapping along to the music, but I tear my eyes away. Chelsea's score comes up, a 13.0, and the red light flashes over to green.

"Let's go, Rey!" Emma calls, but that's the last noise I hear as my gaze lasers in on the end of the beam. Three steps into a roundoff onto the springboard and then backward on the beam, my balance steady, my momentum carrying me into a layout, stepping out, and then into another one. I rise up. Perfect.

And from there, it's just like breathing; my turns flow into each other seamlessly, my arms working around me into the choreography, linking every skill together, and then finally at the end, a perfect triple twist—okay, maybe it's a little bit short, but not too bad.

It's what I came here to do—hit bars and beam—and I've done it.

I pump my fist and yell, "Yes!" before turning to the judges and saluting.

Dani's next. Her eyes are steely, and her mouth is set in a firm line.

"Get it, Dani," I call, and our hands clasp briefly as we pass on the stairs.

My score flashes up, a 14.9, and almost immediately, red switches to green and Dani's up on the beam. She's attacking her skills like a woman possessed. She's angry, that much is super clear, as she hits every skill with authority, not a balance check or a wobble to be seen. She's still pissed about bars, and I don't blame her.

"Whoa," Chelsea whispers at my side, equally impressed.

"Yeah," I agree.

Finally, she's almost done, lining up for her dismount. She throws herself into a back handspring and then another before launching up into a double Arabian, landing and not moving an inch. Stuck.

"Yes!" Chelsea and I shout together and pull Dani straight into a hug when she pops down from the podium with a huge smile on her face.

"Damn, girl," I say, giving her one last squeeze.

Her score comes up as fast as mine did: a 14.4. What the hell? I stare at the judges in disbelief. The entire arena groans in displeasure, and a few whistles of protest pour out from the stands too. That felt like way more than a 14.4.

Dani shrugs, but it's got to sting. She nailed the crap out of that beam routine. "Let's go, Em!" she says, redirecting all of our attention to Emma mounting the beam.

She presses up to a handstand, lifting her entire body weight up onto her hands before lowering her legs into a split and holding for a second, showing the judges just how much control she has. She lowers her feet down onto the beam before standing up, arms raised over her head. Then she flips backward, back handspring, back handspring, into a layout. But when her feet hit the beam, she pops off, straight down to the mat, landing solidly on her feet, almost neatly, like it's part of her routine.

It's not.

That's a fall.

Emma fell off beam.

Shaking her head and then gathering herself, Em climbs right back up, and it's all smooth from there, not even a balance check, but there's no undoing what happened.

Dani screwed up on bars.

Emma bombed on beam.

And now, before we have to rotate to floor, my eyes move

over to the all-around qualifications and there's my name, still at the top.

1.	Audrey Lee	30.2
2.	Daniela Olivero	28.1
3.	Emma Sadowsky	27.8

What the hell is going on?

chapter seventeen

I t's nice to be in the top spot all-around, but that's not really the important thing, especially since we're headed to floor and vault, where Dani and Emma are going to pull ahead of me and the universe will right itself.

My gaze moves from those standings to the individual event qualifications, and there I am, sitting in the top spot for bars and beam. That's what matters. I've given myself a chance to win the medals I set my sights on a year ago, when the doctors told me that I could *try* for the Games, but that there was no guarantee, and that I really probably shouldn't. When Pauline made me downgrade my vault and I wasn't able to tumble with the ease I'd felt before.

"Hey, did you see?" Chelsea says, pulling me out of my thoughts. Thank God. The last thing I need to do is get caught up in everything that went down. She lines up ahead of me as the Klaxon rings, signaling our move to the floor exercise. Her chin juts out toward the all-around standings.

"Yeah, it's a shame I can't just double up on bars and beam," I quip, as a cameraman comes charging toward us to get the shot of our march to the next event.

Chelsea snorts as Sarah and Brooke line up in front of her, and then Emma and Dani join us, one ahead of me, one behind, and a weighted silence falls over the group. They're within a few tenths of each other, jockeying for position to qualify for the all-around final. It doesn't really matter which one of them comes out on top today, but the way both of them are staring straight ahead, their typically excellent posture even more straight and unbending than usual, makes it feel like they're battling it out for that gold medal right here and now.

"Two more," Dani says from ahead of me, and something in my head finally clicks.

Two more events: floor and vault.

My last time competing both of them.

Seriously, are you just realizing that now, Audrey?

I was too caught up in everything, training like this was normal, like everything about this competition was the same as every other competition I've ever been to. Maybe, in some ways, I lost sight of what this actually is.

It's an ending.

"Last floor routine ever," I say, mostly to myself as we drop our things on the chairs near floor and move to line up in front of the judges.

Chelsea turns to me in surprise, her eyebrows lifting. She opens her mouth to say something, but then closes it with a rueful shake of her head. "Just go do your thing, Rey," she says finally.

"You too."

There isn't really time think about it because, as the weakest floor worker on the team, I'm up first, for the very last time.

I close my eyes and breathe, once, twice. A chime sounds in the arena, and then my music begins. "Moon River," clear as a bell, rings through the air, and I'm dancing, and it's like magic as I let the feel of performing in the Olympic arena wash over me. There's no pressure here, nothing riding on this routine except that it's my last and I want to make it a good one. I have to go out and do my routine, like I have a million times before, except I *feel* it, maybe for the first time since the world seemed to tear itself apart around me—around all of us—and we had to stitch it back together again.

I twist in the air in a two and a half to full. I don't stick it, but that's okay because I can even make that step beautiful, pushing up into arabesque and dancing out of it the way I've been taught, and the routine is as much of a blur as the rest of the competition has been so far, but it's also perfect. The crowd is silent for a moment after I finish, and then it erupts for me and I'm breathing hard, but my eyes are closed. I don't want to open them yet. If that was the last time I'm going to dance for them, I want to feel it wash over me.

Finally, I open my eyes and take in the arena, the bright lights, the crowd cheering, and tears start to gather. If this is an ending, it's the best I could have asked for.

"Great job, Rey," Emma says when I race down the stairs, my breath coming in heaving gasps. She's up next. I hug her quickly, unable to get any words out over my desperate need for air, and then move off to the side.

Digging through my bag for some tape, I miss my score coming up, but hear the *ding* of the bell just before Emma's music begins.

"You got this, Em!" I shout when I'm in control of my lungs again.

Chelsea and Dani are pacing in front of me, jogging and swinging their arms back and forth to try to stay warm. The crowd claps along with the music, their thundersticks pounding out the rhythm.

Emma dances and tumbles and sticks the hell out of her landings before finishing with a flourish as the music crashes to an end.

The roll of tape is dangling from my wrist when I hug her and she sits beside me, fighting to catch her breath.

Her score pops up, a huge 14.7, and she nods to herself while I reach out and pull her into a side-hug. That will definitely be good enough for the floor final.

"Just gotta finish strong," Emma says, picking at the tape around her ankles that helped stabilize them on floor but will just get in the way during vault.

Chelsea's swanky routine to "Down in the Valley" has the crowd riled up again, and when she finishes they applaud wildly.

Her eyes are bright and wide as she leaves the floor, waving out into the stands, especially toward the other side of the arena, where a group is decked out in red, white, and blue, someone standing on their seat holding up an American flag.

"This is why I came back," she says, falling into the chair beside me and nudging her shoulder against mine. "There is nothing like this."

Nodding, I look up, into the crowd, around the arena, trying to soak it all in. I'm an Olympian, and that's forever, but I want to remember as much as possible.

Dani's up on the floor, and the crowd roars at her, the same way they have since we stepped into the arena. They clap their thundersticks along to the remixed *The Greatest Showman* soundtrack, even managing to catch and recatch the beat as the tempo changes. Her tumbling is as high and impressive as it usually is, though she takes a big hop back out of her last pass, at least one foot landing entirely outside the boundaries. The line judge's flag pops up to indicate the deduction. It's still a brilliant routine, though, and when she leaps up and lands in a split with her hands raised over her head to finish, we rise along with the fans to applaud.

But it's not over. Not yet.

One more rotation.

"Okay, ladies. Nice job. Let's go," Janet says once Dani has given us fist bumps celebrating our first entirely hit rotation of the day. This fact clearly hasn't escaped Janet's notice if the firm set of her mouth is any indication. Better today than tomorrow, at least.

The Klaxon rings one last time, ending the third rotation and beginning the fourth. We line up together and follow our volunteer around nearly the entire arena, with the thundersticks pounding to the music pumping through the speakers.

"Last vault ever," I say as we stand before the judges to salute them before warm-ups. I mean, I still hate vault. I think I'll hate it forever, but it's the last time I'll do one, and that feels kind of momentous, just like back on floor.

"Make it a great one," Dani says as we jog down the podium to the end of the vault run to begin our warm-ups.

I nod, digging into the chalk bowl and swiping handfuls onto the bottoms of my feet, the insides of my thighs, and the palms of my hands—just enough to avoid slipping off the vault. I race down the runway first, just doing a simple flip off the table, and land on my feet, popping up into the air to eat away the leftover momentum that will eventually propel me into a full one and a half twist.

Walking back to the other end of the run, my eye catches a group in the crowd, the same red-white-and-blue-bedecked section that Chelsea saluted before. It's our parents, all of them, sitting together, clapping their thundersticks as hard as everyone else. My parents are with Emma's, and Emma's agent is with them too. My agent now, I guess, if that deal with Adidas is legit. Chelsea's boyfriend, Ben, is in the row in front of them, a giant Uncle Sam hat on his head. He's holding one end of the American flag, and holding the other end is . . . Leo, with a matching hat.

Sheer force of habit gets me to the end of the vault run and up onto the podium, waiting for the other girls, including Sarah, to finish their run-throughs. I have to physically shake my head to get my focus back, but it doesn't stop my stomach flipping over once and then again when I glance that way out of the corner of my eye.

"I guess you saw him?" Chelsea says from in front of me, where she's waiting for Emma to land and get out of the way.

"Did you know?" I ask, narrowing my eyes at her.

"Ben and I might have asked Janet if it was cool for Leo to stay with him," she says.

"But how did he pay . . ." I trail off as she smirks at me. "You're the actual best, you know that, right?"

"I know," she says, pushing up on her toes and then sprinting full speed at the vault, leaving me behind.

One more round through, and we've all done a warm-up vault, and then I'm left by myself on the podium, first up as the weakest vaulter on the team.

"Now on vault for the United States of America, Audrey Lee!" the announcer calls out.

The light at the end of the run turns green, and I salute, the same way I always have, one arm up, the other to the side, before taking my place on the runway.

One breath in, one breath out, and then I go, as fast as I can: roundoff, back handspring, block off the vault, hurtling into the air, my arms tight against my chest in a full twist and a half, opening up and dropping like a pin onto the mat feetfirst.

"Yes!" I yell, throwing my arms up over my head and then turning to the judges and doing it again. A quick fist pump, and I move off the mat, straight to Janet, climbing up onto the podium. Together we shift the mat and springboard for Dani, and then I'm down the stairs to where the other girls are waiting—everyone except Dani, who's up next.

Emma gives me a quick hug, but she can't linger too long. She's up after Dani.

Dani's Amanar is high and big, just like everything else about her gymnastics, the two and a half twists completed well before she opens up to land. It's maybe a little too powerful, and she has to take a hop out of it. She wrinkles her nose as she salutes the judges. She can do better and knows it.

I give her a tight hug, and we pull apart to bump our double fists together and then turn to look at the scoreboard, Chelsea right beside us.

It's a 15.0, which is a fantastic score and a full point higher than the 14.0 I just got for my absolutely perfect one and a half.

Chelsea reaches out and squeeze's Dani's shoulder, but then she has to leave as well—she's up after Emma.

When Dani's score flashes away and reveals the all-around standings, I have to blink at it once and then again and then a third time.

1.	Audrey Lee	58.2
2.	Daniela Olivero	57.6

Dani's in second.

I'm in first.

Wait, what is happening? My vision flies around the arena, trying to catch one of the many flashing scoreboards with the results from the previous rotation. What did those look like? But there's nothing, just our team score, which sits at the top of those rankings.

Emma's feet pound down the runway, slamming into the springboard, up off the vault, and into the air, one, two and a half twists and landing. She takes a big hop, but it's a good vault, as good as Dani's.

Emma comes down from the podium, her face grim.

I reach out to hug her and she lets me, but it's barely an embrace. She pulls away instantly and then yanks at her wrist guards.

We wait, but not for long.

Emma's score is posted: a 15.0.

Identical to Dani's, but that's utterly meaningless to me.

It's three full seconds before Emma's score disappears, and I feel every single, solitary millisecond of them. My heart pounding, drowning out the sounds in the arena, no thundersticks, no music, no cheering, just the thump of my pulse as my mind spins off its axis.

The standings flash up for the world to see.

1. Audrey Lee   58.2
2. Daniela Olivero   57.6
3. Emma Sadowsky   57.5

Two per country in the final, just two, and I'm one of them.

That dream was dead a long time ago, and now . . . now . . .

Dani's beside me, her arms open, and I fall into them, letting her pull me in and hug me fiercely.

"I'm so proud of you," she mumbles, and I pull away, shaking my head in total disbelief.

I look at the standings again, but they haven't changed.

Then a weight settles into my gut.

Emma.

I spin in place, trying to find her, and there she is, sitting on one of the chairs, her head buried in her hands. Brooke is next to her, an arm around her shaking shoulders. Brooke gets it. She didn't make her final either, but it's different, way different. It's so much worse.

Emma was expected to win this whole damn thing, and now she won't even get a chance to compete.

But I will.

Dani and I turn and greet Chelsea, who finished up her second of two vaults, landing both easily and nabbing a spot in the vault final. Then she's back down with us, and a light of understanding flickers in her eyes.

"Good job, Cap," she says, holding out her fists.

I bump mine against hers, but that's all. For a moment, just a fraction of a second, I resent it. I should be able to celebrate right now, but I can't because Emma's dream had to die for mine to find life again. It's not like she won't be able to compete in the team final and on bars, but still, it's not the same.

Janet's finally down from the podium, where she'd been shifting the springboard and mats with Sarah's coach during the rotation. Her eyes meet mine, and I can see the congratulations there, even if she doesn't say it out loud, but then she moves over to Emma, taking up Brooke's place at her side, speaking to her so softly that we can't hear.

"Now on vault for the United States of America, Sarah Pecoraro!"

She flies down the runway, bounding off the springboard, hands first, and she pops up and off, twisting. Her body is supposed to be fully straight, but instead she's bent way too much at the hips, piking down into the mat. Her hands come out to the mat to catch her momentum, and even though she keeps herself from falling on her face, the deduction will be just as bad.

Her second vault is fine, a nicely executed double twisting Yurchenko, but it doesn't matter. Sarah's Olympics ended the moment she put her hands down.

We hug her tightly, but she moves away toward Brooke and Emma. They sit silently together once Janet stands up and comes over to us.

"Leave them be for now," she whispers, and we nod.

The final Klaxon rings out, signaling the end of the subdivision, and we line up behind the volunteer carrying our sign. It's like we've done all competition long, but it doesn't feel the same—not even close.

We're led straight from the competition floor through a lineup of reporters, but Mrs. Jackson meets us at the edge of the arena and shakes her head at the Olympic official waving us through toward the media.

"Audrey, Chelsea, and Dani only," she says, and the official tries to protest, first in Japanese and then in English, but she just crosses her arms over her chest and then turns away.

"No, I can go," Emma says, sniffling and then wiping impatiently at the tears.

Mrs. Jackson eyes her carefully. "Are you sure?"

"Of course," she says, straightening her shoulders. I want to reach out and take her hand, pull her into a hug, something, but I'm probably the last person she wants to comfort her. I just took her spot in the all-around.

"Audrey, when did you realize you had a chance at the all-around?" the first reporter asks. I recognize her from back at trials. She's the one who didn't get my LL Cool J joke.

"When Dani's score came up and I was still in first, honestly. I still can't believe it," I answer without really thinking about it. My ears are tuned to Emma beside me answering a different reporter's questions.

"I'm disappointed, obviously," she says, "but we came here with one mission: a team gold, and hopefully we got all the jitters out today. I'm looking forward to focusing on that."

"What do you think your chances are of medaling?" another reporter asks me.

I blink back at him. "We'll see. It's gymnastics. Anything can happen. For now, I'm more focused on the team final."

"Did you get any extra inspiration from Leo Adams being in the crowd?"

"I didn't even see him until after floor. I honestly had no idea he was going to be here."

"What are you most proud of today?"

"Oh, my beam, by far. It's the first time I've really hit that routine the way I've wanted to since we designed it last year."

"You designed it with your former coach, Pauline Baker, right?"

At the mention of our coach, my attention flicks back to Emma. She's still talking to reporters. "I'm so proud of Audrey and Dani. They looked great out there. It's obviously not the outcome I was hoping for, but again, the team final is tomorrow, and we've got to focus there."

"Audrey?" the reporter prompts me.

"Right, sorry, I designed my beam routine with Pauline, but Coach Dorsey-Adams has been fantastic in these last couple of weeks, helping me perfect it before the Games."

The reporter raises an eyebrow at my cool answer, but doesn't push and moves on. "What do you have to say to everyone back home?"

Looking straight into the camera, I smile wide. "Thanks so much, everyone, for supporting us! We love you and are so proud to represent you here in Tokyo!"

Moments later, Mrs. Jackson is back and extricates all of us from the reporters with a saccharine smile, leading us away from the media pen and back toward the locker room.

"Will Brooke and Sarah be available to us?" one of the reporters has the fortitude to ask, and I cringe for him when Mrs. Jackson wheels around and glares before answering succinctly.

"No."

chapter eighteen

"Are you sure?" Chelsea asks.

Brooke and Sarah have their bags packed, leos and workout clothes neatly folded into their luggage, toiletries gathered from the shelf in the bathroom we all share.

Sniffling, Brooke swipes impatiently at both her of cheeks. "What's the point in staying? Neither of us qualified."

"Still, it's the Olympics," I say, but the argument is weak. They took a risk, qualifying on their own, not leaving their fate up to the NGC, and it didn't pay off. One missed routine, and that's it. In their shoes, I'd probably be doing the same thing. Who the hell would want to stay here when your dreams aren't going to come true? Why would you want a front-row seat to someone else winning the medal you coveted for yourself?

I glance sideways at the closed door just a few feet away. Emma's in there. Giving her some space seemed like the right thing to do when we got back. Now, a few hours later, she's still in there, and I'm getting worried.

"Guys, I know you're trying to make us feel better, but, like, could you just . . . not?" Sarah asks, keeping her eyes down as she zips up her suitcase.

"Sure," Chelsea says, and we move away into the common area, only to hear the door shutting as soon as we're out of sight.

"Well, this sucks," I say, flopping down on the couch.

Dani joins us from the room she and Chelsea share, ending a call on her phone and sitting down beside me.

Chelsea flips on the TV just in time to see Irina Kareva launching herself off the vault and twisting three times in the air before landing. She's first woman ever to successfully compete a triple on vault, and damn if it doesn't look seriously awesome.

"Jesus," Dani says.

"Who the hell would do that to their ankles on purpose?" Chelsea asks.

I shake my head. "It's the Kareva now, I guess."

My phone goes off, and it's a text from Leo. He's still at the arena with Ben, watching the rest of qualifications. There's no message, but he attached a video of Kareva since they're sitting super close to the vault. It looks even better there.

The crowd is giving her a standing ovation, and I can't lie, I kind of want to join them. It's one hell of a vault, and Irina Kareva is a ridiculously talented gymnast.

The door to the suite opens, and Brooke's dad-slash-coach and Sarah's coach walk in and nod to us.

"Ladies," Brooke's dad says, briefly, but they walk right by us. It has to sting. They made a call, choosing to help their athletes qualify as individuals, keeping them away from the grueling NGC trials process. Honestly, though, even with no medals to show for it, it was probably the right decision. They kept Brooke and Sarah away from Gibby for more than a year. That's worth more than any Olympic medal.

"Girls, it's time," Sarah's coach says.

We stand up when they come into the common area.

"I'll just get Emma," I say, edging out of the room.

I knock gently at the door before opening it slowly. There's a lump in the middle of her bed, completely covered by the blankets, rising and falling in a slow, even pattern.

"Em?" I whisper. "Em, Sarah and Brooke are leaving. Come say goodbye."

Nothing. Not a hitch in her breathing or a groan of acknowledgment.

I glance behind me, where the others are waiting, and then back to Emma. She'll regret not saying goodbye.

"Emma," I try again, stepping fully into the room, my voice louder, trying to break through either the fog of actual sleep or her will to keep pretending.

Still nothing.

I guess that's her answer.

I leave the room and shrug at Sarah and Brooke before giving them both a hug. "Sorry, she—"

"It's okay," Sarah says, nodding. "I get it."

And after good lucks and wishes for safe travels are exchanged, they're gone.

There's a weird kind of emptiness in my gut. I've known them both for a long time, even if we were never super close, but now it's just over for them, and I wonder if I'll ever see either of them again. I'm finished with gymnastics after this, and I have no idea what their plans are for after the Games. Not that I have any idea what *my* plans are for after the Games.

"Cap, cut it out," Chelsea says from the couch.

"What?" I ask, sitting back down, focusing my attention on the TV, where Russia has moved to bars.

"No getting in your own head, not now. We need all our focus on tomorrow."

"How do you do that?" I ask, astounded at her ability to read me.

She shrugs. "Maybe you remind me of someone."

"Damn, look at that," Dani cuts in, nodding to where Kareva is swinging bars on the screen.

"You can beat her," I say immediately, and I mean it. I've watched Dani training up close for nearly a month now. I know what she's capable of. That mistake on bars today was a total fluke. That battle is going to be incredible, and I'm going to have a great view for it.

"First things first," Chelsea says. "We need to beat all of them." Her eyes dart over to the closed door. "Is she going to be able to get herself together?"

"I don't know," I say, "and I don't think I'm exactly the right person to talk to her, but . . . I don't know if . . ." I glance between them. Emma can't be Dani's favorite person, even after she came to her defense during that press conference, and Chelsea might just be a reminder of the all-around gold that, no matter what happens from here on out, won't be Emma's. "Maybe Janet or Mrs. Jackson could . . ."

I cut myself off as the door creaks open.

"Hey, guys," Emma says, her competition makeup completely washed away, her eyes still red-rimmed, but a smile plastered across her face. I shift over on the couch, making room for her.

"Are you . . ." Chelsea begins, but Emma shakes her head.

"I'm fine," she says, sharply, the edge of her smile hardening just a little.

"Okay," I say as she finally sits. I make eye contact with Dani and Chelsea, and we silently agree to just let her be.

"So," Emma says, nodding to the TV. "Did Kareva land that vault?"

"Yep," Dani says, shaking her head, "and it looks good. Way too good."

"Ladies," Mrs. Jackson says, flying into the room, her eyes glued to her phone, "has Emma emerged from her—oh." She looks up, seeing Emma, who sends her an uncomfortable wave.

"Emma, glad to see you up and about," Janet says from behind Mrs. Jackson, giving the other woman a sidelong glance.

"We're watching the rest of quals," I say, trying to divert their attention.

"Good, good," Mrs. Jackson says, still eyeing Emma carefully. "I wanted to say I thought your teal makeup was an excellent choice today, and the media was clamoring for a comment. It's safe to tell them that it's for sexual assault awareness and that you're united as a team behind that cause?"

"Of course," I say and then smile at Dani.

"Excellent," she says, her smile blooming large as her eyes travel over the group of us. "Now, I have some regrettable news."

"What?" I ask, not sure if I really want to know.

"Christopher Gibson gave an interview, and it's . . ." She trails off, shaking her head. "It's not good. I have it here on my phone if you'd like to watch it." She swipes at her screen, clearly getting ready to pull it up for us.

"Wait." I hold up my hand. "Do we really want to watch that?"

"Shouldn't we know what he's saying?" Emma asks.

"It's probably all bullshit anyway," Chelsea says.

"Manipulative bullshit," Dani adds.

"Exactly," I agree. "Manipulative bullshit that we do not need in our heads before team finals."

"So we don't watch it?" Emma asks, looking to me.

Chelsea and Dani's eyes follow hers, and I look up at Mrs. Jackson and Janet, shaking my head. "We don't watch it, and if anyone asks us about it, we say that we haven't seen it and that we don't want to know what he said. Then tomorrow, we do the teal eye makeup again like today, with our black leotards, in protest." I pop up out of my seat and race back into our room, finding the leo in question. "This one."

I hold up a long-sleeved black leotard with a glittery sheen to the fabric and a clear crystal outline of an American flag on the left arm. It might be the most sedate of the set we were given way back at the training center, but we don't need too much embellishment and glitz because tomorrow we're going to conquer the world.

———

When I wake up the next morning, Emma is staring right at me. "Hey."

"Hey, guess what?" she asks, smiling. The smile is fake, but I'll ignore it for now. Emma's a pro, and if ignoring what happened is what's going to help her get through the next few days, I'm going to support her.

"What?" I ask, already knowing the answer.

"Today we're going to be gold medalists."

"Damn straight we are."

Makeup and leos take a little longer than usual because we want to make sure it's all perfect. The four of us have our hair pulled back in buns, and when we're done, Dani pulls out a can of spray glitter from her bag.

"It's gold," she says, smiling widely.

"Yeah, that's happening," I say, holding out my hand. "Someone grab a visor out of my kit. Our hair is going to shine gold in that arena today."

An hour later, we emerge, shimmering glitter in our hair, glossy lips, sharp winged eyeliner, and the teal shadow that's quickly becoming our signature.

"Wow," Chelsea says, studying the group selfie we just posed for on her phone. "We look like we're about to fuck up someone's shit."

"Chelsea!" Janet scolds immediately as she comes out of her room, but then she shrugs a little bit as she looks us all up and down. "She's right. You all look incredible."

I *feel* incredible.

Our white USA tracksuits over our black leos make the look almost chic, and with our team united, everything feels like it's falling into place right when it needs to. We have to go out there and hit our routines, nothing more, nothing less. We're the best gymnastics team in the world, the four of us together, and nothing can change that.

Snapping a selfie, I send the picture to Leo. After a minute, he responds with a level of prose I wouldn't expect from a guy who chucks himself off snowy mountaintops for fun. I refuse to show it to anyone else. The amount of crap I would get for it would be unending.

We board one of the buses to the arena and settle into the back, waiting for another team to join us. The doors open, and it's the girls from Team Canada.

"Oh my God," Dani says, a hand coming up to cover her mouth.

Their whole team is also wearing teal eye makeup, and they've even added teal hair ties to keep their braids, ponytails, and buns in place.

"Wait, okay," Katie Daugherty, one of the Canadian girls, says, holding out a hand, "don't cry because then we're going to cry, and we'll all look totally wrecked when we get to the arena."

"We saw that interview with that asshole, and we wanted to let you know we stand by you," another girl, Tricia, says. "I think the Dutch and British girls are doing this too. The Japanese team actually has teal leos, so they're going to wear them. Romania and China have ribbons for their hair, and Russia has armbands."

"Russia too?" I ask, stunned. I've always had a healthy respect for the Russian team, but they're our fiercest rivals. Having their support is incredible.

"Russia too," she says, smiling. "Everyone."

She's right. Everyone in the warm-up gym has teal somewhere on their leos or in their hair, and when we drop our bags near the floor to start our warm-up routines, almost every single girl and coach comes over to offer us a word of support or a fist bump or a high five. Sun Luli—one of the top all-arounders from China and one of my major challengers for uneven bars gold—gives us all hugs, since the language barrier is way too steep to climb.

233

Even Irina Kareva and her Russian teammates raise their hands to wave to us from the other side of the gym, pointing out their teal armbands and giving us thumbs-ups.

"Crying is bad," Dani says aloud, reminding us all that being leaky messes before we go out onto the competition floor is really not a good look.

"Not gonna lie," I say, sitting down and beginning to stretch out. "This is way better than going to the opening ceremonies."

"Totally," Chelsea says.

Only Emma is quiet. "Em?" I ask, turning to her. I don't want her to feel left out of any of this, especially after what happened yesterday.

"Yeah, definitely," she says with a nod.

Our warm-up session is amazing. That well-oiled machine from Coronado is back and better than ever.

"Great job, ladies," Janet says, clapping as Chelsea finishes off our practice floor rotation. "Let's bring all of this into that arena. Get some water, get cleaned up, and check your bags to make sure you have everything. And above all, stay warm. We go in ten minutes."

"Ten minutes!" a tournament official yells in English and then Japanese, echoing Janet. "Line up, please." He walks over to our team and gestures toward the exit, where the Japanese team has already lined up.

"Okay," I say, taking my spot at the head of the line. "Let's do this."

The arena is packed. Thundersticks have been handed out to the crowd again, and they're banging them together in sync. It's when our line passes closer to the stands that I get a good look at the noisemakers and I realize they're teal too.

Apparently, the whole world is with us, and I am definitely going to ruin my eyeliner before this competition starts.

"Do you see?" Chelsea says behind me, and I nod, reaching back for her hand. She grabs mine, and then I can feel her shift enough to know she's reaching back for Dani, who then reaches back for Emma. We walk hand in hand to the vault and raise our arms together when we're announced to the crowd to acknowledge their support as a cheer as big as the one they gave the Japanese team echoes through the arena.

Dani's first, and the crowd goes insane as the announcer calls, "Now on vault from the United States of America, Daniela Olivero!" Their thundersticks crash together and drown out the sound of Dani's feet pounding down the runway and off the springboard, but the result is clear. She lands and doesn't move and somehow the arena gets even louder. That's a great vault.

She runs down the stairs, pumping her fist at the crowd, and I nearly tackle her with a hug. A 14.8 pops up on the scoreboard, and the crowd actually hisses in response. I was expecting a fifteen, but Dani sometimes bends her knees before she lands; maybe that's what the judges saw.

It doesn't matter. It's still a great score to build upon.

Russia's up next, with Galina Kuznetsova, their weakest vaulter, but still a powerhouse with an Amanar. She lands on her feet but under-rotates slightly, having to hop forward and sideways, trying to make it look like she completed all two and a half twists.

I look to the judges who are scribbling furiously on their score sheets, but wrinkle my nose when Galina's score comes up. A 14.8, the same as Dani, when Dani's vault was so much better.

Okay, so it's going to be one of those days, then. Fine. We'll just be so good that they can't take it away.

"Come on, Em!" I yell up to her, clapping my hands together fiercely to keep from going over and slapping a judge or two. "You got this!"

"Crush it, Emma!" Dani yells.

It's her first competition routine since she didn't make the all-around, and I know how badly she wants to do well.

The green light flashes, and Emma takes a deep breath, before sprinting down to the vault, roundoff, back handspring, one . . . two . . . and a half twists with . . . whoa, a really big hop forward and then another lunging step and then a smaller one. Totally over-cooked, but I get it. After Dani's vault, her adrenaline was probably pumping. It's just, those were really big steps.

I still hug her, but she pulls back, biting her lip, and shakes her head. "Damn it," she mutters.

"We'll get it back on bars."

She nods fiercely, almost like she's trying to convince herself of it.

A 14.3 lights up the scoreboard. It could have been worse, and it's still not as bad as if I'd gone up to vault in her place.

Sitting down, I grab my tape and grip bag, starting to get ready for bars, just as Irina Kareva goes up to the podium. She salutes, the same way I do, one arm up, one arm out. She's going second, so I guess she's not going to use her triple here in team finals, where a fall could cost the team a medal. That's confirmed when she only twists two and a half times and then takes a small hop forward.

She comes down from the podium, high-fiving her teammates, and sits down just one chair away from me, digging into her own bag and emerging with her grips. She looks up, and our eyes meet for a second, and it's kind of awkward. Do I smile? Congratulate her for a great vault? She's our competition, but I've competed against her for years. We know each other even without really *knowing* each other.

I open my mouth to say *good job*, but it's too late—her eyes are flying to the scoreboard over my shoulder.

A 14.9.

Chelsea is already up on the podium waiting for the green light.

"The final vault for the United States, 2016 Olympic all-around champion, Chelsea Cameron!"

The thundersticks are back, pounding in full force when they hear her name.

"You got it, Chels," Dani calls out.

And she does. A nearly perfect two and a half twist with a stuck landing that makes me want to go over and steal the execution judges' score sheets so they can't deduct at all. It would have been impossible for them to see a flaw in Chelsea's vault with the naked eye, it was that good. Except they've seen her vault a million times, and they know she tends to twist slightly off the table and that'll incur at least a tenth of a point deduction, plus whatever other bullshit they think they see to get to the 15.1 that comes up beside Chelsea's name.

Erika Sheludenko is Russia's final vaulter.

"*Davai! Davai!*" the other Russian girls call to her as she pounds down the runway, a roundoff, back handspring off the vault, and then two and a half twists, flying higher and farther than everyone else and landing in a perfect stick. The crowd sucks in a collective breath of awe before it explodes.

Erika races down the stairs and into a sea of hugs from her teammates and coaches. I almost want to hug her myself. That was incredible.

The judges agree when they post a 15.3, and my stomach rolls. We have to be behind.

My eyes zero in on the scoreboard.

1.	Russian Federation	45.0	
1.	People's Republic of China	45.0	
3.	United States of America	44.2	(-0.8)
4.	Japan	43.6	(-1.4)

Not bad, even with Emma's hiccup. Only eight-tenths of a point. We can make up that ground. I tighten my grips and stand up, moving into line so we can march to bars.

It won't be easy, but we can do it, and I can't wait to get out there. I'm going to rock bars and beam and make that deficit into a lead.

"Just like we've been doing in training," I say to Dani and Emma as we stand in a semicircle facing the bars. Russia's Lada Stepanova is halfway through her routine, but I'm barely seeing it. "Just like in training."

"Like in training," Emma repeats, nodding her head.

Stepanova releases into a full-in dismount, landing with just a tiny hop forward, and I turn to Dani. "Get us going."

"Aye, aye, Cap," she says, shooting me a small salute, streaking chalk on her forehead.

When she steps up onto the podium, the thundersticks pick up again, getting louder and louder as she waits to go up.

I'm glad we didn't watch it, but whatever Gibby said in that interview must have been pretty terrible to get everyone—our competitors and their fans—on our side.

"Just like always, Dani," Chelsea calls out to her, but I'm sure the sound is swallowed up by the time it gets to Dani on the podium.

The noise doesn't rattle her at all, and the dumb fluke from qualifications was just that. Her routine is solid, and the crowd roars even louder when she lands, sticking the double layout cold and then waving to them as she jogs off the podium.

A 14.8 for Dani and I can feel our deficit shrinking.

Erika Sheludenko is next for Russia, her dirty-blonde curls pulled back in a bun, but she smiles at the judges before she runs up to the springboard, launching herself up to the high bar and swinging aggressively through her routine. She's a taller gymnast, like me, and her skills look almost wild, but her form is impeccable, just like the rest of her teammates on this event. Thirty seconds of gorgeous gymnastics later, she's dismounting into a full-in—two flips, the first with a twist—and she's done with just a small step on the landing.

Another routine, another hit for Russia.

"Okay, c'mon, Emma," Janet says, as they head up to the podium to chalk the bars, waiting for Sheludenko's score.

It's a 15.1.

"Bring it, Em!" Dani calls to her right before the green light goes on, and Emma shoots us a tight smile before she straightens her shoulders and salutes the judges.

I can tell right away something's off. As she goes to brace her toes on the low bar for a transition up to the high, her foot slips and her hands release way too early. She falls to the mat between the bars.

"Shit!" Chelsea curses, loud enough for the cameras to pick up as Janet leaps onto the podium to check on Emma. My heart is pounding, but I have to calm down. Emma fell, which means we're going to need a big number from me to make up for it. *Calm down, Audrey.* A deep breath in and out helps me settle, and I hope Emma can find the same calm in the next few seconds so she can get back up there.

"I'm fine," she says, standing up and shaking her head. She looks a little dazed, but not injured. "I'm fine," she says again, moving to the chalk bowl and reapplying some to her hands before she comes back to the bars to start over.

"Take a deep breath," Janet says.

Emma inhales and exhales and then nods. She's okay.

Janet retreats off the podium, and Emma salutes again, starting one more time. Everything is better now—her transitions are solid, pirouettes maybe a touch late, but that's picky. She starts to build up for her dismount, a giant into a pirouette and then a release into a double layout, but her timing's off, and she trips forward to her knees when she lands.

A second fall.

Two full points.

"Fuck," I mutter, and since there's a camera right beside us it definitely picked it up.

I shake out my wrists and walk to the stairs. Emma's already down them, and I can see her face. Her red hair is bright against her pale skin—almost translucent in shock right now. I can't even give her a fist bump or a word of encouragement because I'm pretty sure she didn't even see me as she walked past me. Two falls. Two full points.

I manage not to react at all when Emma's 12.0 pops up on the screen for her routine as Irina Kareva salutes and mounts the bars. It defies the laws of biology and physics that she's powerful enough to do a triple on vault, but swings bars like she's lighter than air. And I grimace when she does. Her score pops up, a massive 15.3.

Janet is chalking the bars for me, and I go to the chalk bowl to make sure my grips are perfect. I need to hit this. I'm going to hit this. I hit the routine at trials. I hit it in Coronado. I hit it yesterday. I can hit it now. For the team, because we need it.

A deep breath and then a leap up into the air to start my momentum onto the low bar gets me swinging. I'm into a handstand and then down beneath the bar, body folded in half, legs straddled and toes perfectly pointed before I release up and around to the high bar, turning halfway and catching smoothly, and up into a handstand again, a half turn and a release and catch before flipping right back down to the low bar. And then, making it look easy, I'm straight back up to the high bar, a full pirouette landing at twelve o'clock and letting the judges see it, admire it longingly so they can't find one deduction on it, before I swing down, release into one, two, three twists, land, and stick!

"Wow!" I'm pretty sure I say it out loud before I remind myself to salute the judges.

I make it down off the podium, and the girls are waiting there for me with fists held out for bumping.

Emma smiles before giving me a hug. "Thanks for picking me up," she says and then releases me.

"What are best friends for?" I wiggle my fingers at her, like we used to when we were kids. She wiggles them back, just as my score is posted. A 15.3: exactly what we needed.

"Superstar," Chelsea says.

I smile, sitting down and yanking off the grips and tape around my wrist as the leaderboard reshuffles.

1. Russian Federation	90.1	
2. People's Republic of China	90.0	(-0.1)
3. United States of America	86.3	(-3.7)
4. Japan	86.2	(-3.8)

Dani's beside me, still staring at it, and I turn to her. "It means nothing. We're still in this. Beam and floor and we win. You got it?"

She nods. "I got you, Cap. I got you."

I hope she does, because we're headed to balance beam, where Olympic dreams go to die.

'***ve always been a great beamer, but today we *all* need to be, with this hole we've dug for ourselves.

I open my eyes after visualizing my routine one last time and before turning to Emma. She still looks a little shaken after bars.

"Hey, you've got this. You are money on beam, and you're going to nail this. Dani's going to start us up, I'm gonna hit, and then you're going to bring it home."

She nods with my every word, her shoulders relaxing under my hands. "I can do this."

"You totally can."

We had to count her twelve on bars, when normally her score would be somewhere in the fifteens. We're the best team in the world, but it's not like those other teams are total wastes. They're perfectly capable of hitting their routines, and so far, they have.

Dani's up first, and her beam routine has been getting better and better every time I've seen her do it since trials.

Up on the podium, Dani salutes, and the crowd falls silent. There's barely a sound in the arena except for the floor music of a Canadian athlete. Dani works through her beam routine, tumbling across it like most people walk on the ground. Where I dance on the beam, she attacks, moving through her routine in a way that old-school Romanian gymnasts used to: no hesitation, trick after trick, but seamlessly tied to her choreography, so much so you barely notice that she's doing incredibly difficult gymnastics. Finally, she sets herself and launches into a roundoff and a double Arabian with a decent-sized hop on the landing.

"Nice!" I let myself shout, though I probably should have been focusing on my own beam routine instead of watching hers. I haven't felt this good in competition in a long time. I'm used to having to find ways to distract myself from the pain, but the cortisone is doing a great job of masking that right now, so instead of reverting back to my pre-injury self and blocking everything out, I'm taking everything in.

I give Dani a fist bump as she passes me and waits for her scores. The crowd isn't quiet anymore, a steady stream of "Da-ni! Da-ni!" reverberating from the stands until her score pops up: a 14.4. It's super solid for her, but not quite her best. Still, it's the kind of score I can build on.

The crowd is reacting to Stepanova's routine, but I try my best to zone it out, running through my beam routine in my mind's eye. I swing my arms, going through the motions of every section. Up to the beam, and then my turns, keeping them smooth and connected, aerial sequence, leaps, maintain rhythm, dismount, clean.

Just like in training, Audrey. Just like in Coronado, just like in quals. The crowd is applauding for Stepanova, and I open my eyes, finding Janet in front of me.

"You good?" she asks, and I nod, following her up the stairs, where she carries my springboard to the mat and I mark the beam with chalk for visual cues during the routine: a line for my aerial series and a line for where to set up for my dismount.

The green light flickers at me, and I move to the edge of the mat, narrowing my vision to the springboard Janet set up at the end of the beam. After a quick salute, I run to it, a roundoff, layout step-out onto the beam and then two more following it with no hesitation, traveling across nearly the entire length. I raise my arms to show the judges control, and then it's like something clicks inside of me. It's easy. I almost feel separated from my body, like I'm watching myself perform instead of actually working through the routine. My turn sequence is perfection, not a flicker in my knees, and then it's a few more skills to the dismount, and I can hear my own heartbeat as I take a breath and settle myself and count out my dismount to my pulse: one, two, one, two, hands, feet, hands, feet, triple twist, land, stiiiick—okay, a small step, but still. That was good.

I salute the judges and let out a breath. That's what I came here to do today. I hit bars. I hit beam. Now I can only watch.

My score is up quickly, a 15, and I nod in agreement with the judges, a rare feat. That routine was great, and I'm glad they knew it too.

"Nice job," Emma says, squeezing my shoulders.

"Your turn," I say, wiggling my fingers at her, and she does it right back.

Good. This is where it starts. Emma hits, and we'll be right back in this thing. Russia can't match us on beam if we hit. Galina Kuznetsova is up there now, and even if she does everything she's capable of, Emma can outscore her by nearly a point. We're gonna do this.

The crowd applauds with their thundersticks for Galina as she dismounts, banging them together, though perhaps with not quite the same amount of enthusiasm as they did for me. They're a pretty savvy crowd and know a great routine from a decent one.

Wow, Audrey, conceited much? Oh well, it's the truth.

"You got this, Em!" I call to her just before she salutes, and with three running steps she's up on the beam, her shoulders set, her feet steady, working through her skills, one by one. It's solid. Just like her gymnastics has always been up until yesterday.

"Nice!" Chelsea says when she hits her switch split leap and then swings her arms, gaining momentum to connect it to a back pike, but the word is barely out of Chelsea's mouth when Emma's foot lands half off the beam and she slides down, her hip bouncing off the edge before she falls to her back on the mat.

The crowd gasps in that high-pitched, legitimately shocked way. I want to be shocked, but I'm not. *How is this happening?*

"This is a nightmare," Chelsea mutters.

"Did she just?" Dani whispers.

She fell. Emma fell off the beam. Again.

Polite applause rings out in the arena when she remounts and then works through the rest of her routine, landing her dismount, an Arabian double front, like Dani. She sticks it cold, but that's not going to make up for the fall. She's down three points so far from falls alone, and when she jumps from the podium, she just walks right by me.

Irina Kareva is up on the beam, working through her routine steadily, no wavers or wobbles, and while I'd never root for someone to fall, now would be a great time for her to . . . not hit.

Crap. *Don't be like that, Audrey.* Except . . . one missed routine we might have been able to absorb, but two? Two is not good, especially when her vault score wasn't where it would normally be. *Stop it, Audrey. Don't think. Just . . . keep going.*

Kareva dismounts, and I don't need to see her score to know it'll be great.

My eyes meet Chelsea's, and I'm ready for her to berate me for doing math, but she doesn't say anything, just presses her lips together into a firm line. Dani's chewing on her lip, and Emma? She's sitting on a chair, staring straight ahead, eyes unseeing. Who knows where her head is right now?

Our scores slide into place on the leaderboard, and my heart leaps into my throat. Yeah, this is not good.

It's not even close anymore, and we're not in a battle for the gold or even the silver. That would take a miracle in the form of China and Russia imploding with one rotation left to go. We're a point behind Japan, and while we're stronger than them on floor, a point is a lot to make up, especially . . . especially if Emma doesn't hit. Looking at her now, sitting stock-still on a chair against the competition floor, eyes wide and breath still coming hard, it really doesn't look like she'll be able to stand, let alone get through four tumbling passes.

1. People's Republic of China	134.2	
2. Russian Federation	133.9	(-0.3)
3. Japan	129.7	(-4.5)
4. United States of America	128.7	(-5.5)

"Emma," I start, but she looks right through me, like I'm not even there. "Em?"

"Audrey!" Janet calls out.

"Emma," I try again, but her head drops to stare at the ground.

I give up, moving over to Janet, who slides an arm around my shoulders. "Audrey, can you do a floor routine?" she whispers.

Glancing back at Emma and then over to Dani and Chelsea's desperate faces, I swallow down the panic and nod. I can. For my team, right now, to somehow salvage this day—this day, which was supposed to be a coronation but is rapidly spiraling into disaster.

"I . . . I don't know if it'll be enough."

Enough for bronze. Enough for any medal. We were supposed to win gold, and now . . .

"I'll take whatever you can give us."

"I'll do my best."

"I know you will. You'll go up last, give you enough time to get your mind right."

"Okay." I nod, though I regret that as soon as she turns away from me to tell the judge I'll be replacing Emma in the lineup.

I'd rather go first, just to get it out of the way, but it's too late. There's sweat on my palms that keeps reappearing no matter how much chalk I layer on, and I have to keep moving, my whole body vibrating with tension at what I have to go out and do.

I pace up and down the well between the stands and the competition floor, back and forth, hands on my hips, head down and eyes trained on the neon green carpet that lines the entire arena.

Five full floor routines before my turn.

Don't watch, Audrey, just visualize, every step, every tumble, every turn, every leap. There's no controlling what's happening out there now; just focus and go when it's time.

Except I'm not supposed to be here. I was never supposed to compete on floor in team finals. This was where Chelsea and Dani and Emma were going to bring home the gold and I was going to cheer them on, having done my part. I jog in place to try to get warm.

I send Emma, sitting in her seat, still not responding to the world around her, one final look before I turn and make my way to the raised podium. The final floor routine of the Olympic team final.

"You got this, Rey," Dani says as we pass each other on the stairs.

"Do the thing, Rey!" Chelsea calls from behind us.

"Now on floor for the United States of America, Audrey Lee!" the announcer calls, and the crowd lets out a confused murmur.

I shake my head, removing all the self-doubt, all the tension, everything else. The world narrows to me and the floor. I don't know if the arena is actually quiet or not, but I can hear my own inhale and exhale before the warning beep, and then my music begins.

I dance, doing my best to make sure every flicker of my fingers and point of my toe is taken in by the judges. I can't outscore Chelsea or Dani. I don't even know what I need. I have to stick everything, every pass, every turn, every leap. I have to be perfect, and if there's one thing I've learned in my life, nothing—no matter how hard you try or how much you deserve it—is ever perfect.

I land my final pass and my feet shuffle, an inch, maybe two. I raise my hands and salute to the judges, and I wave to the crowd because my parents and Leo are in there somewhere.

I walk down the stairs, still catching my breath, no idea if it was enough, no idea where we stand.

Dani and Chelsea are waiting for me. Emma is sitting in a chair near the floor, her head in her hands.

"Come on," I say, leading them to Emma. I grab her hand and tug, sliding my arm over her shoulders as she stands. Her eyes are red and watery, her body shaking with what has to be regret.

I lean in, and they lean with me, arms around one another. "Girls, no matter what happens, it's been an honor," I murmur within our huddle. "I love you all. You're my sisters, and I am so, so proud of you."

We break from the circle, but I keep Emma's hand in mine. Janet stands at her other side, an arm around her shoulders. Dani takes my free hand and then finds Chelsea's with her other. I lift my gaze to the board again.

My score is up. A 14.0. That's pretty good, at least for me. Then the board flashes to the team totals.

1.	Russian Federation	177.1	
2.	People's Republic of China	177.0	(-0.1)
3.	Japan	171.7	(-5.4)
4.	United States of America	171.6	(-5.5)

We're one-tenth of a point back.

Fourth place.

Off the podium. That medal I knew was ours when I woke up this morning is gone, and I'll never have another shot at it.

We're the greatest team in the world. I know it with every fiber of my being.

Except we're fourth. We're not gold, silver, or bronze.

We're nothing.

We're ushered out of the arena and to a media session.

"What happened out there?" a reporter asks as I walk past him.

I stop and look him dead in the eye, leaning in toward his extended microphone.

"We lost."

—

We're barely back at the village for more than a few minutes before I get stir-crazy. I don't want to look at my phone or my laptop or the TV. I can imagine what everyone's saying about our performance, and I don't need a million people telling me I suck when I'm perfectly capable of coming to that conclusion on my own.

Emma's in the chair across from me, and Dani and Chelsea are sitting together, silently, on the couch. I'm not sure I've ever not heard them speak for this long. I don't really want to talk either, to be honest. The last thing I want to do is rehash everything that went down. If I could block it out for the rest of my life, I would. Fourth place. It's unreal to me.

The competition is a total blur, aside from that one-tenth deduction on my last pass. I'm pretty sure I'll still be thinking about it for the rest of my life.

Was that what lost us the medal?

No.

One deduction on its own doesn't knock you off the podium, but damn, does it feel like it did.

I still don't understand what happened to Emma. What could have caused that kind of epic implosion from the best gymnast in the world? Was it not making the all-around yesterday? Or maybe it was a fluke? Did Emma have the worst day of her entire gymnastics career at the worst possible time? It's happened to people before. Could it have been the pressure? Maybe it was just gymnastics being hard. We make it look easy sometimes, but it's the hardest sport in the world. Or maybe it was . . .

"It's my fault," Emma says, out of nowhere.

"Em, it's not your fault. It's gymnastics. These things happen," I say, moving out of my chair toward hers and kneeling beside it.

Emma shakes her head wildly. "No, it's not that."

"Then what?"

She takes a deep breath, and then the words come spilling out. "You're all going to hate me, and I'm going to deserve it, but I need you to know . . . why what happened out there today happened. Everyone was so . . . Everyone was there for you, Dani. Even Russia wore those armbands in support, and I . . . I wasn't there for you even though I knew better. I *knew* you weren't lying, and I didn't say anything. Audrey nearly gave up her spot on this team to help you. Mrs. Jackson suspended the entire NGC. Janet put her life on hold,"—she sends each of them, standing just behind us, a tight smile—"and I wasn't brave enough to . . . to tell the truth."

I blink up at her in confusion. What truth is she talking about?

"I was just so scared when I saw you get kicked off the team and then how Sierra and Jaime treated you. I was terrified, and I was making it worse for you and didn't know how to stop. It just felt like it was too late. But when I saw all that support today from strangers, from people who didn't know you or grow up with you or know for a fact that you were telling the truth, I . . . I broke. I knew you weren't lying, Dani. I knew because for the last year, he was doing the same thing to me."

All the air leaves my lungs in one breath, like slipping on the beam and landing on my sternum.

"Em?" I croak, but the sound of my voice must jolt something in her.

She leaps from her chair, holding herself around the middle. Her whole body shakes as the sobs burst forth, and then she's gone, flying out the door.

"Emma!" I call, on my feet in an instant, but Mrs. Jackson blocks my exit.

"I'll go," she says quietly. "We don't want a public scene."

I blink up at her. What does she think I'm going to do, berate my friend for being a victim and surviving? I would never. Is that what Emma thought? Does she really think I'd hate her?

Mrs. Jackson leaves, and Janet is just a few steps behind her.

"I thought I was the only one," Dani said. "If I had just said something, then maybe—"

"No," Chelsea cuts her off. "You're not going to blame yourself for what he did."

"How did I not notice?" I whisper, but they both hear me. "She's my best friend, and I just didn't notice."

"You had your own stuff going on last year, Rey," Chelsea says. "You were hurt."

I was hurt, and I wasn't there. So Emma was left to room alone, just like Gibby tried to make me do at camp and just like he made Dani do at worlds. And that wasn't my fault, but I should have been able to tell. I should have known something was going on with her. I should have been there for her.

I can't sit still anymore. I need to get away.

"I'm taking a walk." I sling my athletes' credential around my neck and leave, not waiting for a response.

They built the Olympic Village on an inlet of Tokyo Bay, and the sticky humidity in the air combined with the water traffic and the planes going overhead really does remind me of home. I want to text my parents, but that would require looking at my phone, and I don't want to do that. I don't need one more ounce of negativity right now, and there's no escaping that on social media. Even random people who have my number won't hesitate to let me know exactly how they feel about what went down today.

Maybe just one message, though.

Can you get here?

I drop a pin and then shut my phone off, burying it in the pocket of my jacket.

Making it down to where the edge of the village meets the water, I sit on one of the benches.

The horizon beckons in the distance. Coronado's five thousand miles away. Home is more than eight thousand. I'm at the Olympic Games, the thing I've been working toward my entire life, and all I can think about is how I want to crawl into my bed back in Queens and let the sounds of cars and ambulances and airplanes and people outside on their stoops and kids playing in the alleyway behind our house drown out everything else. I want to inhale the scent of the laundry detergent my mom uses on my sheets and the aftershave my dad uses in the bathroom.

I want to go home.

The tears come unbidden, not a steady stream, but one at a time. I want to go home. I want all of this to go away.

I'm this team's captain, a title I didn't earn and definitely don't deserve, and the team is crumbling. I have no idea what to do to fix it, and my only solution is to run away. *Great leadership skills, Audrey. Really fantastic.*

"Hey, there you are," Leo says from just a few feet away.

I reach up quickly, wiping away the remaining tears from my cheeks, but he saw them.

"Can I?" he asks, motioning toward the open spot beside me on the bench.

I nod. That's all I'm capable of right now.

"I keep thinking about how this is the same water we left behind at home," he says, nodding out to the inlet.

"Yeah, the ocean is big," I retort and then cringe at the sarcasm laced through each word. He doesn't deserve me lashing out. I asked him to come, and he came. He's done nothing except be there for me, despite, you know, knowing me for, like, five whole minutes. "How did you get into the village?"

"I bribed the guard."

I finally turn to look at him, eyes wide. "Seriously?"

"No, I had my mom sign me in as a guest," he says, heaving a sigh and sliding a little closer. He doesn't reach out for me, so instead I do, leaning my head against his shoulder. He laces his fingers with mine, holding my hand and pressing a kiss to the top of my head.

"Thanks for coming so fast. I'm sorry . . . I can't . . . I can't tell you what happened. It's not my secret to tell. I just . . . I don't know if I can do all of this anymore."

"Whatever it is, I know you can," he says without hesitation, and that surety, that confidence he has in me, is what makes me snap.

"I can't!" I shoot back, leaping up from the bench and whirling on him. "My brain has been going a mile a minute since trials. Like I didn't even have a minute to process any of it and then we got here and now there's way too much time to think and I go over and over it in my head a million times and I haven't even begun to think about what could have happened to me with Gibby if Dani hadn't stopped him and now Emma . . ." I trail off before I reveal too much. "They were depending on me. I was supposed to be their captain, and I can't . . . I can't think . . ."

"So don't think."

"You make it sound so simple," I shoot back and throw my hands out in frustration. "It's not. The only time I can't think is when I'm doing gymnastics, and what if that won't work anymore, because now gymnastics means losing?" My voice cracks, and I'm close to tears, but I don't want to cry. I want to fix this.

"I'm sorry about what happened today. You deserved to win. You deserve every good thing in this world."

That's when something inside me breaks. Maybe like it did for Emma today during the competition. It's all finally too much, and I burst into tears.

He lets me cry for I don't even know how long, but it's a while before my breathing evens and the tears stop coming.

"I'm such a mess, and I'm always crying on you. I'm sorry. I need . . . I don't even know what I need. A distraction, maybe."

Leo raises an eyebrow and stands, holding his hands out to me. "Fine, then I'll distract you. Dance with me."

His totally random suggestion actually makes me stop spiraling. That was the last thing I expected to come out of his mouth. "That's not, like, a euphemism for . . ."

He snorts, but his eyes are twinkling. "No, it's not. I'm asking you to dance."

"You dance?" I ask through a laugh. "You're kidding."

He shakes his head with a rueful grin. "Totally serious. My trainer made me take lessons. He wanted me to improve my body awareness. I took a month of ballet before I begged for anything else, so he signed me up for ballroom dancing."

"And you liked ballroom dancing better?"

"Oh yeah," he says, his smile widening. "The girls there were a lot less uptight than the ballerinas."

At that I throw my head back and laugh, and damn if that doesn't feel good. "God, they must've been like a picnic compared to me."

"C'mon, Rey, don't be so hard on yourself. You're a delight."

"An *uptight* delight," I correct, knowing how unhinged I sounded a few seconds before, but smile despite myself.

"A little bit uptight, but also smart and talented and insanely hardworking and selfless—and is that enough to get you to stop stalling? I could keep them coming, but are you going to dance with me or not?"

"I still don't believe you can dance."

Leo tilts his head like he's accepting the challenge and steps close to me. One hand slides around my waist, coming to rest at the center of my back, and with the softest touch he pulls me closer. His other hand takes mine and lifts it to his shoulder before grasping my free hand with his.

"There's no music."

He smiles again then opens his mouth and starts to sing, in a low tone, slightly off-key, but I'm too stunned to care. "Moon River, wider than a mile, I'm crossing you in style someday . . ." I didn't notice when he started dancing, but instinctively I follow him. It's another moment before I realize that at some point he must have picked up the waltz choreography from my floor routine, because that's what he's leading me through, his steps sure and perfectly in time. He's either an extremely talented dancer or he's been watching me really closely. Or maybe it's both. I shiver as he spins me beneath his arm and catches my hand again easily before moving into the next verse.

His voice struggles a little on the higher notes, and he flushes a bit but then settles smoothly into a more comfortable range, and I squeeze his hand, desperate for him to continue.

He pulls me in closer, our chests brushing lightly, and his fingers twitch at my back. His breath is warm against my temple as he leans in close, still singing softly. He spins me away from him, holding his hand high as I twirl underneath into the same double pirouette from my routine, my leg held up behind me in attitude, like I would on the floor, and when I finish he pulls me in again and this time we're dancing together. His forehead rests against mine as I whisper the final words along with him, "Moon River and me."

We stop dancing and just stand together, breathing each other in. The dance was slow, but my heart is racing, pounding to a rhythm much faster than the waltz. He's still holding me against him, but he doesn't move except for a small twitch of his jaw. Our eyes meet. He's waiting for me. He wants me to know that I can trust him, even if I'm not sure I can trust anyone, even myself. It's a big deal. A really big deal.

I push up on my toes and press my lips to his. His grip on my waist is firm, but he stays passive. He's kissing me back, but letting me lead. I let my teeth gently nip at his bottom lip. He groans from the back of his throat, sending an echoing vibration through me. My skin tingles as his hands fist into the bottom of my shirt, sliding beneath the hem, his knuckles brushing against the bare skin at the small of my back. I pull away gasping. There's something about even that soft touch that sets me on fire. I close my eyes, trying to keep my balance as my head spins from the sensation. His breathing is as ragged as mine.

A perfect first kiss.

"Audrey," he rasps, but he stops with my name.

"You memorized the words," I whisper, still stunned by it all, "to the song."

"I looked it up after I saw your routine that first night of trials. Went to bed listening to it on repeat," he confesses with a shrug and a hand rubbing at the back of his neck. "You were so gorgeous out there, and then we reconnected, and now . . . it . . . it sort of feels like it's about us, you know? Like this was fate."

"I don't believe in fate," I murmur. "Not anymore."

"What do you believe in?" he asks, his voice raw.

His question has me on tiptoe again, and he meets me halfway, this time taking the lead in the kiss, as he did in the dance. His hands slide beneath the back of my shirt, hauling me against him, nothing gentle about it this time. I reach up and twine my arms around his neck, and then his hands are moving, one tangling up into my hair, burying itself in the messy bun, and the other gripping me firmly at my hip, pulling me into him and creating a sharp friction between us. I'm going to burst into a million pieces if he keeps touching me like this.

That thought makes me pull away. We're out in the open and anyone could see us. He seems to understand, his grip loosening, our lips parting one final time.

"When this is all over, Audrey Lee, you and I are going to . . . We're going to have that very serious conversation," he says, looking up over my head, breathing heavily. I can feel his heart pounding and the warmth of his skin seeping through his T-shirt into the palm of my hand. "If you still want to."

I nod, but he can't see me. "I still want to"—I pause, gathering up my courage—"have a serious conversation"—I reach up, laying a hand on either side of his face, guiding his eyes to mine—"with you. Very serious. The most serious."

"Good," he says before smiling wickedly. "So, are you distracted yet?"

I laugh again. It feels so good to do that, and he makes it happen so often that it's like a drug. "You're the worst, you know that?"

"Yeah," he says, slinging an arm around my shoulders and pulling me into his side as we walk back. "I know."

He did distract me, at least for a few minutes, but even as his rough fingertips brush against the skin of my shoulder, it doesn't solve anything. Everything I said was still true, and maybe he thinks, with his charming arrogance, that a distraction is enough.

But it isn't.

Our team is broken, but I'm going to fix it.

I have to, or I'll regret it for the rest of my life.

chapter twenty

I say goodbye to Leo, which maybe takes a little longer than I antici-pated, and then make a beeline to our building. I have a plan—well, more of an idea, really, but it's a good one, and I don't want to waste any more time before bringing the other girls in on it. When I get back to the suite, the common area is empty, but the door to my room is open.

"You're back," I say as Emma moves around the room. The drawers to her dresser are all open, and there are clothes piled on the bed, her suitcase waiting beside them. "What are you doing?"

"Packing," she says, chucking the leos that were carefully folded inside a drawer into the bag and then turning to grab more.

"Wait." I slide into the space between her and the suitcase, blocking her ability to actually pack. "Listen to me for a second."

"It's fine," she says. "I know you feel bad, Rey, but there's no way you could have known what was going on. There's nothing to feel guilty about."

"That's not . . ." I start to protest, but she's right about that. I do feel guilty. Really guilty. "Okay, fine, but take my guilt out of it."

"What?"

"This isn't about me. It's about you."

"Rey, I don't think—"

"According to Leo, we're not allowed to think."

"Snowboarders: so chill."

"I know, right?"

"Audrey—"

"No, just listen. If you want to leave because it hurts too much or because it isn't what you want anymore, that's fine. That's legit, and I don't blame you. But if you're leaving because . . . because you feel like you don't deserve it or you think that what you said before was true, that you're responsible for any of this, then, please, I'm begging you, don't."

"Audrey."

"You're one of the best gymnasts in the world. You've worked your entire life for this, and you deserve to be here. You deserve to give yourself a chance to win."

"But—"

"Dani doesn't blame you. I don't blame you. None of us blame you. The only person to blame is Gibby. I'm not going to give you that whole if-you-give-up-then-he-wins bullshit—"

"That's what Mrs. Jackson said."

"Mrs. J is great, but she's wrong. What you do now has nothing to do with him. It's about what *you* want. What do you want?"

"I want to do gymnastics," she says instantly.

"Well, we just so happen to be at the Olympics, and that's one of the things they do here."

Emma snorts, but I can see a smile—a real one—fighting to break through.

"I don't know if I can go back out there. I don't know if I can face . . . everyone. I blew it in front of the whole world, and I don't want everyone to know why." She's rambling now, but I let her go on. Maybe she needs to get this out. "I'm not like Dani. I'm not as strong as her. I don't think I could take that, but I also want them to know that there was a reason for how messed up I was, that I didn't just choke. But, like . . . everyone thinks I did, and maybe in some ways that's the truth, and that's on me, and now I don't know what to do."

I stare at her in silence. She's right, in a weird, convoluted, context-free kind of way, and I have no idea what to say in response.

"Hey," Dani says from the door, her eyes clearly catching the suitcase but ignoring it, "can I come in?"

"Sure," Emma says, shrugging.

"You are, you know. You're just as strong as me," Dani says.

"I'm not," Emma protests.

Dani moves into the room and glances to me. "Audrey, could you excuse us for a sec?"

"Sure," I say, but before I leave, I reach for Emma and pull her into a hug. "You are strong and you're my best friend and I love you. No matter what you decide, all of that is still true."

Dani closes the door behind me, and I try not to let it gnaw at my gut that when she needs me most, I don't know how to help my best friend.

Chelsea is on the couch, spreading food over the coffee table while Mrs. Jackson and Janet dig into their white Styrofoam cartons with chopsticks. They must have run out for dinner before Emma started packing.

"Here," Chelsea says, handing me one of my own. "Fresh sushi made right in front of us."

"Perks of a Tokyo Olympics," I say. We haven't seen much of the city and probably won't until the competition is over—if at all—but at least we can enjoy the food.

The minutes tick by, and we try to distract ourselves with watching the swimming competition, but aside from admiring how good the guys look slicing through the water, my attention is still focused on whatever is going on behind my bedroom door.

"I assume my son found you?" Janet asks, drawing my focus away.

"He did. Thanks for, you know . . ." I shift in my seat under her steady gaze. For what? Letting me distract myself by hooking up with her son? No, it's more than that. "Thanks for being there this whole time. I know I fought you on some stuff, but you taught me a lot. Mostly that what I'd thought was good coaching my whole life was . . . not."

"You're welcome, though he and I will definitely be having a chat about how he perhaps didn't stay away from you as much as he swore he did," Janet says with a smile, pushing beyond the awkwardness and then changing tracks before it comes back. "He told me, you know, about his training plans. You helped my son find his dreams again, somehow, and I'm sorry we tried to dictate your relationship."

I'm still not really sure I deserve the credit Leo gave me for that decision. It's his Olympic dream, not mine. And the apology? I have no idea what to say to that.

Mrs. Jackson saves me from having to respond. "Leo's going to train for 2022?" she asks, her eyes sliding over me with calculation. "That's interesting."

"Tamara," Janet starts to say, but she's interrupted by the door opening behind her.

Dani emerges first, but Emma is right behind her. Their eyes are pink and a little bit swollen, but other than that they don't look any worse for wear.

"I've decided to stay," Emma says, breaking the silence.

My shoulders relax instantly, and I leap from my seat to hug her. We just stand there, rocking back and forth, squeezing tightly. No one says anything, but whatever tension was left in the room is gone.

"Is that sushi?" Emma asks, with her chin propped on my shoulder. "Can I have some?"

"Yes," I say, pulling away and nearly tripping over myself to give her a plate and a set of chopsticks.

"Thanks," she says as she sits down on the couch.

Janet and Mrs. Jackson look over us, their eyes narrowed. I clear my throat. "Would you guys mind . . . Could I have the room for a second? I need to talk to my team."

Mrs. Jackson quirks an eyebrow at me. "Absolutely," she says, and Janet agrees with a short nod. They take their cartons with them, and then they're gone and it's just us.

"I . . ." I begin slowly, turning to face the other girls. "I have to tell you all something."

The group stops immediately, chopsticks halfway to mouths, a clump of rice falling from Chelsea's lips back into her lap.

"Sorry," I say, shaking my head. "Not that, at least not exactly. It's about when Sierra tried to—"

"Blackmail you?" Chelsea fills in for me, popping the rice back into her mouth.

Nodding, I take a deep breath and then exhale, steadying myself. This is important. "I was going to give up my spot because

Gibby was grooming me, or at least the FBI thought so, and I felt like . . ." I hesitate, trying to keep my cool, breathing in and out slowly and straightening my shoulders. This is a time to be strong, not fall apart. Not again. "I didn't just do it because it was the right thing to do. I did it because I felt like I owed it to Dani for coming forward. I felt guilty that it happened to you instead of me." I nod to her. "And grateful that you came forward when you did. You saved me."

"Rey, that's not . . ." Dani trails off, shaking her head.

"I know, but it's what I felt. And now, knowing that it was happening to my best friend too"—I look to Emma, whose eyes are a little glassy, but she lets me continue—"I just think you guys deserve to know the real reason I did what I did. You deserve the truth."

They don't respond, but there's no anger or judgment or even dismissal in the silence; they're just listening because somehow, after everything we've been through these last weeks, I'm their leader, and my team is waiting for me to make a call.

So I do.

"I . . . I still think we're the best team in the world, no matter what those standings said today."

"You're . . . not wrong," Dani says slowly.

"Obviously," Chelsea adds.

Emma nods.

"Okay," I say, "then we have a week left to show everyone that we're still the best team in the world. There are five more individual competitions before the Games are over, and we're in all of them, two of us in most of them. We can still kick ass, all four of us. Together, just, you know, separately."

Chelsea laughs a little and then smiles a wicked grin. "I like the sound of that."

"So do I," Dani says.

Emma's eyes twinkle at me when she says, "Me too."

"Okay." I nod. "Then it starts tomorrow." I hesitate, looking at Emma, even when I didn't mean to.

"It starts tomorrow in the all-around final," she finishes for me, even if she has to look away as she says it. It can't be easy for her, after everything, that she won't be competing tomorrow. "You and Dani are going to kick ass."

———

There are six of us in the top flight for the all-around competition. Six gymnasts with a realistic shot at winning this thing. We were all within a point of one another in qualifications, and that means there's a chance for each of us to finish the day at the top of the podium, and a chance is all we need.

The arena is the same. The same freezing temperatures, the same buzzing crowd, the same announcer saying everything in English and Japanese. I feel like something should have changed after we left yesterday. That the cosmos should have made something different about the place where we entered as the far-and-away favorites to win gold and exited without a medal.

Dani and I line up with the other girls, and since I'm taller than the three ahead of me in line, I can see beyond the tunnel entrance and out onto the floor, where one of my dreams died yesterday.

Today, though, today a dream I buried more than a year ago has a chance to live again. It was never supposed to be me, even when we were little. Now I have a chance to take home a medal, to *officially* be one of the best gymnasts in the world. I don't even know how I feel about that. There hasn't been enough time to totally process it.

I bounce on my toes, trying to get warm, when Janet and Chelsea show up to take our bags into the arena. Technically, Janet's there for me, and Chelsea's stepped in as Dani's "coach," but since we're in the same group it'll be a team effort.

"Look who's here," Chelsea says, slinging Dani's backpack over her shoulder and nodding up to the edge of the stands that overlook the tunnel. Leo leans on the railing, an American flag painted on one cheek and a teal awareness ribbon painted on the other.

"Nice face."

"Yours too," he says, his smile crinkling the paint job.

"I know," I say, trying to be flippant and failing.

"Own it," he says, crouching down to get near my eye level, reaching through the metal bars between us. I knock my fist against his, then, pushing up onto my toes, urge him closer with my eyes. He leans in and lets me kiss him quickly, but he's Leo, so he doesn't pull away and instead shifts forward and lets it go on for much longer than it should, probably long enough for the cameras to catch us. It's ridiculous. We should not be doing this. We were pushing it the other night at the Olympic Village, but this is way more official, out in public with TV cameras everywhere. And yet I don't care.

A laugh breaks in from behind me, back where the other girls are lined up. I pull away, letting Leo stumble back a bit. He leaves me with a quick eyebrow bounce and a cocky wink.

When I turn around, Irina Kareva and her teammate Erika Sheludenko are smiling in my direction.

"He is cute," Irina says.

"They're gross," Dani says, nudging me with her elbow and then waving me forward. "You've got paint on your cheek."

I scoff in mock offense, letting Dani wipe the paint away with her thumb, barely believing *this* is the conversation we're having right before the Olympic all-around. "Please, we're adorable."

Ana-Maria Popescu chimes in from behind me. "It is sweet. I never have a boyfriend."

Then Sun Luli, who doesn't understand a word of English, smiles brightly from the end of the line and makes a teasing kissing noise that makes us all burst into giggles.

The tension is broken, and as the IOF official walks out of the tunnel to start the competition, we all settle back into line and focus.

We begin to move, following the volunteer with the GROUP 1 sign.

That's us.

Six of the best gymnasts in the world.

Four rotations.

Three medals.

"Let's do this."

We march out to vault, and the déjà vu is nearly overwhelming. I look down at my long-sleeved leo. It's not black like yesterday. It's blue and metallic with sparkles up and down both sleeves. It's a new day and a new chance.

My eyes flicker over the stands as we move up onto the podium to be announced to the crowd. Emma is across the arena behind the bars, an American flag wrapped around her shoulders as she bops her head up and down to the pulsating beats of the music pumping through the sound system. Mrs. Jackson stands beside her, a perfectly practiced and indulgent smile on her face. Leo and Ben are at either end of the row, clearly fending off the curious onlookers with their arms crossed over their chests and their mouths set in stern lines. I have no idea where my parents are sitting, but just knowing they're in the arena is enough.

The announcer runs through our names and, like yesterday, Dani gets a huge response from the crowd, as does Irina, but then so do I. Maybe something about finishing fourth has made our team underdogs somehow? Like losing, plus everything we've been through, somehow made us more likable. Or maybe they're super excited that Japan edged us for the bronze. No matter what it is, I'll take whatever support I can get.

As the judges sit, we sprint down the vault runway to get in our warm-ups. The air-conditioning in the arena is unrelenting, and we have to keep moving to stay warm enough to compete. I do a full twist in my final warm-up and then jump down from the podium to wait my turn. I'm up third this rotation, and Dani's fifth, but unless disaster strikes, I'm going to be dead last as we head to bars. Every single girl in the rotation with me has an Amanar—at least—and here I am with my bullshit baby vault. But I'm here, and that means I have a shot.

Erika Sheludenko is first up, and when she takes off down the run, Irina yells out, *"Davai! Davai!"*

Her form isn't the greatest, but it's still an Amanar, and when she lands, Irina yells, *"Stoi!"* telling her to stick her landing, which she does. Impressive. It's so impressive that I can't help myself and hold up a fist for her to bump when she walks by me. She tilts her head in confusion for a second, but then shrugs and knocks her hand against mine. Dani follows suit, and Erika smiles, this time fist-bumping with a little more enthusiasm.

And you know what, why the hell not? These girls supported us with their teal makeup and armbands and hair ties. We have far more in common than not. If they can put aside the competition to stand for something that we all believe in, maybe we can support one another here and now, doing the thing we all love the most.

Next up is Sun Luli. She's tiny, and her Amanar is clean and stuck too! It's not quite as high or far as most, as her smaller stature gives her a disadvantage in generating enough power to *really* fly. Still, the score that pops up—a 14.7—is a good one, especially since vault isn't her specialty. I can't help it again. I'm right by the stairs, so I offer up my fist again, and she bumps it with a grin. When I turn to head to the end of the vault run, Erika and Irina are congratulating her too.

I'm next, with Ana-Maria Popescu right behind me.

I get the green light from the judges and raise one arm to salute them, and then I'm headed down the run for the last vault I'll ever do—for real this time.

A roundoff, back handspring onto the vault, and I'm up. One and a half twists later, I open up, land, and don't move an inch.

Smiling, I raise my arms in the air and then to the judges before clapping my hands and jumping down from the podium. Chelsea's there to hug me first, with Janet nodding in approval.

Then Erika and Sun Luli are walking to me with their fists raised and smiles on their faces. I give them each a fist bump before I pull at my wrist guards to get ready for bars.

My score comes up, a 14.3. "Yes!" I pump my fist a bit, but then reel it in as I focus on wrapping my wrists.

It's funny, during the team final, when Emma pulled in a 14.3, that was considered a rough vault and the start of the collapse that lost us a medal. Now here I am celebrating the exact same score, a score that might put me on the path toward the medal she was supposed to win. Sports are super weird.

Ana-Maria vaults next, an Amanar, maybe the sloppiest of them so far, but when she lands, her feet don't move at all. Another stick! That's four in a row. The crowd is rumbling in excitement, but you can tell they don't know quite what to make of it. Sticks are rare things in gymnastics nowadays with how insanely difficult the sport has become. Still, so far, it's pretty cool.

"Come on, Dani! You got this!" I yell from my seat where I'm wrapping my wrists, but make sure to extend my hand when Ana-Maria moves toward her own bag on the chairs. She nods to me firmly before we knock knuckles.

Dani's vault is high and clean and powerful. That's the best one yet, and she sticks it too! Holy crap. The crowd erupts, and so do I, standing and applauding with a roll of tape still hanging from my wrist. I jog to the stairs, where she's being congratulated by the other girls, and pull her into a hug.

"That was awesome!"

She smiles, her eyes wide with joy. "That was the best I've ever done."

The judges seem to agree, since it's the best score she's ever gotten too. I grab her by the shoulders and turn her to face the scoreboard, where a 15.4 is lit up beside her name.

"Whoa."

I nod. "Yes. Whoa."

It's Irina Kareva left and her triple-twisting Yurchenko. The Kareva. The vault that everyone thought would propel her to the gold medal ahead of Emma and Dani and the rest of the world.

Except when she sprints down the runway and launches into her vault, she does two and a half twists, sticking it cold, which sends the crowd into apoplexy. Six out of six sticks in one rotation.

But the only rotation I'm interested in is the half twist Kareva didn't do.

Maybe she wasn't feeling good about it in training. Maybe she thinks without Emma around, she's got the gold on lock. Whatever it is, she downgraded her major advantage in this competition, and when I smile and offer her my fist to bump, it might be a little too genuine.

Her score comes up quickly. There wasn't much to deduct, and the crowd buzzes again. A 15.4 for Irina, exactly like Dani scored. They're tied as we all line up to march to bars.

1.	Daniela Olivero (USA)	15.4
1.	Irina Kareva (RUS)	15.4
3.	Ana-Maria Popescu (ROM)	14.8
4.	Sun Luli (CHN)	14.7
5.	Erika Sheludenko (RUS)	14.6
6.	Audrey Lee (USA)	14.3

As we walk, I keep my eyes focused on the bright green floor, trying to drown out everything around me, especially the cameramen who are following us with steady cams, projecting our images out to the world. The crowd is still buzzing from our sticks, but I can't let any of it get into my head. *Just focus on hitting bars like in training, Audrey, and that's all.*

Irina vaulted last, so she's up first on bars. I fiddle with my grips as the Russian superstar salutes and approaches the bars. Russian bars are an art form more than a sport, but their routines sometimes have weird built-in errors. Like a half turn that doesn't make it even close to a handstand and incurs a really big deduction before releasing into a huge double-twisting double-back dismount. She sticks it, giving the crowd a jolt. That's our seventh stick in a row, and they're so into it now.

Kareva was going to try to launch herself into first place with her bars score, but now there's an opening, the second one she's given us in as many rotations. Her score is a 14.7, and that feels about right considering the error.

As she passes me, I offer her a grip-encased, chalky fist to bump, and she hesitates for a second—probably knowing she'd cracked open the door even further—before she lightly taps knuckles with me and moves on.

Her teammate is next, and where Irina opened a door, Erika is trying to pull it shut. She's a great bars worker, and it shows with every perfect handstand and her floaty, almost ethereal, releases. She lands her double layout lightly, like she hopped off a step and the crowd roars with approval. Another stuck landing, and her score is going to be higher than her teammate's.

And it is: a 15.0. That's going to keep her in the race for a medal.

Sun Luli is next, and she blinks first. A great routine full of epic pirouetting and a fantastic release combination that made the entire crowd gasp ends with a short double layout, her knee and shin scraping across the landing mat as her hands go down to catch her. She's in tears before she leaps off the podium and into her coach's arms. It's not my job to console her, but I want to. The judges hammer her. She'd scored a 15.3 during the team final on her routine, and when a 14.2 appears next to her name, it's over for her.

Making up a whole point in two rotations will be next to impossible. That's probably something I should have realized yesterday after Emma fell on bars. Maybe she shouldn't have gone up on beam. Maybe that's where it all went wrong.

But I can't think about that anymore because I'm next. Janet hops up onto the podium to chalk the bars for me while I make sure my grips are tight enough and that I have the exact amount of chalk I'll need to keep my swing light.

"You got this, Rey!" Chelsea screams from just a few feet away, and I let that register with a smile and then block everything else out.

The lead judge nods to me and switches on the green light. I step between the bars, salute, and begin. The scrape of the bars against my grips is perfect as I swing and shift my hands around, launching myself up and over to the high bar, twisting into my pirouettes, one hand and then another before releasing and catching in perfect rhythm. Another handstand out of my last pirouette and I swing down and release into one, two, three twists and stick.

"Yes!" I shout and pump my fist. I'm going to inch up on the leaders and leap over the girls who vaulted ahead of me in that first rotation. I clap my hands together, sending out a cloud of chalk dust before I salute the judges and leave the podium.

Sun Luli immediately approaches, her eyes red-rimmed, but a fist held out to congratulate me.

Instead, I open my arms for a hug, which she steps into gratefully. She's not even sixteen yet; her birthday isn't until December. That's pretty young for your dreams to get crushed.

I'd know. Except that's not quite true anymore, is it? Because here I am, after the injury and Gibby and losing my coach, here I am anyway with girls who've had my back and a boy who makes everything feel perfect and a coach who would never lie to me. I want to tell her all of that, but it's impossible. Even if we spoke the same language, there's not enough time to really make her understand. I hope she does one day.

She releases me as my score pops up—a 15.1—and I nod at it with a smile. That's exactly what I needed to stay in this thing.

A shriek pierces from the stands where Emma and Mrs. Jackson sit, and I smile up in their direction and wave, not really seeing them.

Ana-Maria Popescu is next, and it's tough to watch. Romania isn't exactly known for its bars work, and it's easily her weakest routine. She powers through though, muscling up her skills and desperately trying to keep her swing going through her short and relatively easy routine. She just has to land her dismount, a full-twisting double layout, and her score will be decent enough for her to make a run at a medal. She does, and it's stuck too, which makes the crowd go wild again despite the routine itself.

There's just Dani to go now, and I let out a deep breath before finally taking off my grips. "Come on, Dani! You got this."

Dani wasn't a great bars worker when we were younger, but she's better than decent on them now. Her swing is maybe stronger than what people would call natural for the event, but she always hits her handstands, her releases are high and caught easily, and she sticks her landings.

The crowd chants her name again, "Da-ni! Da-ni!" as she comes off the podium. I'm right there to give her a hug, and the rest of the girls in the rotation offer her their fists as we wait for her score.

Wow. A 14.7 for Dani, and that propels her into a tie for first.

1.	Daniela Olivero (USA)	30.1
1.	Irina Kareva (RUS)	30.1
3.	Erika Sheludenko (RUS)	29.6
4.	Audrey Lee (USA)	29.4
5.	Sun Luli (CHN)	28.9
6.	Ana-Maria Popescu (ROM)	28.4

This is going to be close.

chapter twenty-one

I have to hit my connections. That's what's going to keep me in this. If I hit my connections, even with my floor being super weak compared to everyone else, I'll have a shot. I close my eyes, visualizing my routine like I did what feels like a million times back in Coronado. There are four routines between now and my turn, so that's plenty of time to see it in my head over and over again.

Dani's up first and my eyes open to take in her routine. Before my injuries, I would float through competitions in a laser-focused trance, but after, I'd need everything around me to distract from the pain. Now? Well, I guess something good came from all of that, because I can watch Dani work through her beam set like a pro, not a wobble or a hesitation, one skill after another with perfect ease. She sets herself for her dismount and then launches into an Arabian double front, putting an exclamation point on it by sticking the landing.

"Da-ni! Da-ni!" the crowd starts up again, banging their thundersticks together, waiting for her score. She's their girl, and she's giving them everything they want. I'm not out of it, but not gonna lie, I kind of want her to win too.

I push that thought out of my head as her score is posted. A 14.6. I hold up a fist as she walks past me and she doesn't break stride as she hits it with her own. She knows I need to run through my routine as much as possible. I go through it in my head again, letting my body imitate the motions of each skill, joining them together seamlessly while my feet are still on the ground.

The crowd murmurs in agitation, breaking through my visualization. Something happened on the beam. I let my eyes flicker up to it, and it's Kareva setting herself for her dismount, but she looks rattled. There hadn't been a *thwack* of the mat, so she didn't fall, but still . . .

"Huge bobble, and she almost put her hands down on the beam," Janet says from beside me, quietly enough that no one will hear, except maybe the cameraman who's no more than half a foot away at all times.

I nod and picture my dismount, tucking my arms into my chest, rotating as fast as I can before landing.

That's it. That's the routine I want.

I look up in time to see a 14.3 listed next to Kareva's name.

Wow. That's . . . that's low, like my vault score low.

Kareva comes down from the podium and throws herself into a chair, ignoring her coaches as her teammate goes up to the beam.

Sheludenko's strength is not beam. She almost never falls, but it's rare she gets through a routine without almost falling, and that trend keeps up as she goes into her flight series and barely manages to stay on the beam when she lands her second layout step-out with her shoulders way out of alignment. Waving her arms furiously, she eventually manages to regain her balance, but that's going to cost her majorly. She dismounts and salutes, but the twist of her mouth and the drop of her shoulders tell everyone in the arena that she didn't do what she needed to.

I know it too. I just have to hit my connections. Hit my routine, and I can secure a bronze. A bronze medal in the all-around. Nope, wait, way too early. Can't think about that right now.

Beam first, Audrey. Hit your connections.

The crowd erupts in applause, and it's for Sun Luli, who must have hit her routine. Good for her after that fall on bars. I hope she finishes strong, but, you know, maybe not too strong.

I'm next, and I fist-bump her as we pass on the stairs to the podium, and damn, they gave her a 15.0 for that routine. That's very strong.

But I can be just as strong.

Chelsea is setting up my springboard, and she moves to me, staring me dead in the eye. "Do the thing, Cap."

"Damn straight."

Then she's gone, down off the podium just as the judges give me the green light.

Saluting with a small smile on my face, I begin.

Up to the beam and directly into two layout step-outs. Good. Now my turn sequence. The triple turns into a double as my shoulders shift out of alignment, but my arms don't waver, and I can go straight into an L-turn and then down and up through the full illusion and set. Good.

I lift my chin again heading into the last half of my routine, leaps connected, aerial cartwheel, and a gainer down to straddle the beam. The turn on my back makes the crowd cheer, a soft buzzing in the back of my mind.

And then finally the dismount, I count off, hands, feet, hands, feet, and tightly into a triple twist with a tiny hop to the side, and it's done. I hit it. I salute the judges and smile widely.

I owned it, and when I'm down on the floor again and look up at the scoreboard, that 15.0, matching Sun Luli's score, proves it.

One girl left. Ana-Maria Popescu. And, like me, if she wants a shot at bronze, she needs to hit this beam routine. She's capable of it too. Romanian gymnasts are pretty much born being able to do a beam routine, and Ana-Maria is fabulous. A roundoff to layout full that she lands without a flicker. A standing Arabian that looks like she's got springs on her feet and the beam is ten feet wide. It should be a fun balance beam final in a couple of days if she can bring it like this. She dismounts like I did, with two back handsprings into a triple twist, but she sticks it cold.

It's a great routine, and the judges reward her with a 15.3. That's one hell of a score, and it gets her back into the meet as we go to floor, one of her strengths and distinctly not one of mine.

The scoreboard updates, and there I am, tied with Irina Kareva, with Dani only three-tenths of a point ahead of us. So it comes down to one floor routine. A minute and thirty seconds for each of us to put everything we have out there and see where we land.

1.	Daniela Olivero (USA)	44.7
2.	Irina Kareva (RUS)	44.4
2.	Audrey Lee (USA)	44.4
4.	Erika Sheludenko (RUS)	43.9
4.	Sun Luli (CHN)	43.9
6.	Ana-Maria Popescu (ROM)	43.7

I'm last. Last up on floor. Not last place, thank God, but last in line as we queue up for the march to the final rotation. Dani reaches back, and I grab her hand, squeezing. We're in this together, no matter what.

I'm *actually* ranked second. Second and we're headed to floor. If I can hold my ground, though, not make any major mistakes, maybe a medal is within reach here. The medal that I forfeited to Dani and Emma and even, briefly, Sierra, earlier this year. The medal I thought was impossible.

Dani and I are in the same corner of the floor for warm-ups. She turns to me and holds out a fist. "We've got this. You and me. One more time."

I knock my fist against hers. "One more time."

My floor routine can be beautiful, but it's not difficult, not nearly as difficult as those of every other girl who will go up before me. That's out of my control, though. The only thing in my control is what I do out there.

Ana-Maria Popescu is up, and she's got the crowd clapping along to her music, a bouncy classical piece I don't recognize. It almost sounds like it's from a carnival or circus, and she plays up to the crowd with her dance and her fabulous tumbling. She bounces out of two of her passes, though, costing precious tenths, and she needs every tenth she can get.

I applaud with everyone else, but my focus immediately shifts to Dani, who is at her starting corner, waiting for Ana-Maria's score to be posted so she can begin. She looks cool and calm, but her heart has to be going a hundred miles an hour. She could clinch an all-around gold medal with this routine if she does what she's capable of here.

After everything she's been through, it all comes down to this routine for her, and there is something perfect about that. She suffered Gibby's abuse alone. Standing up on that podium, waiting to begin, she's still on her own. That's the nature of our sport. For all that we make of the team concept and support from our coaches, when it all comes down to it, we have to compete alone. Dani's strong, though. I believe she can do this. I know she can.

The *Greatest Showman* medley pours out from the arena's sound system, and the crowd is immediately into it. They know what's on the line here, and if they can, they're going to cheer her straight to the top of the gold-medal podium. But maybe the moment is too big, because Dani takes a huge hop back and nearly out of bounds on her first pass. Her next pass is better with a small shuffle of her feet on landing, and now she's halfway through and playing to the crowd with her bright smile and broad gestures. She's settled into the routine because now she's dancing through her required leaps and spins like she's in total control, not a toe or finger out of place, not a stumble or a hesitation as she moves across the floor. It's gorgeous.

"Come on, Dani! Finish it!" I shout, trying to get my voice to carry over the crowd, but I'm probably drowned out by the fierce cheering as she lands her final two passes, sticking the last one cold and raising her arms in triumph. She did it. She's done, and if that doesn't win gold, all of Tokyo might riot.

I run up to where she's waiting for her score with Janet and Chelsea, hugging her from behind. She jumps in surprise, but then she turns and embraces me fully. Her body is shaking in my arms, and I can practically feel her relief seeping into my skin from hers.

I can't really celebrate with her yet, though. I still have to compete.

A 14.3 is posted, not quite her best, but it definitely should be enough. She came into the rotation with a decent lead over both me and Kareva.

Irina moves onto the floor, and the fierce look in her eyes as she waits for her music to begin is enough to make me believe that she's going to force the judges into giving her a chance at gold. I'm sure it's going to be a great routine, but I don't want to watch.

I need to focus on what I have to do, just one more time. One more chance to stun the crowd into an awed silence or make them shed a tear or two. I close my eyes and concentrate on my breathing. In and out, over and over again, the world around me fades entirely and I'm suspended, weightless in a sea of black, the meditative state I'd managed to perfect during those wild weeks in Coronado.

Kareva's music ending and the crowd exploding in applause is the only thing that breaks my almost trancelike state, jolting me back to a world full of color and noise.

I move to an empty bit of floor away from the competition and close my eyes. The sound of Erika Sheludenko's haunting ballet music tries to force its way in, but I push it back and replace it with my own. I keep warm, swinging my arms back and forth, lunging out with one leg and then the other. I'm going to need every ounce of energy left in me for this floor routine.

Next is Sun Luli's "Ride of the Valkyries," where through sheer force of will she manages to transform herself from a sweet teenager into a fierce warrior, but still, I push it aside. More deep breathing, and I start to walk around, keeping my routine in my head, my tumbling, the dance sequences, the leaps and turns all blending seamlessly into one expression of artistry for the judges.

The music comes to a crashing halt, and I open my eyes. She salutes and waves to the cheering crowd.

One floor routine. My last floor routine.

I march up to the podium before her score is even posted. I don't want to see it, and I won't be able to from where I am, beside the carpeted springs that will help me determine my fate.

The crowd applauds whatever number the judges give her, but I look straight ahead until the red light switches to green.

My arms open wide as I move out onto the floor and settle into my starting pose. A soft tone warns me that my music is about to start before the twangs of a cello plucking out a rhythm lead me into another universe, one where I don't have to talk. I can let the music play and use my body to tell everyone exactly what I'm feeling. To dance like I did yesterday with Leo, letting the world melt away and creating our own little universe where we're the only ones that matter.

My two and a half to full is perfect, and I push up into arabesque to show the judges exactly how much control I have before moving on to another corner with an Arabian double front, leaping up out of my landing and dancing across the floor. Maybe there's a twinge in my back as I hit my third pass, but who cares? This is the last time I'll do this, and somehow that makes the routine even better, the subtle reminder that one day soon the cortisone will wear off entirely and all of this will be nothing more than a memory, but damn if it won't be a beautiful one.

The music has almost run out, and the crescendo is building as I stare across the floor for my last pass, a simple double back. One breath and then two, and I run into a roundoff, back handspring, launching myself into the air, flipping backward twice, bent at the hips, but my legs tucked, and I land with the smallest shuffle of my feet, almost identical to how I finished my routine yesterday. Funny how fate works sometimes.

The music fades, and I end with a flourish, reaching up into my ending pose. My chest is heaving with the exertion, but I barely feel it. That was the best I've ever done. The best I'll ever do. And it was perfect, not because I didn't make any mistakes—I'm sure I did—but because of what it took to get here, all the pain and suffering, all the angst and worry, every ounce of blood, sweat, and tears for the last fourteen years, and it all came down to this, and *that* is what makes it perfect.

I salute the judges, but also the crowd that carried me through it, and taste the tears sliding over my cheeks onto my lips. Dani's right there, and I launch myself at her.

"That was beautiful," she whispers into my shoulder. She's crying too. There's so much crying. No one ever told me it would be like this, that it would be this perfect. More perfect than I could ever imagine.

Now we wait, beneath that scoreboard again, clutching each other's hands, as I try to catch my breath. The standings will reset themselves into medal order a moment after my score comes up. We'll know immediately. I hold my breath. This is it.

chapter twenty-two

1. Daniela Olivero (USA)	59.0
2. Audrey Lee (USA)	58.9
3. Irina Kareva (RUS)	58.3
4. Ana-Maria Popescu (ROM)	58.2
5. Sun Luli (CHN)	58.1
6. Erika Sheludenko (RUS)	57.9

One-tenth.

The difference is one-tenth of a point, like in team finals, but winning a silver medal feels a whole lot better than losing a bronze. It's also the highest all-around score I've ever gotten, even before my injury. It's the best I've ever done in the most important competition of my life.

Can't ask for more than that, can you, Audrey? To do your absolute best on the day you needed it the most?

I never thought I'd make it that close, and maybe someday I'll wish away a deduction here or there, but right now I can't find it in me.

I won silver. I *won* it. I'm an Olympic medalist, and no one will ever be able to take it away from me.

Chelsea is closest to me, and I let her pull me into a hug.

"Great job, Cap," she says, squeezing me tight.

A few feet away, Kareva collapses to the ground while her teammates console her, and Dani is sobbing into Janet's shoulder. As much as this means to me, and it means a lot, I can't even imagine what's going through her mind right now. I can't muster up even an ounce of resentment. Dani won, and that in and of itself is an inherent good thing, like the universe is righting itself after all the shit it's thrown at her.

"I did it," she manages to cry out between gasps of breath. "We did it." She turns to me, and I pull her into a tight hug.

"You were incredible. You were *golden*."

"Oh God, that's so cheesy," she yells, swatting at my shoulder, but I smile. "I'm so proud of you. You were amazing, you pushed me so hard today. And that last routine? Rey, that was beautiful."

The arena is shaking around us, everyone on their feet screaming and clapping, singing along as Queen's "We Are the Champions" reverberates through the speakers. Dani stands up on the podium and waves wildly to the crowd, and they somehow get even louder, roaring back their approval. Then she waves me up, and a photographer tosses us an American flag. We wrap it around our shoulders, holding out the edges so everyone can see. We're the two best all-around gymnasts in the world, and soon we'll have the medals to prove it.

We can't celebrate for long. Competition officials quickly usher us out of the arena, and we're escorted back to the tunnel by a volunteer. Irina leads the line, still in tears, Dani behind her, sandwiched between us, where she'll be on the medal podium. We wave to the crowd as we exit the competition floor.

Mrs. Jackson meets us down there, quickly handing us the USA's official medal ceremony outfit. "I didn't want to give these to you girls beforehand. I didn't want to jinx anything," she says, holding out a deep navy-blue jacket with USA stamped across the back in white and matching blue bottoms and white sneakers to complete the look.

Apparently, Mrs. Jackson isn't actually a robot and believes in things like superstition and jinxes. Who knew?

We quickly pull on the outfits, and then she stands back and smiles at us. "Ladies, you look fantastic, and I . . ." She hesitates, looking away for a moment, taking a deep breath—wow, not just superstitious, but emotional too? "I am so proud of both of you for everything you've gone through to end up here. Remarkable."

She reaches out and hugs Dani, and I press my lips together, trying to hold back my own emotions. My makeup is probably already a wreck, and I don't need to make it worse. Mrs. Jackson pulls away from Dani and hugs me next before stepping back and nodding at us.

"Now, I also thought you might need this," she says, reaching down to the floor and holding out a small makeup kit.

I smile widely. "This is why you're my favorite, Mrs. J. My absolute favorite."

We sit cross-legged on the floor of the tunnel, and I do Dani's makeup first. "Can you believe this?" she whispers as I take her by the chin and flick two perfect wings of eyeliner atop her eyelids.

"Of course I can." It's the truth, almost. "Well, I believe you won, but me? I'm not sure I'll ever believe what just happened."

Dani laughs a little, but then grows serious. "Do you think he saw?" she asks, but I don't answer because she's still talking. "I hope he saw. I hope he saw me winning without his sick, twisted ass on the floor. I hope he knows I did this despite him."

"He knows." I look her dead in the eye. "And he's going to rot in a cell for the rest of his life, and you're an Olympic gold medalist."

Dani sniffs and squeezes my hand back. "I'm so happy we did this together. I'm so glad you were the one out there with me."

Warmth pulses through my heart. It's something I've never felt before with anyone except Emma. Real friendship, sisterhood, the kind of bond that will never break.

We both nod and then sit in comfortable silence as I finish up her makeup. There's nothing left to be said about it. It almost feels like closure, the kind so many survivors rarely get, a complete and total triumph over their abuser. She won. He lost. The end.

I'm halfway through cleaning up my own makeup when I see Irina waiting with her coaches. I catch her eye and point at my liquid liner and then lift a shoulder in suggestion. It takes her a moment before she nods, and I can understand her hesitation. But then she says something to her coach, who looks stunned, and makes her way over to me. I hand her a cleanser wipe and finish my own face before turning to her.

"Like you," she says and closes her eyes.

"No problem."

And fifteen minutes later, we're lining up and marching back out onto the floor with our faces free of tear tracks and that cat eye I'm quickly making our team signature perfectly applied. The three best gymnasts in the world, one Russian and two Americans, separated by less than a point on the scoreboard, but with far more in common than what divides us.

The walk to the floor is short, and the announcer introduces the members of the IOF that will be presenting us our medals. As soon as he announces their names, I forget them, because the announcer is calling our names now, and it's surreal.

"The winner of the bronze medal, representing the Russian Federation, Irina Kareva!"

"The winner of the silver medal, representing the United States of America, Audrey Lee!"

"The winner of the gold medal and Olympic Champion, representing the United States of America, Daniela Olivero!"

It's all such a blur of kisses to both cheeks and well wishes, the sweet scent of Japanese apple blossoms from the flowers they hand us before the satisfying weight of the silver medal is around my neck. I pick it up, the round silver disc that declares me an Olympic medalist. It's the most beautiful thing I've ever seen.

"Ladies and gentlemen, please stand for the national anthem of the United States of America!"

I turn to the end of the arena, where our flags are being secured, and put my hand over my heart. I've never been an especially patriotic person, but my entire body starts to tingle and break out in gooseflesh when the orchestral version of "The Star-Spangled Banner" starts to play. I'm fighting tears—and the destruction of the work of art that is my eye makeup—when Dani's free hand rests on my shoulder from the gold medal platform, squeezing lightly.

We're here together. We won together, and that's forever.

———

The pace of the Games is unrelenting. Less than twelve hours after the all-around, we're back in the warm-up gym at the arena. It's the first day of event finals—vault and uneven bars. Dani is running through some conditioning since she doesn't compete today at all. She'll head up to the stands to watch us compete just like Emma did yesterday.

Tomorrow is the last day of the women's competition: beam and floor.

For me, it's bars today, beam tomorrow, and that's it. My Olympics will be over, and I'll have to . . . do something else with my life, I guess. I'm still not really sure if I'm ready to deal with that. In fact, I know I'm not.

I push it to the side as I start to stretch out. The bars final isn't until after vault, but the other seven finalists are here too. If you look at our qualifications scores, we're all within a few tenths of one another. We're in for a great competition, and it's going to be a close one.

My phone blings to life on the mat beside me, and I grimace, ignoring it.

"Don't look at it," Emma says, settling beside me, stretching her legs out in front of her, pointing and flexing her toes over and over again.

"I'm not," I assure her, and it's the truth. At least, I stopped looking after the first few notifications. Apparently, there are some people out there who think that Dani's gold and my silver aren't legit because Emma didn't get to compete against us. Yeah, the two-per-country rule sucks immensely, but the trolls have made it about anything and everything other than gymnastics, from a conspiracy of political correctness focusing on Emma's skin color versus mine and Dani's, to the Russians bribing the judges into eliminating Emma, giving Kareva a clear path to gold, only to have it backfire in competition. "Have you?"

"Yeah, it's bullshit, all of it," she says, "and I told them so."

"What?"

We haven't exactly talked about it, the fact that I got to compete for the medal she was expected to win.

"I posted that I didn't belong in the all-around final and that everyone should stop giving you shit. I choked when it mattered, twice, and that's that."

"You didn't choke, Em; you were dealing with a major trauma."

"I'm going to talk to the FBI," she says, basically ignoring what I just said. "After I talked to Dani, I thought about it, and I'm ready to tell them what happened to me. Mrs. Jackson is going to set up an interview after we get home."

"If you feel like you're ready."

"I am," she says simply.

This is the Emma I remember, cool and calculating, never letting anything rattle her. The mental strength it must have taken to get her mind to this point is totally beyond me.

"Em?"

"Yeah?" she asks, looking up from bending over her knees, her hands pulling at the arches of her feet.

I want to say something profound, something that lets her know just how glad I am she's my best friend, and that we've come through this together, but that might make us cry, and we don't have time for that right now. We have to compete soon and kick the rest of the world's ass on uneven bars.

"I'm really psyched that you'll be out there with me when I win bars."

She snorts and lets it turn into a chuckle, but doesn't say anything, just shakes her head and keeps stretching.

This is good—better than good, it's normal.

Emma stands up, shaking out her limbs, and jogs away. I'll join her in a minute. It takes me a little longer to stretch out.

"Nice, Chels," Janet calls from over by the vault, where Chelsea and the girls who will compete in a few minutes are warming up.

Mrs. Jackson has totally embraced athletic chic while at the Games: a new tracksuit each day and matching sneakers.

"Audrey," she says, "good luck out there today. I know you'll make us proud."

"Thanks, Mrs. J."

"I've been meaning to ask, have you thought about what comes next? Janet informed me of your unfortunate situation regarding your injuries, and since you can't compete in the NCAA . . ." She trails off.

"There's been some sponsorship interest, but honestly, I haven't had time to talk about the details with my parents."

"Sweetheart, you've been trending worldwide since qualifications. Sponsorships are wonderful, but not what I'm talking about."

I tilt my head in confusion. "Then what?"

"I've watched you these last weeks. You're a natural leader, quick on your feet, hardworking—"

"Mrs. J—" I try to cut her off.

"Modest," she jokes, with a knowing grin. "You're the first Korean American to win an all-around medal in the history of these Games."

"Really? I didn't know that."

"I know you didn't, but it's a big deal. You're a big deal, Audrey Lee. Don't forget that. No matter what happens in the next few days, you've made history here. Your life will be a whirlwind for the next few months, but when things calm a little, if working with the USOF is something you'd be interested in, please reach out."

"But Emma or Dani—"

"Both have plans to compete in the next quad," she finishes for me.

I'm out of excuses.

"I'll think about it."

She lifts one perfectly shaped and filled-in eyebrow. "Excellent."

———

We can't watch Chelsea compete on vault because as soon as they're finished we have to march straight out for bars. I can listen to the crowd, though, and hear the announcer call the competitors' names.

Chelsea qualified first, so she'll go last.

The minutes tick by as I run through my bars routine in quarters and then halves, rotating with Emma. The crowd has been groaning and cheering as gymnasts have fallen or hit, and then finally . . .

"Now vaulting, for the United States of America, Chelsea Cameron!"

The arena falls to a silent hush before giving way to feet pounding down the runway. I close my eyes, picturing her hitting the springboard and then the vault, wrapping herself in tightly for the two and a half twists, and—bam—sticking it!

The crowd explodes, and the noise ricochets into the concrete tunnel where we wait.

One down. One to go.

Whatever her score is, it must be good, because the thunder-sticks are pounding, matched only by the roar from the crowd, before the announcer calls out again. "And now the second vault from Chelsea Cameron."

Her Rudi is almost as good as her Amanar, and I close my eyes again, waiting for the sound of a vault and then the crowd's reaction.

She's running, and I can see it in my head, left, right, left, right down to the vault, full speed off the board, hands first to the vault with a *thwap*, and then it squeaks in protest, taking her weight and sending her flying into the air, one and a half twists, the motion try-ing to force her body out of the straight line, but her training allows her to hold before she lands with a *thwack*.

A wave of thundersticks bouncing together and cheers follow.

That's gotta be a hit.

But what does it mean?

It's an agonizing few minutes of uncertainty.

"And the final standings in the vault final," the announcer says. "In third, Lou Ting from the People's Republic of China. In second, representing the Russian Federation, Erika Sheludenko . . ."

"She won," I say, and Emma nods.

". . . and in first place, from the United States of America, Chelsea Cameron. Ladies and gentlemen, please join us in celebrating our Olympic medalists."

We keep training, trying to stay warm as the frigid air pumps into the gym, just as it has all week. Quarter, half, and then full rou-tines, over and over again. Critiquing each other as we go, just like we have since we were little kids.

Emma lands her final warm-up routine and looks to me for a cor-rection, but I shake my head. "I'm really glad you're still here, Em."

She quirks a grin at me. "Yeah, me too. Now, you're up."

The sounds from medal ceremony travel back into the training gym, and I swing through my bars routine one more time with "The Star-Spangled Banner" rattling in my ears.

Maybe, not too long from now, it'll be playing for me.

"Okay, girls," Janet says, coming in from the arena, where the medal ceremony is wrapping up. "I trust you're ready to go?"

Emma looks to me, and together we nod.

As we line up to march in, Chelsea walks past us, gold medal still hanging around her neck, a bouquet of Japanese apple blossoms clutched in her hands, and tear tracks over her cheeks.

There's no time for congratulations, but she turns to us and says, "You got this, girls!"

"And now, the uneven bars finalists!" the announcer calls to the arena, and the thundersticks start up again as the lights go dim and a spotlight follows us out onto the competition floor.

We head straight for the uneven bars podium, and when my name is announced, the roar in return is way louder than I expected. I guess I've made an impression on them.

The Klaxon sounds, and we move down the stairs, leaving Michiko Nakamura, the eighth-place qualifier, up on the podium to perform her routine.

I'm up last, and I'll know exactly what I need to win this thing, but I already have an Olympic medal, and it's one I never thought was within my reach. Anything beyond that is gravy.

Oh, who the hell am I kidding?

I want this gold medal. This was the gold medal I came to the Olympics for, back when I didn't think I'd make the team, back when an all-around medal would have been a laughable, insane pipe dream. I came to Tokyo for this bars gold, and I want it. I want it more than anything I've ever wanted in gymnastics. I am the best bars worker in the world, and it's time to prove it.

Emma's beside me as we sit down in chairs lining the competition floor, Janet directly in front of us, watching the routines. I let my gaze wander over the crowd and make eye contact with Dani, who is just a couple of rows up to my right. She sends me two thumbs-ups and mouths, *You got this!*

I smile back and then, with a deep breath, try to relax as much as possible, keeping my eyes trained toward the bars but not really taking in the routines being performed.

I make an exception for Emma's. It's the first bit of competitive gymnastics she's done since she fell off beam in team finals.

"C'mon, Em," I call out as she salutes and stares at the bars. Then, with a deep breath, she goes.

I hold my breath for the entire forty-four seconds of her routine, and it's flawless, exactly the way she's been training all along. She releases into her double layout, body arched, and lands upright, feet unmoving. That's it. The last routine of her Olympics, but it was damn good.

As she comes off the podium, the tears in her eyes have already started to fall, and I wish there were time to do more than hug her quickly and fiercely, but there isn't.

It's my turn. I haven't even glanced at the scores. Who cares what everyone else did? If I do my best routine, if it hit, I'll be an Olympic gold medalist.

The judges give me the green light, and I salute and begin. A swing on the low bar to get started before I'm up into a handstand, holding and then folding myself down and around the bar with my legs extended out, toes pointed to perfection, and then I'm flying backward up to the high bar and twisting halfway to catch it cleanly. Another handstand, held to show control, before I swing down and release, turning and catching again. Then up into another hand-stand, a pirouette and down, letting go, twisting one, two, three times, and stick.

That's it.

It was perfect.

I salute and send a practiced smile at the judges before leaping down from the podium to wait for my score. My name is going to slide into the top of the standings like Dani's did yesterday and Chelsea's did less than an hour ago.

And then it doesn't.

1. Emma Sadowsky (USA)		15.4
2. Audrey Lee (USA)		15.3
3. Irina Kareva (RUS)		15.1
4. Erika Sheludenko (RUS)		15.0
5. Zhang Yan (CHN)		14.9
6. Katie Daugherty (CAN)		14.8
7. Michiko Nakamura (JPN)		14.6
8. Luo Ting (CHN)		13.1

One-tenth. Again, just one-tenth.

Somewhere in the routine, I'm not even sure where. Maybe a toe wasn't pointed or maybe my legs briefly slid apart on a transition or maybe it was that handstand before my dismount, but when my score lights up the board, there's my name in second place behind Emma's, who is hyperventilating in the corner, and I have to settle for silver.

There's so much about it that feels wrong. Yesterday, I knew without a shadow of a doubt that I'd won my silver medal and not lost a gold, but this? This feels like losing, maybe even more so than it did in the team competition.

And, damn, does it hurt.

But I can't let it hurt right now. I have to hug my best friend. I am so happy for her—really, honestly happy for her, even as the surreal truth weighs down on me that she's an Olympic gold medalist and I'm not.

I hug Emma and hold her tight while she sobs into my shoulder, crying the happiest tears of her life. "I'm really proud of you." She pulls away, smiling, and then lets Janet embrace her too.

Barely holding it together, I march back out of the arena. Chelsea is there, standing with the other vault medalists, and she immediately draws me into a hug.

"You were great," she says, but it doesn't help.

Everything about standing on the silver medal podium again feels wrong, from watching the American flag rise in the gold-medal position, knowing it's not for me, to listening to the anthem play while Emma sings softly behind me.

I have one more chance tomorrow, one more shot at fulfilling my dream of a gold medal, and of course, it's on the balance beam, where Olympic dreams go to die.

eo's visiting us in the village. We're lounging on the couch in the common area, curled up next to each other, our legs intertwined, the calloused tips of his fingers gently stroking against the point of my hip. I'm relaxed for the first time in way too long, and unconsciously, I check my phone.

Big mistake.

Huge.

#SilverGirl.

Silver Fucking Girl.

Ugh.

I swipe through into my social media accounts, and it's everywhere. There's even a viral tribute video set to Idina Menzel's cover of "Bridge over Troubled Water," the last moments of my all-around floor routine lining up exactly with the "sail on, silver girl" lyric. I don't know who originally made the connection, but there's no stopping it. This is who I am now: Audrey "Silver Girl" Lee. Famous for coming in second place.

Both Sarah and Brooke have texted me congrats, and that makes it feel even worse, since they're sitting at home, and I bet Sarah would be super happy with a silver on bars after not being able to compete in the final at all.

It doesn't help that there's a message from Sierra there too.

Congrats, Silver Girl. You definitely deserved it.

She's totally embraced my new moniker, and damn that bitch for knowing exactly how much it would hurt. I wonder if I scroll past her message, if there'll be a near identical one from Jaime, but I'm not in the mood to find out.

"It's a good thing," Leo says, trying to help as I grip my phone a little too hard before slamming it down on the couch cushion. "Look at what they're saying. They think it's awesome that you've won two silvers." Tilting my head at him in disbelief, he sighs. "I know *you* don't think it's cool, Rey."

"It is cool. I just . . ." I lean back against his shoulder and sigh. "I didn't know how much I wanted that gold until I lost it."

He doesn't correct me. He doesn't say that I won a silver and didn't lose a gold, and damn if I don't love him for it.

Whoa.

Love?

I tense in his arms, and he must feel it, so he squeezes gently at my hip, drawing me closer. I'm not complaining, but still . . . holy crap.

Love.

Whose crazy brain came up with that word? The panic must play across my face, and even though he has no idea where it came from, he still reaches out with his free hand and takes mine, pressing a soft kiss to the back of it and then to the inside of my wrist.

"You have another chance tomorrow," he says softly, "and I know you're going to be great. You're always great, Audrey, even when you're not perfect. *Especially* then."

My heart twists. Okay, maybe *love* is the right word. The right word, but still incredibly terrifying and way too fast and not something I'm ready to say out loud. Not for a while, at least, but still, the feeling is there, and that's kind of amazing.

I prop my chin on his chest, looking up into his eyes. "I can't believe all this is over tomorrow. After everything we've been through, it's all going to end."

"Not everything is going to end," he whispers.

"No, not everything. We finally get to have that serious conversation."

"I hate to break this to you, Audrey Lee, but I think maybe we've been having it this whole time," he says, smiling down at me.

I snuggle closer. "Of course we have."

The door to the suite opens, just a crack, and Chelsea's voice calls inside. "Everyone decent?"

I roll my eyes and then stand up to stick my tongue out at her. But really, they've been great since yesterday, giving me my space. They all have gold medals now, and I don't. It's not a good look to be jealous of your friends' success, but clearly, they get it. They get me.

"What's up, Chels?" I ask, pulling my hair up into a ponytail, feeling Leo stand behind me.

"There was a news conference back home," she says, walking into the room with Dani. Emma, Mrs. Jackson, and Janet come through the door behind her. She turns on the TV and swipes a video from her phone to the larger screen.

A reporter is speaking into a mic with a large courthouse behind him. ". . . I can confirm that though he maintained his innocence after his arrest and in a live interview as the Tokyo Olympic Games began, Christopher Gibson, the former head coach of USA women's gymnastics, has today pled guilty both to charges related to tampering with an athlete's drug test and to a variety of offenses related to sexual assault."

Immediately, my thoughts go to Dani and Emma, who are silently staring at the screen, and my ridiculous nickname and not having a gold medal are suddenly the least important things in the world. That monster is going to jail, and we're still here, despite everything, untarnished by it all; in fact, maybe we shine a little brighter for it.

Dani takes a deep breath and releases it. "Good," she says and looks away from the TV.

"Damn right," Emma says.

It doesn't seem like either wants to talk about it. I meet Chelsea's eyes behind their backs, and she shakes her head just once. We're on the same page, and we let it go. When they're ready to talk, they will. Or not. We're good with either.

"Okay, ladies," Mrs. Jackson says, turning off the TV. "It's time to go."

Our last day of competition. The beam final and the floor final: one last chance for each of us to medal.

One more routine, and that's it: I'm done.

Okay, Audrey, finish strong.

———

The arena is comforting in its consistent tundra-like temperatures and the slightly stale taste of recycled air. It's the sixth day in a row I've stepped into this massive structure, and part of me has a weird sense of affection for it. It's the last place I'll ever do competitive gymnastics. Today, I even love the stupid frigid air, because it means that I get to be a gymnast.

There aren't many girls left in the warm-up gym. There's a lot of overlap in these finals. Beam and floor tend to be complementary strengths in our sport. Beam's first, though, so anyone not competing in it, like Chelsea and Dani, wanders off to stretch out and keep warm while they wait. The rest of us head to the practice beams.

This final is going to be brutal. The beam workers at these Olympics are out-of-control good, and while I know I can compete with them, it all comes down to my connections once again. I don't have the electric tumbling that Ana-Maria Popescu can do or the ability to put my feet together side by side with room to spare, making the beam seem huge in comparison, like Sun Luli. I have to hit my skills and keep going, no hesitation, let it all blend together into a beautiful dance for the judges and keep their pencils off those score sheets.

There's a normalcy to all of this now, almost like we all train together in one gigantic international gymnastics commune. The girls we've been competing against all week have somehow, in the midst of the fiercest competition of our lives, become our teammates. We work in order, like a team would prepare for a competition, rotating one after another doing pieces of our routines before finally putting it all together as we hit the ten-minute warning the officials give us.

I grab some water, give my hair one last coat of hairspray, and then line up with the seven other girls who are going to fight me for every thousandth of a point today. As we march out into the arena, I feel it building again, the want. I want this gold medal. I want to go out on top. I wanted that bars gold too, though, and that didn't exactly work out. I try to push it back, but it's too late. I let the want in, and there's no getting rid of it now.

We're announced to the crowd. They seem more subdued than in the last few days. Maybe the realization that it's all coming to an end has hit them too.

I'm up sixth, so when the Klaxon sounds to end warm-ups, I head down off the podium with seven other girls to sit and wait while Erika Sheludenko from Russia gets the green light from the judges.

Some people think that you can tell how a beam rotation is going to go by how the first athlete's routine goes. It's the same reason why teams tend to put up their most solid performer first, the girl most likely to hit, so that the day doesn't turn into a splat-fest.

So when the crowd groans as Erika misses her foot on a back handspring into a layout and falls to the mats below, I want to groan with them. That is not a good sign. Not at all.

Then Elisabetta Nunziata from Italy goes up, and the same thing happens, a fall on a switch split leap, and the nervous energy in the arena begins to permeate everywhere.

My leg starts to bounce up and down on its own. I don't want to watch this. I don't need to put two—I cringe as Han Ji-a of South Korea falls on her front tuck mount—three falls into my head before I go up there with my last shot at an Olympic gold on the line.

"Breathe, Audrey," Janet says, breathing with me.

I follow her, breathing in and out and the tension in my bones starts to seep away.

Three routines. Three falls.

Three fewer scores at the top of the standings for me to try and pass?

Not that I want to dance on anyone's grave or anything, but I guess I'll take it.

The universe begins to right itself, though, as Natalia Cristea, one of Romania's best on beam, tumbles and leaps her way to a clean routine.

It feels like the air is back in the arena, and we can all breathe again when her score, a huge 15.0, pops up on the board.

Well, then, that's the mark to beat.

I stand up and stretch my neck in one direction and then the other. Time to get this done.

Sun Luli is up now, and I'm right after her. I raise my arms over my head, making sure to keep my blood moving.

She hasn't had the best Olympics. She came in with super-high expectations, but she finished fifth in the all-around and fourth on vault. Maybe I shouldn't be too pissed at the Silver Girl thing. I know what it's like to finish fourth, and I imagine fifth isn't exactly fantastic either.

I want her to hit her routine. I want her to medal. I look to my left. Irina Kareva is preparing for her routine—she'll go last. To my right, Ana-Maria Popescu is waiting too. She'll go right after me, and I want them to medal too. We've all earned it. We all deserve it. Every girl here has the talent and has put in the time and the effort for this.

That doesn't mean I still don't want it for myself, though.

I want this more than anything.

Sun Luli nails her routine. I applaud and offer her a fist bump as she passes me, coming down from the podium while I go up.

Okay, this is it.

My last chance.

Whether I hit this routine or not, it's over, no matter what.

Might as well make it a good one.

Janet sets up the springboard for me as we all wait for Sun Luli's score.

"You've got this, Audrey," she says.

"I do."

My eye catches the scoreboard as the score appears. A 15.2. That's not just good. That's fantastic.

Breathing in then out, I wait for the green light from the judge.

I can be fantastic too.

On the green light, I salute before I turn to face the beam one last time.

Then I go, a roundoff, back handspring into a layout step-out and then straight into two more, layout step-out, layout step-out, and I rise up standing tall without a flicker, lifting my chin again to show how in control I am of that combination.

I fulfill a few requirements, connecting a leap with another, and then it's the real test—my turn sequence. I release a breath again and spin, one-two-three, a triple turn into an L-turn, leg up and one rotation around and down into a full illusion, my leg kicking up and over as I rotate in one spin and set. Another lift of my chin, and this time I let myself smile. That was perfect.

I step lightly to the end of the beam. Halfway there. I'm so close, but I push that thought aside, pointing my toe out in front of me, setting up for the last major connection of my last routine. An aerial cartwheel—no hands—straight into a split leap, switching my legs in the split as I fly through the air and land softly before kicking out a leg and flipping backward into a gainer, down to straddle the beam. I lift my chin again, and the smile is wider before I sit back and spin, kicking my legs out and around and hearing the crowd whoop in reaction. I press my hands into the beam and lift my body up into a handstand before standing tall to set up for my dismount.

My final dismount.

The last skill I will ever do.

No, Audrey, don't think. Just breathe and go.

My eyes laser down at the beam where my feet are pressed together. I raise my arms over my head and let all my training, every drop of sweat from the last fourteen years, guide me backward, hands then feet, hands then feet and up, twisting, body line tight, legs extended, toes pointed—one, two, three twists, and land. I don't move. I stand there and let the wall of sound explode out from the stands, thundersticks and voices uniting together into the most electric roar I've ever heard.

It's the last dismount of my career, and I stuck the ever-loving shit out of it.

Finally, I let myself exhale—a shaky rattle in my chest—and turn to the judges to salute. The crowd is still cheering, so I wave to them as I leave the podium.

I need to sit and breathe. I need to hug my teammates. I need to thank my parents. I need to kiss Leo. I need to tell Janet and Mrs. Jackson how much I appreciate them.

First, though, I need my score.

Was it enough? It was good. It was great, even, I think. I don't know. Sun Luli was great, and Ana-Maria and Irina still have to compete, and they're great.

The crowd must see my score before I do, because the reaction is instantaneous and fierce.

"The score for Audrey Lee of the United States: a 15.4!" the arena's announcer calls out.

That's even more than fantastic.

Janet claps and then pulls me into her side, squeezing my shoulder, because we can't fully celebrate yet. There are two more routines to go. Irina and Ana-Maria have gymnastics left to do.

And as that thought flickers through my mind, that's when the tears spring. They have gymnastics to do, and I don't. I never will again.

No matter what happens and no matter what color medal I wear at the end of this—and I am guaranteed a medal now—it's over.

Gymnastics is over.

Maybe life is just beginning, though.

Ana-Maria is up on the beam, and she is amazing. That layout full isn't any less impressive after an entire week of watching her nail it over and over again, and her triple twist is as good as mine.

Janet's arm around my shoulders tightens a little bit as Ana-Maria salutes the judges and comes down the stairs. I pull away from her, and when Ana-Maria's finished hugging her coach, I offer her my fist, which she bumps in celebration.

The crowd applauds and cheers, and I have no idea how they're getting the scores before us, but then the announcer calls out, "And the score for Ana-Maria Popescu of Romania, 15.3!"

She's in second.

I'm still in first.

One routine left. Irina Kareva. Of course it is. Of course it comes down to us.

I've edged her out all week, silver over her bronze in the all-around and then again on bars.

I don't want to watch, but at the same time I have to.

One routine.

My fate tied to someone else for the rest of our lives.

Silver or gold?

chapter twenty-four

I take a breath when Irina mounts the beam and force myself not to hold it. She's brilliant, the kind of gymnast with no real weakness. But gymnastics is hard, and even the best of us can falter, if only in the smallest of ways.

So when she launches into her dismount, a roundoff into a full-twisting double back, and she takes a huge hop backward, then a second, much smaller step to steady herself, I know.

I know without a shadow of a doubt that I was better. My routine was as difficult. I didn't make a mistake up on the four inches, and neither did she, but I stuck my dismount cold, and she did not. I knew during bars too, though, and look how that turned out. So despite knowing deep in my soul that it's mine, that everything I worked for is about to culminate in a gold medal—even if it's not the one I thought I'd win—I still wait and wait and wait.

The crowd is restless. The thundersticks start up again, beating out a rhythm as they urge the judges along.

And then they're reacting, but I have no idea what their screams of joy mean. Are they celebrating Irina's victory or the final routine of my gymnastics career earning gold?

"The score for Irina Kareva of the Russian Federation: a 14.9!"

I collapse straight down to the floor. My legs give out in the way I'd always feared they would before my dreams came true, but this is the kind of collapse I can live with, because it's over now. It's over, and I won.

I'm an Olympic gold medalist.

Janet is crouched down beside me, an arm around my heaving shoulders. I'm not crying, just shaking. It doesn't feel real.

Three medals.

Two silvers.

One gold.

I can't believe it.

"You did it," Janet murmurs over and over again. There are feet surrounding us on the floor, probably cameramen, and I don't want to deal with that right now, but there's no avoiding it.

The cameras give way, but only just, and there's an Olympic worker trying to get me to come with her. Her face is twisted with frustration as she tries to guide me to where Ana-Maria and Sun Luli are standing so we can march out of the arena together to prepare for the medal ceremony.

I pull away from Janet, and just over her shoulder, Leo is at the edge of the stands, crouching down to get as close as he can. He smiles, and that's all it takes to send me running in his direction. He stands, offering his hands to pull me up. I find my footing and grab hold of the railing before kissing him lightly. The crowd starts screaming like crazy, so I can only assume one of the cameras is beaming the footage up onto the big screen hanging from the top of the arena.

Finally, breaking the kiss, I glance to the side, and embarrassingly enough, my parents are right there. Leo gives way to them, and Mom reaches me first, hugging me fiercely before Dad comes in over the top and completes the circle. I can't hear what they're saying, but it doesn't matter. I just hug them tighter.

Taking pity on the poor Olympic volunteer tapping my ankle from below, desperate for me to come down, I release my parents and jump out of the stands. I follow the volunteer, a girl not much older than me, who looks super relieved she didn't have to, like, pull me down herself.

I march out with Ana-Maria in front, Sun Luli behind, waving to the crowd with both hands.

Mrs. Jackson is waiting at the entrance to the tunnel with my medal ceremony clothes, like she did for the all-around. "I thought you'd be needing this today. I"—she hesitates—"I'm so glad it's gold, Audrey. Truly."

Her eyes are a little glassy, and her smile trembles a bit.

There's no time to respond; I'm being guided away again, this time back out into the arena toward the floor, where Chelsea and Dani will compete in a little while for the last three medals of the Games.

The arena is dark, spotlights twirling around as we approach the floor, and then finally the lights come up, and the crowd cheers when they see us emerge from the darkness.

"Ladies and gentlemen," the announcer says, translating his last words from Japanese. "Your Olympic balance beam medalists!"

We're led to the podiums and my heart leaps as I stand behind the highest one.

"Winner of the bronze medal, from the People's Republic of China, Sun Luli!"

She moves up onto the podium and waves to the crowd.

"Winner of the silver medal, from Romania, Ana-Maria Popescu!"

Ana-Maria steps in front of the podium and kisses Sun Luli on each cheek before moving to the second-highest step.

"Winner of the gold medal and Olympic Champion"—my breath catches; that's me—"representing the United States of America, Audrey Lee!"

Chills run through my every nerve ending as I hug Sun Luli and then air-kiss Ana-Maria on each cheek, adding a hug for good measure. She expected to win this gold, and I know better than anyone what the agony of silver medal regret feels like.

Finally, I step up onto the top podium and exhale. I'm trying to take in everything. I think I actually manage to see my parents up in the crowd, Dad waving an American flag around like a maniac, Mom openly sobbing. This is for them too.

The official from the IOF congratulates me in slightly broken English and presents me with the same Japanese apple blossoms we were given for our other medals. Then, finally, a bronze medal is around Sun Luli's neck and a silver around Ana-Maria's, and when I bend ever so slightly to allow the gold medal to be put around my neck, everything clicks into place.

This is how it was always supposed to end, from the depths of despair to the highest mountaintop, all in the space of a week, and I can't believe I managed to make it happen.

We're turning to the flags now, and it might be some digital recording someone pressed play on—the same one from when I stood a step down from Emma yesterday—but it feels more like a full orchestra sitting off the floor playing every bar of "The Star-Spangled Banner" just for me.

I sing along, and the tears start to gather in the corner of my eyes. I don't fight them or wipe them away, but keep singing, because this moment isn't forever. It's right now, and right now my dreams have come true and I want to feel this with every fiber of my being.

". . . and the home of the brave," I sing finally, and my voice cracks on that last note.

The crowd roars its approval and we wave again, lifting the bouquets of apple blossoms in the air to salute them back. Then there are pictures together, and pictures separately, before being led from the floor down back to the tunnel and into the mixed media zone, where reporters are waiting. I can't even really see any of them, it's all just a blur.

"Audrey, how do you feel?"

"Numb, I think?"

"Did you know you'd won when you stuck that landing?"

"Absolutely not. I didn't know I won until I actually won."

"You're the first Korean American gold medalist in gymnastics! How does that feel?"

"It's incredible. I'm so proud to represent so many people who have dreams like mine, and I hope I can inspire them to go for it! I might be the first, but I don't want to be the last!"

"Audrey, what do you have to say in response to Christopher Gibson's guilty plea?"

I stop and blink at the reporter who asked it. He's the same shithead from our pre-Olympic press conference. Before I think of a response that would make Chelsea proud, I'm shuffled along down the line by Mrs. Jackson, who seemed to appear from nowhere.

"Thanks," I say as she escorts me straight out of the lion's den and back into the warm-up gym. The girls competing on floor have been escorted out into the arena, and someone's music is already playing.

"Here," she says, handing me a bag. It has a Team USA polo and tracksuit pants in it. "Put those on."

Emma's with her, already dressed in the same outfit, and immediately I understand what they have in mind. I switch out of the medal ceremony clothes to my tracksuit, still over the leo I wore for beam. One way or another, we're going to finish these Games out there on the floor, together, as a team.

I hesitate for a second before taking off my medal. Mrs. Jackson has a wooden box for it.

"I won't let it out of my sight," she promises.

I nod, and then together, Emma and I sprint through the tunnel. Janet meets us at the entrance and comes off the floor, somehow understanding that we all need to be together for these last moments. We flash our credentials to security and head straight for the chairs by the floor podium, where Chelsea and Dani are waiting to compete.

Somehow, it feels like a different place entirely from where I just received my medal.

"Good, you're both here," Dani says, reaching out and squeezing my hand. "You were amazing."

"Seriously incredible," Chelsea adds, fiddling with the tape at her wrists. I glance up at the scoreboard. Four girls have already gone; four more to go.

The scores are reasonable, but nothing that Chelsea and Dani can't match or pass. I breathe a sigh of relief. I want them to have what I did: one last moment of glory.

Chelsea is up next, and when her music starts, she performs with the casual confidence of an athlete who has accomplished everything she's ever set out to in her sport.

It's her victory lap.

She keeps her deductions to a minimum on each pass and dances with reckless abandon in a way that forces the judges to take notice. The crowd, whose thundersticks are clapping along on the downbeats, cheers her along. She has them eating out of the palm of her hand, and when she lands her final pass—the last of her career— she changes the usual choreography at the end of her routine to a simple bow to the crowd before she blows a kiss, a farewell to the fans and to the sport.

I scream along with everyone else as they rise to their feet to give her a standing ovation. Chelsea salutes the judges and then races down the stairs. Dani gives her a quick hug—she still has to go up and perform one last time—and then I embrace her tightly.

"Feels good to be done, doesn't it?" I ask.

"It feels amazing," she says.

I nod, because that's something I didn't realize I'd feel when I was finished. Joy and sadness, obviously, a little bit of fear, but also a tremendous amount of relief. Our entire lives have been about gymnastics for so long, there's satisfaction in knowing that it's over, and, as scary the unknown can be, that it's time to move on.

Chelsea's score comes up, a 14.3, which slides her into first place for now, with two competitors left. She's going to medal. It's just a matter of what color.

Sun Luli is up next, and there is something about that girl, an innate sweetness, that forces you to root for her, especially when she's using all four feet nine inches of herself to command every eye in the arena into believing she's a Norse goddess choosing who lives and dies while she dances and tumbles to "Ride of the Valkyries." She finishes with a flourish, and while I'm not sure I really want her to pass Chelsea—no, I definitely don't—I can't help but smile when she does.

Chels is gracious about it, giving the younger girl a fierce hug when the 14.4 comes up and Sun Luli's name replaces hers at the top of the scoreboard.

Just Dani left now, and as soon as the opening sounds of *The Greatest Showman* burst through the speakers, the crowd is on its feet, dancing along as she pulls everyone into the music with the incredible tumbling she's always been known for and the stunning control that brought her that all-around gold two days ago. It all goes by in a blink, and she's landing her final pass with an emphatic stick that she makes look easy.

She's going to pass everyone and stand on that top podium again. Not because she deserves it for all she's been through. No, Dani Olivero's going to win because she is the greatest gymnast in the world.

—

The suite is quiet. Janet is down at the dining hall grabbing lunch for us, and Mrs. Jackson is off scheduling media appearances for us tomorrow. Leo and Ben are off making dinner reservations for us so we can celebrate tonight as a team. For now, it's just the four of us, alone, maybe for the very last time.

It's barely one in the afternoon, and yet so much has happened that it feels like the sun should be setting in the distance. Instead, most of the athletes are out training or competing, and here we are, finished. That flame we·didn't get to see lit at the opening ceremonies won't go out for another week, but for us, it's all over. Tomorrow, our arena will be set up for the men's competition and after that for basketball, barely resembling the place where we experienced the highest highs and the lowest lows of our careers.

Maybe that's for the best. After all, we're moving on too.

We don't have to pack yet. We won't fly home for another two days at least. Tomorrow, we'll sleep in a bit and then spend the rest of the day with the media, maybe take in a few of the other events. We'll smile and talk about how proud we are of one another and of representing our country, and maybe I'll score some sponsorships and endorsements. I'll probably answer a billion questions about Leo, and we'll avoid questions about Gibby, and then at the end of it all, we'll go to sleep in this suite one more time before it becomes nothing more than a memory.

And with that thought, an idea pops into my head.

Leaving the girls in the common room for a moment, I move into my room and gather up my medals, all safely nestled in their boxes.

Carefully, I take the two silvers and place them down on the common room's wooden table before I lay the gold between them. The others understand immediately and follow my lead before returning with their own medals: two golds for Dani, a bronze and a gold for Chelsea, and one final gold for Emma. We arrange them on the table, making sure they all touch, their ribbons tangled together almost like they're embracing. Perfect.

There are only four of us, and we won eight medals. That's almost half the total individual medals you can win in Olympic gymnastics. We swept the golds in event finals and owned these Games, just like I said we would. We showed the entire world exactly what we're made of.

I take a picture and add it to a post, but then I sit down and really think about what I want to say before I begin typing out a message to the world.

The words come slowly, but they do come.

What our team has been through was impossible. Yet here we are. We did it. As amazing as this ride has been, I hope it never happens again. I hope no one has to go through what we did these last few weeks. But it's more than a hope. I know it'll never happen again because we won't let it. Tamara Jackson and Janet Dorsey-Adams won't let it. And Dani Olivero, my hero, the bravest person I know, and Chelsea Cameron, who I've looked up to my whole life, but never more than these last few weeks, and Emma Sadowsky, the best friend I've ever had and my sister in all the ways that matter, won't let it. Sarah Pecoraro and Brooke Cohen, Olympians forever, won't let it. And Jaime Pederson and Sierra Montgomery, who thought they had to choose between their lifelong dreams and a friend, won't let it. I won't let it happen again. And I defy anyone to look at this picture, to look at what we've accomplished together, and tell me that we're not the greatest team in the world.

I send it out into the universe and turn off my phone.

The other girls are done posting too, and we stand there for a moment in silence, staring down at our medals, the embodiment of everything we've been through and everything we've accomplished, physical markers of these days we spent together in Tokyo, our Olympics suddenly at an end.

"What's next?" Dani asks.

Chelsea grins, her eyes twinkling playfully. "Only the rest of our lives."

"Oh, is that all?" Emma laughs.

I look at each of them, at these girls, at these competitors turned teammates turned sisters.

"I can't wait."

acknowledgments

So many people had a hand in bringing this book to life, but there is only one place to start. To Alice Sutherland-Hawes, my brilliant agent, you believed in me and in this story before anyone else and I am forever thankful for your support, your expertise, and your friendship. To the whole team at Madeleine Milburn, you are truly the best in the business and I am so happy to be a part of your family.

I'm not sure if I believe in fate, but Julie Rosenberg, working with you on this book was most certainly meant to be. Your insight and enthusiasm for this project were apparent from the start and only seemed to grow as we went along. I still can't believe my luck in getting to work with someone who truly understood the story I was trying to tell and had all the tools to help it shine brighter than I could have ever imagined. You are a brilliant editor and I'm so proud of the work we've done.

To the team at Penguin Young Readers and Razorbill Books: Alex Sanchez, Casey McIntyre, Kim Wiley, Marinda Valenti, Gretchen Durning, Jayne Ziemba, Felicity Vallence, and Bree Martinez. You are the most incredible group of professionals and I am so grateful to be even a small part of it! And to Vanessa Han and Theresa Evangelista, I am more than happy for this book to be judged by its cover forever. It is perfection. Thank you.

People think that writing a book is a solitary activity, but I truly could not have done it without my early readers and idea-bouncer-off-ers, gymternet and writing community types: Lauren Hopkins, Madelyn Glymour, Holly Glymour, Kaelyn Christian, Erin Marone, Cindy Otis, Hannah Stuart, Jessa Swann, and Meg Lalley. Your feedback and encouragement never ceased to spur me on and keep me going. To Mark Benson, thank you for always being the other half of my brain. To the rest of the Writerly 2019 folks, Tabitha Martin, Jean Malone, Krista Walsh, Christian Berkey, Megan Paasch, and Angi Black, you may not know how much you helped bring this book into the world, but just being with you all was an incredibly inspiring experience and I'm so grateful for it.

My students are a constant source of inspiration, but I'd be remiss if I didn't send extra thanks to Katie Daugherty, Sarah Pecoraro, and Erica Sheludenko. I'm sorry your fictional gymnastics counterparts didn't succeed, but I have no doubt you will all do great things in this world. Thank you for making every day I served as your librarian a joy. To everyone in my ESM family who traveled this rollercoaster with me, especially Mike Doyle, Michelle Heaney, Colleen Korte, Victor Correa, and Bonnie Rubin. You make going to work like coming home.

As always, Mom, Dad, and Annie, I could not do any of this without your unconditional love and support. You can't choose your family, but I wouldn't choose anyone else.

And finally, to my readers, thank you for taking this journey with me. I hope you laughed, cried, and cheered with Audrey, Dani, Chelsea, and Emma. I'm so proud to share their story with you.

AUTHOR NOTE

A gymnastics fan all my life, I've been extremely fortunate to get a peek behind the curtain of the sport. These opportunities have been incredible and wide-ranging. I've sat with Olympic gold medallists' families during a national competition, attended two Olympic Trials, appeared on the famous gymnastics podcast GymCastic, live-streamed an all-access conversation with two Olympic coaches, and covered the sport during the 2016 Rio Olympics for Fangirlish.com.

My experiences have given me tremendous insight into the world of elite gymnastics, and one thing has remained true throughout: I am continually inspired by the incredible dedication of the athletes; the supportive parents, family and friends and most of all—the relationships between the truly awesome young women who rise to greatness by dedicating their lives to this sport, a sisterhood unlike any other.

That being said, *Break the Fall* is entirely a work of fiction, though it deals with issues like sexual assault that are, unfortunately, true to life. If you are affected by any of the topics, you can find links to support on the next page.

Jennifer Iacopelli

SUPPORT

Break the Fall is a work of fiction. Audrey Lee and her teammates are fictional, but many young people struggle with issues including sexual assault. Help is out there. For more information on where to find support, you could consider the following sources:

The Survivors Trust

The Survivors Trust is the largest agency for specialist sexual abuse services in Europe. They offer a free and confidential helpline to any survivor anywhere in the UK and Ireland that feels like they need to talk. If you want to discuss what happened to you or just call for a chat, helpline volunteers will be there to listen.

Call free on **08088 010 818**

Childline

A private and confidential service for young people up to age 19. Contact a Childline counsellor about anything – no problem is too big or small. **Available 24 hours**.

Call free on **0800 1111** *or talk online at* **www.childline.org.uk**

Mind

Offers advice and confidential support to anyone experiencing a mental health problem. Helplines are open **9am–6pm** on weekdays except for bank holidays.

Call on **0300 123 3393** *or find them at* **www.mind.org.uk**

Samaritans

Confidential and emotional support for people who are experiencing feelings of distress, despair or suicidal thoughts. Lines open 24/7 and 365 days a year.

If you need a response immediately, it's best to call on the phone.

Call free on **116 123** *or find them at* **www.samaritans.org**

Frank

Offers facts, support and advice on the use of drugs and alcohol. Lines are open 24/7.

Call on **0300 123 6600**, *text* **82111** *or find them at*
www.talktofrank.com

Jennifer Iacopelli was born in New York. Growing up, she read everything she could get her hands on, but her favourite authors were L.M. Montgomery and Frances Hodgson Burnett, both of whom wrote about kick-ass girls before it was cool for girls to be kick-ass. Jennifer writes authentically about sports; she covered the Rio Olympic games in 2016 and has made several featured appearances on the famous gymnastics podcast, GymCastic.

You can find Jen on Twitter:

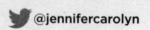 **@jennifercarolyn**